Seasoned With Grace

Seasoned With Grace

Nigeria Lockley

Urban Books, LLC
97 N18th Street
Wyandanch, NY 11798

ISBN 13: 978-1-62286-810-0
ISBN 10: 1-62286-810-2

First Trade Paperback Printing August 2015
Printed in the United States of America

10 9 8 7 6 5 4 3 2 1

This is a work of fiction. Any references or similarities to actual events, real people, living or dead, or to real locales are intended to give the novel a sense of reality. Any similarity in other names, characters, places, and incidents is entirely coincidental.

Distributed by Kensington Publishing Corp.
Submit orders to:
Customer Service
400 Hahn Road
Westminster, MD 21157-4627
Phone: 1-800-733-3000
Fax: 1-800-659-2436

Dedication

While writing this book, I learned that grace comes in many different forms, and one of those forms is friendship.

I dedicate this book to my girls, who have watched me grow, cried with me, and embraced me, no matter what state they have found me in: Maxie Rodgers, Stephanie Charles-Marc, Shaniqua Wilkerson, Latasha Cordera-Belk, Alisha Noid, Tania Louisdor, and Cassandra Allard-Souter.

And to my sisters-in-Christ, who have prayed for me, over me, have fasted with me, and have encouraged me in the Word: Myriam Skye Holly, Sarah Adams, and Shenetta Purnell.

Acknowledgments

First and foremost, I have to give God all the honor and glory for bringing me to this point, for blessing me with this gift, and for trusting me to minister to the hearts of people in this fashion.

William Lockley, my loving husband and partner for this journey, thank you for bearing with me as I ride this wave.

I especially want to thank Myriam Skye Holly for remaining a loyal supporter and beta reader, and for being my cover girl (she helped me select the image for the cover).

I want to thank my soul sis and fellow Christian fiction author Unoma Nwankwor for connecting with me and encouraging me. Thank you, Berta Reddick Coleman, for being a great accountability partner. Our talks come with the perfect blend of comfort and whip cracking necessary for me to get it done.

Michelle Chester, of EBM Professional Services, thank you for taking me on and getting me through this process smoothly. You edited my work and allowed me to maintain my dignity throughout the process; you were responsive, organized, and personable. Every author needs an editor like you.

To my supporters, thank you for welcoming me and my work into your world. I pray that you are edified and entertained.

But unto every one of us is given grace according to the measure of the gift of Christ.

—Ephesians 4:7

Chapter 1

The sound of Young Thug's cartoonish intonation and the infectious chorus of his and Rich Homie Quan's hit song "Lifestyle" snapped Grace King out of her alcohol-induced slumber. She squinted to read the screen of her iPhone. "Ethan Summerville," she read slowly before tapping the green telephone icon to accept the call from her attorney slash agent slash everything. Throughout the years, Grace had come to rely on Ethan. To Grace, it seemed like no one understood her except for him.

"Hello," she grumbled into the phone.

"Grace Terisha King, I know the reason that you are late to this meeting is that you're still in bed."

"No, I'm up, Ethan."

"You know what my mother used to tell me when she caught me in a lie? Lying lips are an abomination unto the Lord."

Grace mustered up enough strength to sit up in the bed so that she wasn't completely lying, just telling a little half-truth. Those half-truths had taken her far. The half-truth she'd told the bouncer—that her friend was drunk and needed her help getting out of the club—had enabled her to finagle her way into the VIP section of the 40/40 Club, where she was discovered by Bleeker Kios, the head of Fresh Faces Modeling Agency. Her friend had been drunk and had needed her help, but she'd passed out with her head on the bar. From there, Grace had parlayed that half-truth into a prosperous modeling career.

"You can't continue to do this," Ethan said when she was silent.

"Do what?" she asked, slapping her thigh. Sometimes Ethan's paternal and overbearing nature frustrated her, and it also made her think of all the things she'd left behind, like family, namely, her father, whom she had once considered herself close to.

"You cannot continue to walk out of nightclubs, inebriated, and expect to book legitimate jobs. It's all about branding, and no one wants you associated with their brand. These proceedings were supposed to begin at eight, and it is now nine o'clock. The judge has been calling here every hour on the hour since six a.m., trying to determine why it was exactly that she didn't lock you up, and why it is that she shouldn't lock you up now."

"So . . . what?" Grace shrugged her shoulders. "Am I not supposed to enjoy myself ever?"

"Not when you're trying to break into the world of acting. Tell me which producer wants the drunken girl on page six on their billboard."

"Page six?"

"I knew you were not out of bed. You're on page six of the *Post,* page two of the *Daily News.* And I'm sure they have a shot of you in every free paper that exists in New York City as well. If you keep this up, your star is going to nova soon."

Grace ran her fingers through the long blond bang she'd had sewn into her short pixie cut as she digested what Ethan was telling her about her career. Since she'd left home at sixteen, the only thing she had had was her career.

"Grace, just hurry up and get down here to sign this plea deal before Judge Laramie comes down here to arrest you herself."

"All right, Ethan," she whimpered into the phone before hanging up.

It took everything inside of Grace to fling her legs over the side of her bed. She rushed out of her bedroom, skirting over her platform pumps, Michael Kors jeans, her white shirt, and the fuchsia blazer she'd worn last night. Her feet slapped the parquet flooring on the steps of her condo as she headed to the door to fetch the newspapers.

Grace hated disappointing Ethan, and she really didn't want to see her bad side in print, but she needed to see the photo that might get her sent to jail. She cracked the door slightly to make sure there were no paparazzi in the hall trying to get the exclusive candid shot of her that magazines like *Them* and *Soundoff* loved printing—models with no makeup.

After verifying that the coast was clear, she pushed the door open wider and collected her loot—the *Times*, the *Daily News*, and the *Post*.

Grace tucked the *Daily News* under her arm and placed the other papers on the small brown marble-legged table near the door. She walked into her living room and pressed the button on the remote sensor for her window treatments. Slowly, the white panels rolled back and revealed Central Park. From her condo, Grace could see the ice skating rink, the pond, and a group of children escorted by three adults. The adults pointed at the pond, and the children scribbled on their yellow notepads.

Why didn't I become a schoolteacher or a librarian or someone who was responsible and able to contribute to society in a meaningful way? Grace thought.

It crossed her mind that maybe she should have completed high school and opted for a normal life. On the other hand, Grace had to admit she loved the perks and the pay that accompanied being a top model, but after delving a little too far into the dark side of things, she found herself constantly fighting for air.

Taking a seat Indian style on her red Italian leather sofa, Grace peeled back the first page of the paper and read the caption that accompanied her photo: *A fall from Grace: Supermodel Grace King, best known for strutting her stuff, reaches an all new low as she stumbles out of Greenhouse after what onlookers said was "a night of binge drinking."*

Onlookers? What onlookers?

After reading the caption twice, Grace allowed her eyes to stray to the photo. She swallowed the image of her long limbs awkwardly contorted. Her legs curved inward, with her kneecaps touching each other and the sidewalk; her right arm was bent slightly to break her fall; and her left arm was tied up in the hands of her friend Chela, another model, who had somehow managed to escape the photogs. As if that was not enough to highlight her fall, the editors had been gracious enough to provide readers with a photo of her on the catwalk for Zac Posen during Fashion Week, in case they didn't have a point of reference.

Grace's eyes darted back and forth from the inset picture to the photo of her collapse on the sidewalk.

"How did you get all the way down there, Grace?" she asked herself, speaking the words.

The buzzer on the intercom interrupted her moment of quiet contemplation.

"Yes, Arnie?" She stared at the dome of her doorman through the intercom camera and wondered why he didn't wear the hat that accompanied his uniform to hide his premature balding.

"Good morning, ma'am. Your car is here."

"Good morning, Arnie. Could you please stop calling me ma'am? Your Christmas bonus is depending on it. And please send the car back. I did not call for a car. It's probably another one of those lousy photogs trying to lure me outside while I'm looking crazy so they can post it on TMZ."

"Ms. King—"

"Grace," she insisted.

"Grace, Mr. Summerville sent this car to take you to his office."

Grace smacked herself on the forehead. She'd totally forgotten the reason why she had bothered to get out of the bed this morning.

"Let the driver know I'll be down in half an hour."

"Yes, ma'am . . . Grace."

"Thank you, Arnie."

Grace made a mad dash for the bathroom. She took a two-minute shower, like she used to when she was homeless and used the showers in the parks department to get cleaned up. Either she'd ask to use the restroom and then hop in the shower or she'd sneak in with a crowd of teenagers walking in for their after-school program, a time when they were really busy.

She wiped the fog off her mirror with a towel, spiked up the front of her hair with pomade, and covered the dark circles around her eyes with concealer. *Let's make the most of today. All you have to do is a little bit of community service, and you'll be back on top.*

"Britney, T.I., Chris Brown." While slipping into a gray A-line skirt and an oxblood peplumed blouse with sheer shoulders, Grace called out the names of celebrities who had behaved badly recently yet had managed to make a comeback.

"This is not a death sentence," she proclaimed aloud, sealing the ankle strap of her black patent leather Mary Jane red bottoms. "It's just another part of your journey." She pulled her navy blue Burberry cape over her head and checked herself in the mirror. Grace smoothed a stray strand of hair and spoke to her reflection. "What doesn't kill you can only make you stronger," she declared before walking out the door.

She continued to mouth clichés and life-affirming statements on her elevator ride down to the lobby and during her car ride to Ethan's downtown office in an attempt to block the thoughts of darkness that threatened to besiege her entire day and the rest of her life. These words had gotten her through so many other trials; she was depending on them to be enough to steer her through this.

Chapter 2

Grace crossed her legs and leaned back on the chocolate-brown leather couch next to the window in Ethan's downtown office. She stared down at the pedestrians hustling to and fro.

"You cannot sign these documents from all the way over there, and you certainly can't read the conditions of your probation, which include community service, through those sunglasses. Please take a seat over here, Ms. King." Ethan pointed to the mini conference table located in the opposite corner of his office.

Grace gingerly slid off her oversize, wide-rimmed sunglasses, pushed herself up from the couch, and asked, "Where do you want me, Ethan?"

"Just take a seat near Ms. Johnson." He pointed at the stenographer. "The court sent her over here to record these proceedings."

"Well, let's just get this over with." Grace plopped down on one of the aluminum and white leather, three-legged swivel chairs at the black matte conference table. "I don't care where I have to do my time at," she announced.

"Then you'll have a great time at Mount Carmel Community Church."

Grace drew her lips up so that they nearly met her pointed nose. "A church?"

"Yes, a church. They run a plethora of community outreach programs that you can assist with," Ethan explained as he joined Ms. Johnson and Grace at the conference table.

"You couldn't find anywhere else for me to go?"

"Excuse me, Mr. Summerville. I'm sorry to interrupt," said Ethan's secretary, Alice Wyatt, through a crack in the door. "Ms. King's latte is ready, and I brought a bottle of water for you."

"Come on in." He waved his two fingers back and forth, granting her permission to enter.

"Ethan, I'm not doing community service at a f—"

"Grace!" Ethan shouted, halting the onslaught of expletives she was prepared to release on him. "That potty mouth of yours is how you wound up in my office."

Grace rolled her eyes. She wondered when he was going to stop throwing her situation with Pamela Di Blasio in her face. Three years had passed since she cursed out Pamela and got sent to Ethan's office on the third floor of Stars Unlimited, a one-stop shop featuring entertainment law, publicity, management, and a talent agency.

When Pamela started managing Grace nine years ago, Ethan was fresh out of law school. She was one of his first clients. Back then it was only paper and the lawyers with more seniority would handle her issues. Once she began racking up troubles and charges, everyone in the agency pushed her off on Ethan.

Pamela was the last to jump ship. When she did, the only thing she said between Grace's obscenity-laden monologues was, "Ethan will now be managing you. I'll take care of the contracts immediately, and if you don't leave my office now, I'll also be drawing up a lawsuit against you for harassment, which I will have sent right down to his office."

"Spending some time in a church is precisely what you need," Ethan said.

"Why?" Grace asked, smirking at him.

"The church would be the perfect place for you to do your time," Alice said, shoving Grace's latte at her. Alice had never been a fan of Grace and her wild antics, and she was sure to demonstrate that whenever she had to deal with Grace. "What you need is an exorcism in your mouth. I hope they do that there."

Slamming her latte on the table, Grace rose from her chair. "And you need to be punched in the face, Alice."

Ethan clapped his hands. "All right now, let's break this up, ladies."

"Did you get that, lady?" Alice shook her hand in the direction of the court reporter. "She just threatened to assault me."

"I think that what we all need right now is a little prayer," Ethan suggested.

"Don't you think you're taking this whole born-again thing a little too far?" Grace said, rolling her eyes. Although Ethan had given his life to Christ three years ago, he was still in what Grace called the "honeymoon phase." It was her least favorite phase—that time when every new convert worked viciously to push his or her newfound salvation onto anyone within earshot, just like a new bride thinks all her friends should be married as well, that is, until the groom starts coming in late or, in Grace's case, when God stopped answering her prayers. The moment she felt that God wasn't listening, she stopped talking.

"Ms. Johnson, we're going to take a break from these proceedings to pray," Ethan said to the court reporter.

"May I join you, Mr. Summerville?" Ms. Johnson asked hesitantly. "I'm an usher at Mount Moriah Baptist Church, and I'm a huge fan of Ms. King. I really hope to see her make it out of this all right."

Another one? I am surrounded. What is this? A Holy Ghost ambush? Grace could not recall the last time she'd been around this many Christians, and she wanted to keep it that way.

Ethan rose from his seat at the conference table, removed his tortoiseshell-rimmed glasses, and smiled at Ms. Johnson, revealing the dimple that decorated his square jawline. "Please join us," he said, with his arm extended in her direction.

She slid from behind her stenotype and jumped to his side.

Ethan and Ms. Johnson joined hands like they had attended a few prayer vigils together in the past. The sight of Ethan holding hands with another woman made Grace cringe. Despite the fact that they'd shared nothing more than the occasional dinner, and the only dates they'd been on were all appointed by the courts, in Grace's eyes, Ethan was all hers. She snatched his right hand with her left and stretched out her right hand toward Alice, who folded her hands when she saw Grace's palm.

"Alice," Ethan said with a raised eyebrow and in that fatherly tone he used that made every woman at the firm do whatever he said. "Let us look to heaven."

Grace held back her groaning. *I am going to use this exercise in futility to work on my acting. Just imagine that there is a God and that He cares about you.*

Grace turned up the corners of her mouth in an innocent smile, nodded her head at Ethan first, and then lifted it toward the ceiling to face God, who, she believed, had turned His back on her long ago.

"Lord, we come before you as humbly as we know how to seek your help. Lord, we don't know why, but everything in our lives has led us to this moment in time, to being together in this room. Please have your way and work this situation out to your honor and your glory. Guard our hearts from doing evil, and keep our mouths from speaking evil, in Jesus's name. Amen."

Ethan released both Ms. Johnson's and Grace's hand from his firm grip. Ms. Johnson licked her lips and offered Ethan a wide grin.

"Mr. Summerville, this is not my place to say, but if you'd like me to . . ." Ms. Johnson delicately placed her hand on his shoulder and traced his sharp profile with her eyes before going on. "Would you like me to strike the exchange between your secretary and Ms. King from the record?"

Grace observed Ms. Johnson.

"Ms. Johnson—" Ethan began.

"Candace." She blushed.

Alice and Grace exchanged looks of shock when they realized what was taking place in front of them.

"Uh . . . can we get on with this?" Grace asked loudly, trying to break up the love connection that was forming.

"Yes, let's move forward. Candace, if you would be so kind as to strike that exchange from the record, I'd—no, we'd—greatly appreciate it," Ethan said, allowing his brown eyes to linger on Candace.

Grace's eyes widened as she took in this scene. She returned to her seat at the conference table. Reclining in her chair, with her hand resting on her throat, she deflected her gaze to the Romare Bearden print that hung on the wall. Candace didn't appear to be the brash, flashy type of woman Ethan was used to dealing with as an entertainment attorney. Maybe that was why her nude lipstick, her simple diamond studs, and the glow that had surrounded her since she walked in intrigued him.

"Do you need anything else, Mr. Summerville?" Alice asked. Ethan shook his head, and Alice cut her eyes in Grace's direction. "What about you, Lindsay Lohan?" she asked with a slight smile and a jingle in her voice.

"Since we just finished praying, I'm not even going to entertain you." Grace waved her hand at Alice. She crossed her legs and wrapped them around each other like twisted vines, then turned her attention back to Ethan. "Please, continue."

Alice exited on cue, and Ethan sat back down at the conference table and returned to the particulars of her probation.

"You cannot consume any alcohol or take any drugs. Is that clear?" He removed his eyeglasses and stared hard at Grace. "Well, do you understand the conditions of your probation?"

"Yes. I just don't understand why I have to do my community service at a church."

Ethan got up from his seat at the table, walked over to Grace, and perched on top of the table. He rested one of his hands on her hand and caressed it.

"What I am about to say is going to hurt you."

"I can take it." Grace swallowed hard, shoring herself up. "Whatever it is, I can take it."

"Right now you're like tainted beef. No one wants to touch you."

Sinking into the chair, with her eyes closed, Grace let her head fall limp. *How could a single slap turn into this?* she wondered. She replayed the night in her head to see if she had missed a GO LEFT sign.

The music thumped in my head. Scantily clad girls were gyrating on the dance floor, while DJ Tony Love hollered, "Who's going to turn it up in here?"

All I did was tap her on the shoulder.

"I don't do autographs at this hour, sweetie," announced Soriah Sommers, the latest reality TV train wreck, shaking her twenty-six inches of Indian Remy in my face.

Since Soriah couldn't take a hint, I squeezed into the small space that existed between her and my date for the night or the week. I had not yet decided what to do about Lance Weston, the newest VJ on BET.

"Excuse me!" Soriah shouted.

"You're excused. Exit stage left," I replied. Lance and I pointed to the dance floor in unison while cracking up.

"Don't nobody play me like that," Soriah snickered at me.

"Keep it moving, sweetie," I said.

"Do you know who I am?"

I turned around to face her. "Keep it moving, Soriah. I'm not the one."

Lance whispered, "Chill, chill, chill," into my right ear, and Soriah barked threats into my left ear. The shots I threw back with Lance and the pounding of the bass seemed to speed everything up. All I could hear was the voices of chipmunks. Before I could stop myself, my fist was in Soriah's mouth.

"Grace . . . Grace? I thought you said you could handle this," Ethan charged, disrupting her meditation on the past.

"I can."

"I was able to get you a position at my church, Mount Carmel Community Church, so that I can monitor you."

With the flick of her wrist, she waved her hand at Ethan and rose to a standing position. Grace peeked over her shoulder to make sure that Ms. Johnson was watching as she stood in front of Ethan and adjusted his tie. She scooped his bearded face into her hands. "You just want to be close to me."

Ethan swatted her hands away from his face. "Please take a seat. This is a legal proceeding. Here are the terms of your probation. Please read over them and sign it. Then we can send Candace on her way, but not without lunch. Candace, would you like to join me for lunch? You've been so patient with us."

"I'm sure that Candace has to hurry back to the court-house. Don't you, Candace?" Grace asked forcefully, attempting to compel her to reject Ethan's offer.

"I am awfully hungry."

"Enough said. Let's wrap this up so that we can eat," Ethan said.

"Shouldn't we go over my itinerary for that new Tim Story film before breaking for lunch? What did you have in mind, anyway? I'm in the mood for some sushi," Grace said.

"I really wanted to talk about that later." He looked up at Grace, then over at Candace again.

Grace felt like a pot of seething water had spilled inside of her as Ethan turned from taking care of her to getting to know Candace. With every word he uttered, his eyes slowly shifted to Candace.

"Let's do it now. She already knows all my business, anyway."

"You've been cut from the film. They're replacing you with Chanel Iman. You're too much of a liability," Ethan revealed.

Grace sucked her teeth.

"Now, about lunch. Candace and I are taking a lunch break. There are no breaks for a star. I have an interview set up for you at the office of *MadameNoire* at twelve fifteen, and after that I need you to go home, get a good night's rest, and be ready in the a.m. for community service. Let's just deal with this and discuss the film situation when you've got it together." He rubbed his palms together and smiled at Candace instead of Grace.

Crossing her arms in front of her chest, Grace sat down and sulked her way through the rest of the formalities, wondering what Ethan hoped to gain from dining with a mere stenographer, when Grace had been in front of him all this time.

Chapter 3

Candace's eyes searched the menu at Bryant Park Grill for a dish she recognized, hoping to avoid making significant eye contact with Ethan. The more she looked into his eyes, which seemed to be filled with amber, like a lion's eyes, and studied his chiseled features, the more he began to resemble a bronze version of the statue of *David*.

"The lamb kabobs are great for an appetizer," Ethan said.

"I don't know," Candace said, sliding the small cross pendant dangling from her neck back and forth.

"What's to know?" Ethan asked, waving his muscular arm in the air, signaling for a waiter. "Just try them."

She marveled at his confidence. *He knows he's the head.*

"May we have an order of lamb kabobs, the Caesar salad, and . . ." He peered at her. "Do you like seafood?"

She nodded her head.

Finishing off the order, he added, "Give us the Bryant Park Sea Grill as well. That should be good. Lobster, shrimps, and scallops."

"This is a really nice restaurant, Mr. Summerville. I feel a tad bit underdressed," Candace noted while pushing up the sleeves on her black and gray spotted cardigan.

"You look fine." Ethan's fingertips grazed hers. He took a sip of his water and loosened the knot on his tie a bit. "Please, call me Ethan. How long have you been a stenographer?"

"For only about six months."

"No wonder I've never seen you around," he said, smiling like he'd just found buried treasure.

"I usually work with Judge Franklin on depositions and civil trials. When I saw my name on the board for this case, I was so excited. The other stenographers told me Ms. King was a real riot, but I just see a hurt little girl," Candace said, summing up her first encounter with the infamous Grace King. "She seems to really love you, though," she added to gauge what was really going on between them.

Ethan shook his head adamantly. "It's not love. It's more like codependency. Everyone at the firm says I enable her, and at the same token, now that she's not the same bright-eyed girl they rolled in fresh off the street, no one wants anything to do with her. I'm getting pretty tired of *The Grace King Show* myself."

"While there's life in the body, there's still hope," Candace said, smiling.

"Yeah." Ethan shook his head in agreement. "That's why I sent her to do community service at my church . . . so that she could get saved and I can keep an eye on her. I don't have too much left in me. If she messes this up, that's it for me. There's a lot more I hope to accomplish in life besides chasing after Grace."

Their appetizers arrived just as Candace was about to launch into a speech about the power and necessity of forgiveness. She noshed on her lamb kabob, savoring the peppery flavor of the tender shreds of lamb. And though she tried to hold back, the spirit demanded to be let out.

"Ethan, I know this is not my place, but may I add my two cents?"

Ethan placed his hand on hers and squeezed it. "Please feel free to share anything with me." From the glimmer in his eyes, Candace understood that he was asking for more than her opinion. He was asking for her.

"Jesus never gave up on Judas. Knowing who Judas was and knowing the intent of his heart well in advance, Jesus still ministered to him. Jesus still accepted his kiss, even on the night of his betrayal."

"Grace and Judas are totally different, and me and Jesus . . ." Ethan laughed a little. "Well, there just ain't no comparison there."

Without restraint Candace jumped on Ethan's slight spiritual deficiency. "God's hope for us is that through this gift of faith and our ministry, we will live up to the fullness of Christ. Ephesians four, thirteen, more or less," she said, shaking her hand. "Grace and Judas aren't different. Both of them have been oppressed by the enemy in need of salvation and had the opportunity to sit at the feet of the Son of God. They who are led by the spirit are the sons of God, brother. Let the spirit lead you so that you can lead her to salvation."

Ethan scratched at his neck. He was definitely perplexed by what she'd just said, and from the looks of it, he was trying to grasp the magnitude of her words. Throughout the rest of their lunch, as they stuffed themselves with Caesar salad and the abundance of soft chunks of lobster, scallops, and jumbo shrimp, Ethan tried to digest Candace's wise words.

"Will there be anything else, sir?" the waiter asked, collecting their dishes.

Ethan glanced at his watch. "My lunch hour is almost up. Give the lady anything she'd like and charge it to this card." Ethan withdrew his Amex from his back pocket and handed it to the waiter.

"I'm not impressed by things, Mr. Summerville."

"Me either. I am really impressed by you, and I hope that you are at least mildly impressed by me. You have a fresh perspective on the scriptures, and you really helped me to see that right now I'm not meeting God's standards in this area of my life. Candace, is it all right with you if we exchange numbers? I'd like to spend more time with you."

A current of heat coursed through Candace's body, a sure signal that her creamy cocoa-butter complexion was turning rosy. She patted her cheeks, then covered her mouth to mask her smile.

"I would like that too." She clutched her forehead. None of this was like her. She didn't go out to lunch with strange men or exchange numbers with them after one conversation. She usually wasn't this bold, but that prayer changed things. The prayer that Ethan had led in his office had moved her and had opened her eyes to a treasure. She thought of a picture she'd seen this morning on one of her girlfriend's status update. A portrait of a man's hands folded, with the words "A real man knows how to talk to God" superimposed on top of it.

Candace had taken every word of his prayer to her heart and had asked the Lord why was she here, and when she'd opened her eyes, she'd seen something different about Ethan. He was a prime cut. Not just in the looks department. She'd checked her flesh at the door when she first spotted his six-foot-two frame strutting through the lobby before he escorted her upstairs.

After that prayer, she had thrown away the "Keep me, Lord" prayer she whispered in the lobby of Stars Unlimited and had determined in her heart to show him she was the helpmeet God had created for him.

Chapter 4

Grace stared at the gold knobs on the doors of Mount Carmel Community Church. She turned her back and took three steps toward the curb. She was supposed to report to church on Tuesday, the day after the sentencing. It was now mild, fog-filled Thursday, and she still wasn't ready to walk through the doors of Mount Carmel.

You have to go in. Go in, or go to jail. She weighed her options. "I can handle the chains. I can handle the jumpsuit. I don't know if I can handle twenty-four hours of women," she said aloud.

Slowly, she walked back to the doors, then turned around again and leaned against them. "I can't do this. I'm just going to call Ethan. . . . I can't disappoint him, but . . ." she murmured.

"But now is the acceptable time for salvation," a woman said to her through a crack in the door.

"What?"

"The Lord led you here for a reason."

"Yeah," Grace said smugly, nodding her head. "He led me here to do community service, not to be indoctrinated."

"Are you . . . ?" The woman gasped deeply. "No. You're not!"

Grace turned around to face the woman completely. She raised her oversized sunglasses, giving her a full glimpse of her face.

"Grace King. Come in, come in," the woman said, quickly opening the door to the church.

Grace stepped into the vestibule of Mount Carmel Community Church and gave the woman who had greeted her a blank stare.

"I'm Sister Connie Bryce. I'll be your tour guide for the day. I'm sure Brother Ethan filled you in on all the various ministries we have. Which one do you think you'd like to take part in?"

With a turned-up nose, Grace replied, "Lady, how many times do I have to tell you that I'm just here to do my time?"

"Where the spirit is, there is liberty. We'll help you find just the right ministry for you to participate in so that you can grow."

Grace cocked her head to the side and wondered if Sister Bryce had heard a single word she'd said. Either she was so high on the Holy Ghost, she could completely disregard Grace's noxious attitude or all the material she had on was affecting her hearing. Her ankle-length plaid skirt and her peach-colored, short-sleeved turtleneck reminded Grace of yet another reason why conversion was not on her to-do list. *It's so unfashionable.*

Grace was giving Sister Bryce a little extra flavor, hoping she'd send her home, forcing Ethan to find a more suitable place for her.

"Follow me this way to the basement, where we do our food ministry, Fishes and Loaves Ministry. I told Pastor that I thought it would be best for you to try your hand in every ministry until we're able to discern your gift."

Grace grabbed Sister Bryce's fleshly arm, stopping her in her tracks.

"I don't think Brother Ethan explained to you clearly why I'm here, but it's not to minister, and my gifts are right here." Grace waved her hand at her face and patted her breast.

"Ow, the blood of Jesus, Satan, the Lord of hosts rebukes you in the name of Jesus." Sister Bryce shook her hand in a flourish in Grace's face. "Nothing happens by chance. If you are here, you were sent here for a divine purpose. You shake those things all you want. They come standard with every model, and some of us are blessed enough to get a little extra." Sister Bryce straightened her back, pointing out that she had received a double portion of Grace's gift. "Though the world values those, they don't mean nothing in the Kingdom. Now, understand this—" she waved her index finger in the air—"Everything we do here is a ministry designed to help us exercise our faith and draw people closer to God."

With that, Sister Bryce turned her back and proceeded to walk toward the altar. Grace remained stationary in the middle of the aisle. *I know she don't think she's about to put no oil on me. I didn't come here for all this.*

"Is you coming or not, little girl? We got the Lord's business to attend to, and He doesn't wait for anybody."

Grace dragged her feet as she followed Sister Bryce to the altar and then down the steps on the left side of the pulpit.

"The steps on the right lead to Pastor's office. He's away at a pastors' summit this week. As soon as he returns, I'll introduce you. Come on now. We got to get ready for the lunch crowd," Sister Bryce said, pushing the door open to reveal Mount Carmel's expansive basement.

Twelve long banquet-style tables occupied the basement from wall to wall. Each table was covered with a scarlet tablecloth, and vases filled with marbles and fake flowers served as decorations. The walls were covered with framed verses from the Bible, written in calligraphy. One scripture captured Gracie's attention. Ephesians 4:7. *But unto every one of us is given grace according to the measure of the gift of Christ.*

God must have measured her present with a short stick, Grace mused, considering her plight.

"You like that one?" Sister Bryce asked, nudging Grace with her elbow. "Let me show you my favorite." She grabbed Grace by the wrist and dragged her to a picture frame and read the scripture aloud. "'Like as a father pitieth his children, so the Lord pitieth them that fear him.' Psalm one-oh-three, thirteen. That's awesome love, isn't it?"

"Some fathers don't pity their children. Some fathers are the demise of their very own children," Grace replied, thinking of her very own father, Thomas King. After not seeing her since she was sixteen, he had sought her out only five years ago, after seeing her on the cover of *Sports Illustrated*, to berate her and tell her how unchristian it was of her to pose near naked on the cover of the magazine. To which she had replied, "I'm not a Christian. I'm Grace King."

"Well, Grace King, are you ready to do some service for the King of Kings?" Sister Bryce asked with raised eyebrows.

"Yes, ma'am," Grace said softly. It was way too difficult for her to maintain her abrasive attitude in the face of Sister Bryce's kindness.

Sister Bryce led Grace to the far end of the room and into the kitchen, which housed several ovens and refrigerators. "This is a full-service meal ministry. We serve a three-course meal for lunch and dinner, and it includes appetizers, an entrée, and dessert."

"All of that?"

"The Lord blessed us last year, when one of our old members returned. She's a famous chef. You probably heard of her. Cynthia Barclay."

Grace shrugged. She'd never heard of her, and she wasn't interested in making any new celebrity friends.

"Well," Sister Bryce continued, "she donated the money to fund this ministry, and she ran a Bible-based cooking class to help members feed their mind, body, and spirit."

"If this ministry is so important, why isn't she here now?" Grace wondered aloud.

"She went back to Virginia to run her restaurant, but she left a ton of recipes, and her class is what launched this ministry. Lunch is usually our busier time. That apron and hairnet over there are yours." Sister Bryce pointed to the blue and white apron with a floral print and the hairnet that sat on top of one of the silver counters in the kitchen. "You can hang your coat up on the rack in the corner near the door."

"I'll do anything except wear this hairnet." Grace held it up between her index finger and her thumb as if it were a dirty sock.

"Why? You too good to wear a hairnet?" a woman asked, creeping up beside Sister Bryce.

"Grace King, meet Sister Thompson," Sister Bryce said, pointing to the woman standing beside her. "Sister Thompson, this is Ms.—"

"I know who she is," Sister Thompson sneered, placing her apron over her neck and tightly fastening the strings around her waist. "She's that drunk model that likes to fight." She snickered, staring straight at Grace.

"What? You too good to do what us common folk do?" croaked a voice from over Grace's shoulder.

Grace peered over her shoulder at a tall woman with broad shoulders who had a gold ball stuck in her nose. Clearly, she had not given up her old lifestyle entirely yet.

"Grace, this is Sister Marva Puck. Sister Marva, this is Grace King."

"I know who she is." Sister Marva brushed against Grace's shoulder as she walked past her. The enmity she exuded was stronger than her cheap knockoff perfume.

"Excuse you," Grace muttered.

"No, you're excused," Sister Marva replied. She held up one palm in Grace's direction and angled her shoulder slightly to face Sister Bryce. "Sister Bryce, we don't need her help. She's only here, pretending to care, until she gets her image cleaned up." Sister Marva pivoted on her worn-down heels and looked Grace in the eyes. "I'm no fool. I know what you're up to," she stated, wagging her finger in Grace's face.

Grace swatted Sister Marva's hand out of her face and stepped closer to her. Through clenched teeth she responded to Sister Marva's accusation. "You must be a fool, stepping to me like that."

"Whoa, whoa!" Sister Bryce waved her hands in the air and yanked Sister Marva back a few inches. "There'll be none of that in here today."

Grace felt like Sister Bryce was staring right into her soul as she made that announcement. This church thing wasn't her thing, and there was no way on God's green earth, or on any other planet that He had created, that she was going to take nonsense from anyone.

"You're right, Sister Bryce. There'll be none of that in here today, because I'm definitely not staying here." Grace flung her hairnet at Sister Marva and strutted out like she was on a runway in Milan.

How am I going to explain this to Ethan? she wondered as she walked up the steps to the pulpit to exit the church. Ethan wasn't going to be pleased. *I can handle him. I can definitely handle him.*

Chapter 5

"You can't just walk out, Grace!" Ethan shouted, slamming his palms down on his desk. "Fridays are supposed to be fun days. I'm not supposed to hear bad news on Fridays. That's always the precursor of a working weekend."

"Ethan, I did what was best. It was either that or I was going to slap what little bit of Holy Ghost that woman had in her. Find me another placement."

"'Find me another placement.' 'Get me a role in the next Tyler Perry movie.' 'Get me a spring roll,'" Ethan whined in a shrill voice, trying to impersonate Grace. "I am not a maid, concierge, or some lackey you can just bark at. I'm a lawyer. The last lawyer left in the building who will deal with you." He stepped out from behind his massive desk, walked over to her chair, and sat in front of her, on top of the desk. "You are standing on your last leg, Grace King, and if you plan on making a comeback, this is where you must begin." He scooped up her hand and held it in his.

The tender touch comforted her in more ways than one. She rested her cheek on the back of his hand.

Ethan fingered the edges of her short hair. "Look at me."

Grace stared up at him. She licked her lips, prepping herself for the kiss she'd imagined they'd share more than once.

"We are going to get through this, like we always have, but if we're going to make it through this"—he leaned in closer to her perfectly puckered, pouty lips—"you're going to have to listen to me."

Contorting her gazelle-like neck, Grace positioned herself to receive him. Between her court dates, mandated therapy sessions, and now community service, she didn't have much time for her two favorite things—booze and hot guys. Right now Ethan would do, with his chiseled chest and muscular arms. Grace traced the muscles in his arms with her eyes, cutting through the silk blend of his Thomas Pink orange button-down shirt. In an instant Grace stretched her long arm out and wrapped her fingers around Ethan's arm.

"Mr. Summerville, Candace is on line two," his secretary blared over the intercom, interrupting the nearly perfect kiss, which Grace needed.

Ethan shook himself out of Grace's grasp, hopped off the desk, hitting his hip bone on the edge, and scurried to his desk chair. He snatched the phone from its cradle.

"Hello, Candace," was all Grace could make out. She listened intently as Ethan's voice dropped to a hushed tone, so that he sounded like he was speaking over a Boyz II Men track. Grace leaned back in her chair, flung one of her long legs over the other, and repeatedly kicked the desk, jerking her knee. After a few kicks Ethan finally acknowledged her impatience. With one palm over the receiver, Ethan mouthed to Grace that she needed to give him one minute.

"That sounds really great. Can we discuss this over dinner?" he asked, wrapping up his conversation with Candace. "I have a client in the office right now. Serafina around six? See you then." Ethan slipped the phone back into the cradle that sat on his desk. He looked in Grace's direction, but the faint glare in his eyes indicated that his thoughts were somewhere else.

"What do you have to discuss with Candace at Serafina? Does she even like Italian food?"

"That's none of your business, Grace."

"Is she trying to get you to help her cousin ManMan get out of jail?" Grace quipped.

"I don't ask questions about the men you date or about their intentions, so don't you dare do it to me, Grace King. What you are going to do right now is go to the church, apologize to Sister Bryce, and serve some food. We need some photos of you doing community service out there so you can start cleaning up your image."

Grace looked down at the diamond bezel around the face of her watch. "As appealing as that sounds, I have a lunch date."

"With who?" Ethan removed his glasses and rubbed the bridge of his nose.

"That's none of your business, Mr. Summerville." Grace pulled the gold chain strap of her purse around her body, lifted her olive-green scarf slightly over her head, and pushed her glasses tightly against her face, trying to hide the hurt Ethan's remark had caused. "When you send a camera crew down there, let me know, and Grace King will be there, feeding the poor and cradling suckling babes in my arms."

"You're going back there this evening to help serve dinner." Ethan let his glasses fall onto the desk. "I'm not hiring a camera crew. There are probably some plants in there already, using their camera phones to get a picture of you. Someone posted a photo of you on CelebrityDaily.com." Turning to his computer, he punched in the address of the celebrity sighting and gossip blog. "Searching for Grace. Supermodel Grace King in front of Mount Carmel Community Church in Harlem, pleading with the doorkeeper to let her in," he said, reading from the computer screen. Ethan turned the monitor around so that it faced her. "You may not think anyone is watching, but everyone is, and a majority of them are hoping you get it together. I'm praying that you do."

"Do they really want to see me get it together, or do you want to mock me?" Grace stood. "You know something, Ethan? One thing I've found to be true in this life is what my mother told me when I was a little girl. She said, 'Trouble don't last always, and when it seems like it does, I've discovered that there's nothing a mimosa can't wash away.'" With that, Grace waved good-bye, as if she was parting with a friend, and walked out of the office.

"Excuse me," Grace called to the young waitress from across the room. "May I please have another?" She raised her empty champagne glass in the air, shaking it from side to side.

"Are you allowed to drink?" Junell Pierce asked.

"Junie, I'm grown," Grace replied in response to her best friend's question. She set the champagne glass on the table and rested her hands beneath her chin. "I can do what I want."

"That's not what I heard," Junell said, flipping her long straw-colored locks over her shoulder.

"What did you hear about moi?"

"I heard that you're not supposed to be drinking, and you're doing community service at some church up in Harlem for, like, a year."

Grace slapped her thigh. "Dang, girl, how do you know all my business? I think you're taking your role on that detective show a little too seriously." Grace chuckled.

"If anybody should know, you should know that people in the industry talk, and right now everyone is talking about you, Grace King." Junell pointed a long manicured finger at Grace.

"Fill me in." Grace scooted to the edge of her seat. "What are they saying?"

"A lot of people are saying you're washed up and you're a liability." Junell pointed at Grace. "But you and I," she said, placing her hand on her chest, "both know that is not true. What does Ethan have to say about this situation?"

"Let's not talk about Ethan right now, please."

Junell took a forkful of her salad, then dabbed the corners of her mouth with her napkin. "Did Ethan drop you as a client? I know a great lawyer. He's not going to manage you or act as your agent. He will only represent your interests in legal matters, but he's good. Do you want his card?" She fished for his card in her boxy, magenta calfskin Céline bag. "How could he do this to you now, in the midst of all this?"

Grace stretched her hand across the table and grabbed Junell's arm before she could extract the card. "It's fine. Ethan did not drop me, but he's been acting funny toward me lately."

"Funny? How?" Junell threw back the last bit of alcohol left in her glass and signaled for the waiter.

"He's been kind of distant." Grace shook her hand from side to side. "I think it's because of this girl he's dating," she said, curling her lips in disgust at the thought of Candace and her cardigans.

"Dating?" Junell gasped, choking on the word. "Ethan's dating? It's not you, and it's a female?"

"Yes."

"I had him pegged for either a closeted homosexual or madly in love with you."

"We were both wrong," Grace said as flatly as possible, trying not to reveal her bruised ego and crushed heart.

A waiter interrupted their chitchat to bring them full glasses of mimosa. "Ladies," he said, bowing before them after placing the long-stem glasses on the table. He locked eyes with Grace and smiled at her, licking his lips. She reciprocated with a flirtatious smile of her own. His blue-eyed gaze seemed impenetrable, making it hard for her to determine the extent to which she could use him or the extent to which he planned on using her.

"You are absolutely divine," the waiter whispered to Grace.

Junell responded to his compliment, preventing Grace from spouting one of her famous seductress phrases. "While the compliment is appreciated, she's saving herself for marriage, young man. Thank you." Junell waved her hand at the waiter like she was swatting at a mosquito.

"Junie!"

"Don't 'Junie' me. You cannot sit up here and expect Ethan to save himself for you, and you're over here, giving away free samples of the merchandise. I'm praying for you, child."

Sucking her teeth, Grace replied, "Not you too. You know, Ethan started praying during the meeting when were supposed to be reviewing the terms of my probation. That's how he met ole girl."

"Ole girl?" Junell raised one eyebrow. "You don't have to say it like that."

"I'm sorry, but I didn't grow up in the Hamptons, speaking proper English." Grace twisted her lips and leaned back in her chair. Junell's middle-class upbringing often served as a source of contention between the two women, and now was as good a time as any for Grace to deflect the conversation away from the idea of her conversion and the frightening idea of Ethan dating..

"You're overreacting. They haven't even been dating that long." Junell laughed and flipped her hair again. "You just got sentenced on Monday. Today is only Friday. And please send the papers to my lawyer so you can sue me for growing up in a house with two parents so that I can testify to how ghetto Wydanche really is. All that glitters ain't gold. I'm sorry you had to learn that on the streets, but we all learn it somehow. Now what you need to do is get yourself together before Ethan gets serious with 'ole girl,'" she said, using air quotations.

"I don't care what he does."

"Liar. If you didn't care, we wouldn't be discussing this." Junell folded her arms and leaned back in her chair, like she'd just closed another case on her detective show.

"I'm not discussing it. You are. I'm drinking." Grace threw back her mimosa.

"Seriously, Grace, you need to do what you have to do to get right. Maybe you should go to church with Ethan."

"Why is everyone trying to do a Holy Ghost intervention on me?"

"This life you're living isn't working, and I know you think no one in the world loves Grace King, but I do, and I don't want to see you in the streets, in rehab somewhere, or on some god-awful reality show." Junell and Grace both shuddered. "It's getting late, Grace."

Glancing at the face of her cell phone, Grace said, "Junie, it's only one o'clock."

Junell reached across the table and put her hand over Grace's. "No. I mean you're getting too old to be living your life so recklessly, especially in this industry."

"Chile, please." Grace sat up straight and crossed her legs. "I'm only twenty-six."

"How many times have you been twenty-six?" Junell and Grace both broke out in laughter in response to that question.

The other patrons stared at them. They weren't the typical businessmen at lunch, the clientele that Billy's catered to, which made the restaurant the perfect place for a model and an actress to step out of character and be themselves without any fear of being caught on camera or accosted by some crazy fans.

Grace clutched her chest to catch her breath and tried to count how many times she'd turned twenty-six since her actual twenty-sixth birthday. Four times. *Have I become one of those washed-up stars who are still clinging to their youth, without a hope or a prayer of ever regaining that fame?* She stared at her friend. They'd both entered the industry at the same time. On the same day.

We were sitting in the waiting room of Fresh Faces Modeling Agency, nervously shaking our slender legs and biting our fingernails, awaiting a big break.

Junell's mother, Mama June, popped her daughter's hand and said, "Don't do that. Who is going to want to see them grubby little fingers in a magazine? I know I wouldn't. Even if you are my daughter, I wouldn't buy no magazine with you on the cover and those nails look-ing like that." She tapped me. Would you?" she asked.

I turned around and said, "I don't know, ma'am."

"Of course you don't know. You can't think straight with all that makeup on," Mama June said, laughing. "Girl, did you get jumped by a bunch of clowns? Where's your mother at?"

"I don't know."

"Did you come here all by yourself?" Mama June asked.

"Yes, ma'am. Do I look really bad?" Both Mama June's and Junell's heads bobbed up and down.

"Come here, little girl. Mama June is going to fix you up real nice." Mama June did just that. She used her makeup wipes to cleanse my face and then applied a little primer, foundation, blush, and a peachy-colored lipstick that shone against my dark skin. "Pass me the mirror, Junie." Mama June took the mirror from her daughter and held it up in front of my face.

I loved the fresh face that stared back at me and the glowing eyes. "Thank you, ma'am. I look beautiful," I gushed.

"Don't thank me. You look like that on account of God, your mama, and your papa. All I did was clean you up a bit so we could see your beauty. I'm Mrs. Pierce, but you can call me Mama June, and this is my daughter, Junell."

The agency signed two girls that day—Junell Pierce and Grace King. They went on shoots together, shopped together, roomed together when they went to Milan and Paris for Fashion Week, but somehow Junell had managed to advance unscathed and had smoothly transitioned into acting. Junell already had two motion pictures under her belt and had just secured the lead role on a new detective series, *Bloodshed*. The more Grace thought about it, the more it infuriated her that Junell had made it and she hadn't. There was no way Grace was going to mention that she'd been dropped from Tim Story's latest project. Junell could find that out the same way she had found out about her sentence.

"What's wrong, Grace?" Junell asked.

"Nothing." Grace bit down on the corner of her lip. "I was just thinking about things. Junie, how did you make it out in one piece?"

"If it had not been for the Lord, who was on my side, I don't know where I would be today."

Grace rolled her eyes and signaled the waiter for a refill. If she was going to have to sit through a sermon, she wanted to at least have a drink in her hand.

"I'm serious, G. Without God's mercy and protection, I honestly don't know where it is exactly that I would be. He kept me in many situations that would have killed somebody else. Remember Darnell? Every girl needs a bad boy. What a lie from the pit of hell. That Negro almost killed me and nearly destroyed my career, but God . . . but God . . ." Junell began to stomp her foot as she proclaimed God's good works in her life.

"Calm down, Shirley Caesar Jr., before you get us thrown out." Grace chuckled.

"It's not funny, G. Jesus really did a work in my life. You were there. If nobody else knows, you know how messed up I was. You should attend a service or two while you're working at that church, or come with me to church. You know, Mama June's been asking for you."

Grace thought about what Junell had just said. *If nobody else knows, you know how messed up I was.* It was true. Grace had seen Junell at her worst. She'd held Junell's hair back as she threw up in the toilet, she'd seen her sniff a few lines and even pop some ecstasy, and yet here Junell was, preaching to her. Grace's perfectly arched eyebrows formed a furrowed line in the center of her head. Either God was a real jokester or He didn't care about Grace at all. The more she pondered the situation, the more infuriated she became. Junell was no different from Grace, yet it seemed as though she'd received more grace than Grace.

"Check please," Grace called out, announcing her imminent departure.

"Are you done already? We didn't even have dessert yet," Junell protested.

Wrapping her scarf around her neck, Grace replied, "I'm going to go and get my life together, as you suggested, Junell." Grace reached into her Chanel purse, withdrew two hundred-dollar bills, and pushed them across the table to Junell. "This ought to cover my damages."

Junell pushed the bills back to Grace and said, "Only the blood can do that."

Chapter 6

Grace crept up to the side entrance of Mount Carmel, where the people who were being served entered. As a precautionary measure, she had donned an olive-green cape, with the hood pulled over her head, and a set of oversize Marc Jacobs sunglasses to conceal her identity. If she had to be relegated to church duty, she could at least do it fabulously.

She didn't want to return to the church; Sister Marva's attitude and her own attitude were the ingredients for a dirty bomb, and the impact of the blast was guaranteed to be worse than an explosion in Times Square. Grace pounded on the door vigorously for at least ten minutes before Sister Bryce cracked the door open.

"We don't begin serving dinner until seven o'clock. You've only got another thirty minutes to wait. You can have a seat in the park across the way or join the people in the sanctuary for prayer." Sister Bryce listed her options without looking up.

"Sister Bryce, it's me, Grace." She lifted her sunglasses up and down like she was playing peekaboo with a baby.

Sister Bryce opened the door and playfully slapped Grace's forearm with the dishrag she held in her hand. "Why didn't you say something immediately? You gotta make yourself known and your presence felt, child. I know you know that."

"You certainly made your presence felt when you came to the door. 'We don't begin serving dinner until seven o'clock.' I bet you had your hand on your hip when you said that."

"I most certainly did," Sister Bryce said, laughing. "You ready to serve dinner? I mean, are you truly ready?"

Grace was banking on either someone from the talent agency's public relations department calling and issuing an apology for her or Ethan phoning in advance to clean things up. The grave look on Sister Bryce's chubby milk-chocolate face meant that no such call had taken place and that it was up to Grace to apologize for her own mistake. *There's a first time for everything.*

Clearing her throat, Grace stood up straight and stared directly into Sister Bryce's dark brown, doe-shaped eyes. If she was going to apologize, she had to come correct with Sister Bryce. "Sister Bryce, I'm sorry about what happened yesterday." Grace's conversation with Junell and her immeasurable debt loomed before her. She didn't want the blood of Jesus to pay for her or speak for her. As much as it was killing her to be in a church on a Friday night and to apologize, Grace had to be humble. "I can't say that it won't happen again. That other sister was really working my nerves, and I did not want to get into anything."

"You can't let everybody push your buttons. You can't let your emotions always get the best of you." Sister Bryce slid Grace's sunglasses off her face. Normally, Grace wouldn't allow anyone to touch her, unless it was a man, but there was something motherly and humbling about Sister Bryce. Maybe it was the stern yet tender note in her voice or the sincerity in her eyes. It had been a long time since Grace felt like someone sincerely cared for her.

"In the position you're in, everyone wants to get something out of you, and then there's Jesus, waiting for you to let Him put something good in you. No matter what nonsense you see or hear the saints do, don't let nobody run you out of the church. *Nobody.*"

Grace wished somebody had told her that when her mother told her that she was a shame to Christianity. Fifteen years had passed since Grace had gotten pregnant, aborted her baby, and abandoned the church, yet the wound still felt like a knee that had just been scraped. *Raw*.

Feeling her belly tighten, a sensation that was almost always followed by an hour-long session of weeping, Grace took control of the conversation.

"Yes, ma'am. I'll keep that in mind the next time I see Sister Marva."

"That's all the Lord needs, a willing spirit to work with, and I will keep Sister Marva far away from you."

"You better keep her very far away from me." Grace recognized Sister Marva's type. Sister Marva thought she ruled the roost, and she was willing to do anything to get someone who had disrupted the pecking order she'd established out of the way. Now, Grace King was definitely not one for following rules, orders, or for being treated like anyone's subordinate.

Grace followed Sister Bryce through the dining room and into the kitchen. Her floral-print apron and black hairnet were still waiting for her.

"Where are the plates and silverware?" Grace asked, staring at the rows of food in heated silver containers.

"Since the people are coming out of prayer and it's a school night, we don't do the fancy table settings. When they come in, Sister Marva distributes the plates and silverware, rather the plasticware." Sister Bryce pointed to a rolling cart with paper plates and sporks sealed in small ziplock bags with a napkin, salt, and pepper. "You just give them what they ask for. Tonight we're serving braised chicken, baked macaroni and cheese, black-eyed peas with brown rice, steamed broccoli and carrots, corn bread, and banana pudding for dessert."

If Grace didn't have to work so hard at thirty to stay within the 120-pound zone so that she could still have some viable modeling options until her acting career kicked off, she would have hooked up a plate for herself.

"Please start removing the lids," said Sister Bryce. "I don't know where Sister Marva is, so I'm going to wheel the paper plates and plasticware out and start opening the doors. You think you can handle it back here?"

Grace shook her head while tying the strings of her apron. She secured her hairnet, then did just as she had been instructed. Once the doors were opened, the room filled up almost immediately. Mothers plopped some of their young ones at the tables and directed them not to move. The elderly parked their canes and walkers at their tables, then lined up at the counter.

Grace's heart ached at the sight of the small children who stood before her, shaking their plates, with their eyes fixed on every movement of her hand. She recalled how difficult it was for her to find a meal when she went off on her own. She gave every child who stepped in front of her three scoops of whatever they asked for.

"Grace, you're too heavy-handed with that spoon. Just give the children one scoop, before we run out of food," Sister Bryce said, reprimanding Grace as she reentered the kitchen. "Sister Marva's here now, so let's get this line moving."

Grace tried her best not to give out more than the mandated single serving and to ignore Sister Marva's jabs for the rest of the evening. The line dissolved after an hour and a half. Then Sister Marva focused her attention on dumping out the gravy-lined pans. Each trip she made across the acid-washed tiles, Sister Marva huffed and rolled her eyes at Grace. Grace assumed that Sister Marva's huffing and puffing was supposed to serve as some sort of command for Grace to assist her. Instead,

Grace followed Sister Bryce's lead and took a seat on a banged-up metal stool. She leaned back and rested her elbows on the steel countertop behind her and tried to convince herself that she could handle this new life.

"You all right?" Sister Bryce asked before she began taking a bite out of a hearty chicken thigh.

"You never ask me if I'm all right," Sister Marva complained to Sister Bryce's back while she stared at Grace. Her eyes were hard as stones.

Sister Bryce made a slight turn and responded to Sister Marva's accusation of favoritism. "I asked you if you were all right after you completed your first night of serving, just like I'm asking her." Sister Bryce maneuvered herself back around to face Grace. "So, what do you think?"

Grace thought there was no way that she was going to make it another 364 days doing this. Tonight was almost as bad as the three months she'd spent working at McDonald's. On her final day there she'd dumped all the ingredients on the counters and the floor of the kitchen. The onions, the pickles, the tomatoes, and the shredded lettuce. She did not belong in any situation that required her to be hospitable to other human beings. It might have taken some time, but she'd grown accustomed to the life she'd created for herself, and most days she liked it. However, there was no way in the world she was going to admit to that in front of hawk eyes.

"Sister Marva, go and check on the people. Make sure everyone has what they need, and don't forget to distribute the Bibles, tracts, and the church's schedule. Grace and I will take care of the kitchen."

When Sister Marva walked out the side door, Grace dropped all pretenses, pulled off her nude patent-leather pumps, and began scrubbing the pans Sister Marva had begun piling up in the sink.

"This is a nice little program y'all have here, but I don't know if I can do this."

"Well, serving people in those heels would prove to be difficult for any one of us. Tomorrow you better put on some sensible shoes, like these." Sister Bryce stuck her leg straight out and hiked up her skirt a bit to model her tri-toned gray ballet flats.

"The only thing I know how to serve is style," Grace said, holding her head up high. "I don't own any flats, and I most definitely do not plan on purchasing a pair just to satisfy our judicial system. It's just hard being here, watching hungry families and the elderly pile in here for one meal that can carry them only through the night. What are they going to do tomorrow?"

"Let God worry about feeding His people." Sister Bryce rose from her metal throne and added her plate to the pile of dishes Grace was scrubbing. "What you need to worry about is how to keep those dainty little hands of yours smooth. Put on some gloves next time. The Lord fed them tonight, and He'll feed them tomorrow, just like He did the children of Israel in the wilderness. You ought to be pleased to be an instrument of the Lord."

Grace turned her eyes back to the suds before her. She hadn't asked to be a part of the Lord's trio of servers. She'd rather be sipping champagne at the Monkey Bar or have her head buried in a sweet libation from the Sugar Factory. At the bare minimum, she'd go for a cup of the wine that they sip during Communion, but she didn't think Sister Bryce was about to heed that request. After a few moments of scrubbing in silence, Grace recalled that Sister Bryce had mentioned some other ministries she could try. Maybe one of them ended early enough for Grace to both do her time and get home and at least indulge in a glass of wine.

"Sister Bryce, on my first day here you mentioned that there were other programs that I could participate in."

Sister Bryce was now sweeping. She didn't look up from the small pile of stray food she'd collected. She just hummed, "Uh-huh . . ."

"I was thinking maybe I could try my hand at one of those tomorrow."

Sister Bryce paused and leaned on the top of the broom handle before answering Grace. "Most of our other ministries are very interactive, hands on, and would require you to take on some type of authority and responsibility. From our Woman at Well weekly meetings to the adult reading classes, all our other ministries require you to lead."

The word *leadership* put a smile on Grace's face. The idea of being in charge gave her something to look forward to upon returning to Mount Carmel. That and not having to wear a hairnet.

Sister Bryce approached Grace and placed one hand on Grace's shoulder. "Before you can lead, you have to serve."

Chapter 7

By her third night at Mount Carmel, Grace had gotten her emotions in check. She cringed only on the inside when she had to put the hairnet on, and she cut her eyes at Sister Marva without cussing or storming off. And she'd mastered the art of the single-spoon serving.

That night Sister Bryce and Grace filled the plates side by side. The line was rolling along like an assembly line at Ford until some man stood in front of Grace at the counter and just stared at her. His hands were construction worker hard, his body was whittled to Tyrese perfection, and his face was Hill Harper handsome. His deep-set brown eyes felt like lasers against her skin, and his slight stubble enhanced his raised cheekbones. Before the drool actually started running out of her mouth, Grace reminded herself that this was a food ministry program and he wasn't serving. He was receiving. That meant that while he met all her physical requirements for a man, he certainly did not come close to the minimum seven-figure-salary criterion she had set for even her one-night stands.

"What's the holdup?" someone shouted from the back of the line.

"Brother Horace, tell the woman what you want, or keep it moving. This ain't no line at a museum," Sister Bryce scolded.

"Sister Bryce, the scripture is true. Every good and perfect gift comes from above," he said, still holding Grace under arrest with his stare.

"Is that the new Christian pickup line?" Grace snapped.

"Leave that girl alone, Horace," Sister Bryce ordered.

"I don't know what it is about you women that makes you think everything is about you. I was talking about that braised chicken. May I have a breast please?" Horace retorted.

Grace could not ascertain whether he was trying to be fresh or serious with that last remark. Avoiding Horace's eyes, she slapped a breast on his plate. "You're not my type," she whispered so that only she and Brother Horace could hear what she was saying.

"My Lord can fix that," he declared, then walked away with his plate full.

Grace tried to fight the desire to watch him walk away.

"If you bite down on your lip any harder, you gon' have a hole in it. Pull it together, girl. This is a church," Sister Bryce said, popping the side of Grace's leg with a spoon.

"Who is that?" Grace inquired, whispering over her shoulder to Sister Bryce.

"Oh, he's a regular here. I'm shocked he didn't try to hit on you Friday night. That is Brother Horace Brown—Mount Carmel's most eligible bachelor."

Grace was shocked as well. How could such a large serving of fineness get past her radar? Besides being a fashion connoisseur, Grace liked to consider herself a master appraiser of the male species. She could recognize the finest man in the darkest place, so missing Horace on day one was perplexing to her. The more she thought about him, the larger her interest in the possible uses for him in her life grew. He could serve as a wonderful diversion, one that would make her sentence fly by, or he could become her new favorite pastime, now that drugs and alcohol were off the table.

Grace shook herself and asked Sister Bryce if she could be excused. In the privacy of the bathroom, she splashed cold water on her face and slapped herself a few times. *He can't even buy you a meal, Grace. With those lips, who'd be thinking about eating?* She doused herself with cold water again and looked in the mirror. All she could see was Brother Horace's toasty skin. She couldn't shake his hypnotic eyes, his commanding gait, and his wide back. *Get it together. It hasn't been that long since you were with a man.*

Her little pep talk didn't work. Brother Horace was still on her mind, so Grace pulled out her phone to call the one person who could always—well, almost always—get her thinking in order.

"Ethan, what took you so long to pick up?" she demanded after the fifth ring.

"I can't talk now, Grace."

"Ethan, I need you."

"Grace, I'm sure it can wait. Are you at the church?"

"Yes."

"Then you can't get into that much trouble."

"That's what you think. There's this guy here. He looks like—"

"I'm way downtown with Candace. Jesus is closer, so try praying. Don't forget you have anger management tomorrow morning. Bye," Ethan said hurriedly before hanging up on her.

Grace frowned at her iPhone. *No booze. No boys. No Ethan.* Why on earth would she pray to the Lord, when He insists on torturing her?

With her attention still focused on the screen of her phone, which was now dark, Grace walked out of the bathroom with her head down and bumped right into the chest of Horace. Her phone fell from her hands and hit the floor.

Both Horace and Grace stooped down to retrieve her telephone. Horace's arms were slightly longer than

Grace's, so he was able to pick her phone up first. He let it dangle in his open palm. Grace snatched her phone out of his hand and stood up straight.

"Next time you need to watch where you're going," she barked.

Horace licked his lips and stood up straight as well. "I *was* watching where I was going. I've been meaning to bump into you around here. You were the one so engrossed in your little gadget that you didn't see me."

Grace tucked her phone into her back pocket. "So, what do you want now? An apology or something?"

"No. Allow me to apologize for interrupting that important exchange. Given the time I just interfered either with the exchange of the most romantic texts or in the late-night negotiations of some major business deal. I'm sorry. I promise I'll do my best to stay out of your way, Ms. King." Horace raised both of his hands in the air.

Even if either one of those notions of his were true, Grace still would not be able to find fault with those deep-set eyes and those plump lips.

"Grace. You can call me Grace." She extended her hand to prove to Horace that she bore no hard feelings about what had just gone down.

Horace gathered her hand into his and raised it to his lips. He pressed his lips into the back of her hand and focused his eyes on her. The ardor of his gaze arrested her, and Sister Bryce's high-pitched reprimand set her free.

"Brother Horace, leave that girl alone," she said, slapping his shoulder with the rag she was carrying in her hand. Horace released Grace's hand and held his head down while Sister Bryce slapped his shoulder blade a few more times with the rag. "Since you're so good with your hands, you get out there and help take out this evening's trash, you rascal."

"Yes, ma'am," Horace said, standing at attention.

"Grace, I came to check on you because you were taking so long. I wanted to make sure you were all right. Had I known Brother Horace was over here harassing you, I would have been here sooner."

"Don't worry, Sister Bryce. I can handle myself," Grace said, staring directly into Horace's eyes.

"It's not you I'm worried about. Come on and let's get the tables cleaned and the chairs put away. This ain't no social club." Sister Bryce pointed at Horace. "And, you, don't you mess with this girl. She's here for a reason, and she doesn't need to get involved in any trouble."

"Sister Bryce, I don't want to tell any lies in the house of God. I don't know if I can stay away from her."

Chapter 8

Grace's eyes darted from wall to wall and from corner to corner in Dr. Sternberg's office. His degrees from Hofstra and Yale hung neatly in matte black frames on the wall behind his desk. Every paper and folder was meticulously stacked one on top of the other—not a thing was out of place. "They think I'm the one who needs professional help," she mumbled, counting the number of pens in a jar that read SMILE—IT COULD BE WORSE on the table, which was equivalent to the number of notepads beside them. After an uneventful weekend, Monday had rolled around again and had led her here.

"You must be the remarkable Grace King," Dr. Sternberg said from behind her.

Grace took a few steps farther into the room, allowing Dr. Sternberg some space to enter his own office. He stood beside her, jammed his hands into his pockets, and surveyed his office along with her.

"No one has ever referred to me as remarkable, but I certainly am the one and only Grace King." She waved her hand above her head, as if she were presenting herself to an audience as a prize on a game show.

"Please take a seat, Ms. King. You're paying me by the hour." Dr. Sternberg motioned toward the sofa.

"By the hour? I'm going to have to speak to someone about this. I didn't sign up for this. Why should I pay for it? You see, stuff like this gets me so—"

"Angry?" Dr. Sternberg said, completing her sentence.

Grace nodded, then slid into a cucumber-green leather chair with an angled back, crossed one leg over the other, and rested her arms on the armrests.

Dr. Sternberg took a seat in an identical chair just a few feet away from her.

"Would you like to hang up your coat?" He pointed toward a wooden coatrack just over her shoulder.

Grace opened the top button of her camel hair coat. "I don't think I'll be here that long. Who's your interior designer?" Grace's eyes scanned the room. The cool green color palette and the art deco furniture were a great fusion of soft and hard. "I really like the way you have this place decorated. I was thinking about having my condo redecorated while I have all this downtime."

"I'm completely booked until December." Dr. Sternberg smiled.

"You did this?" Grace asked, wiggling her finger in a circular motion.

"I most certainly did. I selected a color palette based on the colors that are least likely to induce rage, studied a little feng shui, and tried to select the most beautiful items I possibly could."

"So, you basically trick your patients into not being angry. Check please." Grace held her hand in the air.

"No. I just try to create a safe and serene place for my patients to feel comfortable sharing intimate details about their life with me, a total stranger. Then, gradually, they enter into group therapy, and if their mind isn't right, this just won't work. There's something about being surrounded by beauty that lulls you into a state of calmness," Dr. Sternberg explained.

Grace doubted that he was usually this forthcoming with his patients. Clearly, this little talk was nothing more than a ruse to gain her trust and confidence.

"Is it working, Grace?" he asked eagerly.

Grace looked around the office once more before putting her stamp of approval on the place. "You did good, Doc."

"Thank you. Now let's get down to business. We both know why you're here."

"You think you can cure me?"

Doctor Sternberg rubbed the bald spot in the center of his head. "There is no cure for anger. However, it can be curbed. Stand up." He stood and waited for Grace to join him. He walked her over to a closet and opened it. A large, round, ornately decorated mirror hung on the inside of the door.

"Look at yourself."

Is he crazy? I know what I look like.

"Doc, did you read the file? I'm a model. I look at myself all the time."

"Do you ever get an opportunity to look at yourself, or do you look only at a stylized version of yourself, all primped and posed the way that some curator of style has positioned you, like you're an artifact in a museum? Do you ever get a chance to look Grace King in the eye? Have you ever—"

Grace held her hands up in the air, forming a T, in front of Dr. Sternberg's face, signaling a time-out.

"Dr. Sternberg, I appreciate your concern, but don't you think that you're jumping in the deep end of the pool a little early? You don't even know if I know how to swim. May I at least take off my coat?"

Bowing in concession, Dr. Sternberg backed up a bit, providing Grace enough room to remove her coat and stretch her long limbs.

"Are you ready now?" he asked after she had set down her coat. "I promise to take it easy on you. I'll ask you just one more question."

Grace ran her hands along the sides of her one-piece floral jumpsuit, then adjusted the red leather belt she wore midwaist to emphasize her waist. The sweat on her palms made the jumpsuit's pants stick to her legs. *All you have to do is look in the mirror. Lift your chin and straighten your back,* she reminded herself after tucking her hands into her pockets. Slowly, she raised her head, leading with her eyes.

"What do you see?" Dr. Sternberg asked in a whisper.

She took a quick inventory of her face. Her pores appeared to be growing, and she'd put on a few pounds. They hadn't caused her to lose the contour in her cheeks yet. All the nights she had spent staring at the ceiling, trying to figure out what her next move should be, had prompted some bags to collect under her eyes.

"What do you see?" Dr. Sternberg asked again.

"A tired model."

"Not what do you do, but what do you see?" Dr. Sternberg stepped behind her, disappearing behind her tall frame. He squeezed her arms and jerked her body a bit. "Look at yourself, Grace. What do you see when you look at yourself?"

The word seemed to be spray painted across the mirror—*mistake. Mistake* was all she could see. Closing her eyes was no help. The word *mistake* reverberated in her ears like a gong. Cold shoulders and hushed whispers were imprinted upon the backs of her eyelids, along with the word *mistake.*

"What do you see, Grace?"

When she opened her eyes, the word was still there on the mirror.

"A mistake," she said dryly. "When I look in the mirror, I see a mistake."

Chapter 9

Grace pounded the pavement as she headed up Lenox Avenue, toward 125th Street, to meet Junell for lunch. Since Junell's show, *Bloodshed,* was filmed in New York, they tried to meet for lunch as often as possible. After the eye-opening encounter she'd had at anger management the previous day, she wasn't in the mood for small talk or for the mini-sermons that Junell always seemed to have prepared every time they talked. Nor had she been in the mood for the guilt trip Junell would lay on her if she canceled. Thus, she had decided to head on out, regardless of her mood.

A walk usually made her feel better, although it didn't feel that great in pointed-toe heels. Grace noted all the new construction and the renovation being completed on the brownstones that lined Lenox Avenue. She hoped to one day own one of those brownstones and to have a cute little family to go with it. First, she'd need a husband.

Having a husband was no longer a necessity for most women. There were plenty of women opting to be single parents today. *No, sir, that ain't for me,* Grace decided, watching a woman lug a stroller in one hand and a baby in the other down the steps of a brownstone. She preferred the stability, the help, and the warmth that a man could bring over independence. The only problem Grace had—besides being involved in one too many public brawls—was finding a husband, especially now that Candace had Ethan under what seemed to be some kind of love spell. Being forced to spend all her time serving food at Mount Carmel was not conducive to finding a mate, either.

"Grace! Grace!"

Grace stopped walking and scanned the dust and scaffolding, searching for the one who had called her name. Brother Horace emerged from between some scaffolding, with his bulky arms on display in a sleeveless gray shirt. Most of his clothes were covered in splotches of white paint and a coating of dust.

"Nice jacket," he said as he ran his fingers down the lapel of her jacket.

No one was allowed to even breathe on her custom-made Balenciaga motorcycle jacket, yet all she could think about was how cute Brother Horace looked in his hard hat.

"What are you doing walking around here with no bodyguards?" he asked.

"Do you think I need someone to guard my body, Brother Horace?" Grace added a little extra arch to her back.

Smiling, Brother Horace removed his hard hat, giving Grace a direct view of his sumptuous brown eyes. "With a body like that, someone should be watching you."

"Brother Horace." Grace lightly slapped him on the chest, fabricating a look of innocence. "Are you being fresh?"

"Yes, I am. I'm saved, not dead. I know a good-looking woman when I see one."

"Wow."

"Don't act so shocked. I know you know you're one of God's greatest endeavors," he said, licking his lips. "I'd like to see more of you, Grace."

"Yeah, I'll see you on Wednesday at the pantry."

While his directness and confidence aroused the butterflies in Grace's stomach, there were two big warning signs that flashed before her eyes. One, his bank account was way too low, so there'd be no romantic getaways to Golden Bay beach in Malta and no suites at the Mandarin Oriental. And then there was the whole "man of God" thing. She'd already experimented with romance in the church. It was the greatest romance she'd ever known and the worst heartbreak she'd ever felt. If Grace had been allowed to continue dating her then boyfriend, David, if their relationship hadn't ended because he was forced to put his career in the ministry before his feelings for her, she wouldn't be so full of distress right now, she thought. Loving a man of God wasn't a roller-coaster ride that she was about to step willingly onto again.

"I have to go, Horace. I was on my way to meet a friend for lunch before you stopped me." She walked away without saying good-bye and refused to look back, even though she could feel his eyes locked on her every move.

Grace scuttled her way up the next three blocks to the restaurant, then plopped into the seat across from Junell at their table on the sidewalk.

"Why are you out of breath? Paparazzi or crazed fan?" Junell asked, pushing a glass of water at Grace.

Grace took a gulp of the water and fanned her cheeks a little before she began speaking. "It was neither. I'm so glad to see you, Junie."

"I'm glad to be seen. I hope you don't mind eating alfresco. It's been a while since I've had a chance to eat alfresco, and with this gorgeous weather, it works out perfectly. Sixty degrees is the perfect temperature for September. I'm so over summer. I ordered you a shrimp po'boy, and I ordered the pulled pork for me. Is that okay?"

"A shrimp po'boy? Do you know how many calories that is? And you ordered pulled pork?"

"You're not working now, so why are you counting calories? You could use a little meat on those bones," Junell said, reaching over the table and pinching Grace's slender and toned triceps.

"Girl, who am I fooling? I'm not working right now, or anytime soon. I suppose I can indulge a little." Grace smiled widely at Junell's round face. There was a certain warmth that Junell emanated. "Now, I have an excuse. Unemployment will make you consume carbs in mass quantities, but when did you start eating pork? Or are you still in character?"

"Since I found out I was pregnant. We tried to keep it under wraps until I hit the three-month mark, which is today. Grace, can you believe it? I'm pregnant!" Junell raised her arms in the air, doing a double fist pump.

Grace didn't move. Her heart prompted her to celebrate, to get ready to throw a baby shower that rivaled Kim Kardashian's baby shower. Meanwhile, her mind told her, *Don't you move! Don't you even crack a smile for her. You have no reason to be happy. She's having a baby not you.*

"Aw . . . G, I'm sorry." Junell rubbed the back of Grace's hand. "It's not too late for you to have children. Just because you had an abortion doesn't mean the Lord won't bless you with a baby someday."

"Well, what is He waiting for? It wasn't my choice to have an abortion. My mother and father convinced me that it would be best for me and for the father."

"What did the father think?"

Grace paused as the waiter arrived with their food. Right now she did not need someone looking for a come up to overhear this story and leak it to the press. The waiter took his time placing their plates gently in front of them. Then he snapped open their cloth napkins and poured them each a fresh glass of water. Grace knew he must have recognized her or Junell and was delivering the best service he could in order to walk out with a handful of cash.

"What would you ladies like to drink?"

"I need something strong," Grace said, peeling off her leather jacket. She looked at the list of cocktails, skipping over all the ones that ended with *ini* or had some type of fruit as an ingredient. "Gimme the Down in the Delta."

Junell looked at her over her drink menu with both of her eyebrows raised.

"Don't look at me like that, Junie. The strongest thing in it is gin. We both know I can handle a little bit of gin. She'll stick with the water," Grace said, turning back to the waiter. Grace snatched the drink menu from Junell and shoved it and her own menu in the waiter's hands. "Thanks, love." She patted him on the rear end, sending him away.

"You're not off the hook, Grace. What did the father think?" Junell said, pressing, as she propped her elbows up on the table and rested her head on her hands—a sure sign that she wasn't going to let this conversation go.

"We never really discussed it. He was being prepped to go into the ministry. We'd talked about getting married once I graduated from high school, but then I got pregnant, and his parents and my parents came down on me like a sledgehammer. The way they explained it, I would be responsible for ruining three lives." Grace held up her thin fingers and counted off. "His, mine, and the baby's. I didn't want that."

"What do you want now?"

"A drink." Just as Grace made her declaration, the waiter arrived with her drink. Grace stirred the ice in the glass. "I mean, you know the rest of that story. I went from the clinic to being on my own, and that wasn't the wisest choice. I was a sheep available for any wolf to devour."

Grace's statement was incorrect. Junell didn't know everything. She didn't know the things that happened on a set to young girls with no chaperone. Mama June had always been there for her.

"So, what's next? You usually follow up a drink with a man. You know, you can't keep running around with every Tom, Rick, and Larry and expect to have a family."

"Wait a minute. Who the heck is Rick? It's Tom—"

"Sssh . . ." Junell put her fingers up to Grace's lips like she was a five-year-old. "These lips are holy, and I'm not about to fix them to say some nonsense. You do know that the Bible says we're going to have to give an account for every idle word we speak, right?"

Grace twisted her mouth up to the side and sipped her Down in the Delta through a skinny red straw. There was no way a God who was supposed to be so complex would waste time counting her words.

"Listen, Grace, it says it right in Matthew twelve, thirty-six. Furthermore, He knows what you're thinking anyhow. So, you better just get it together, girl. How are things going at the church?"

Reclining farther in the square-backed chair, Grace took a long sip of her drink and let out an exaggerated sigh.

"Who is he? That sigh is most often followed by a 'Girl, you just don't know' story."

Horace's eyes and sly grin penetrated Grace's mind. The church was no longer just synonymous with pain in her head; it was now synonymous with a feeling that she could not yet name. Her attraction to Horace felt more magnetic than just a sexual response, and that was unusual.

"There's no 'Girl, you just don't know' to go with this story. His name is Horace, and if I had to guess what the name Horace means, I'd say it means hot, handsome, and flirtatious."

"Horace means timekeeper."

"How do you know that?"

Junell pointed at her tummy. "I've already begun the hunt for a great baby name. I'm not doing any of the out-of-this-world celebrity baby names, and I'm not doing the ghetto throw together of any combination of letters to make up a unique-sounding name, like Junell. Enough about me. We'll have plenty of time to talk about the baby. We have another six months to discuss all that, God mommy. What I want to know is, why am I just now hearing about him?"

Trying to drag this out for as long as she possibly could, Grace took a heaping bite of her po'boy and stuffed into her mouth a little shrimp that had fallen onto her plate. She had not mentioned meeting Horace, because she didn't feel like there was anything to tell about the six-four hulk of a man whom she'd met on a food pantry line. She would not have mentioned his name if she hadn't bumped into him during her walk over here. Or would she?

"Stop holding out." Junell tapped the tabletop, demanding more info. "You already know how simple Michael likes to keep things, not to mention he's away on business again. In the beginning it seemed like a wise choice to get married to an international real-estate magnate, but now . . ." She tsk-tsked, shaking her head from side to side. "Now I have to live vicariously through you. Spill the beans on this brother. Is he a minister? A deacon? Be careful. Those deacons are a little shady sometimes."

"Thanks for the info, but I don't have to worry, and you shouldn't get too worked up about Horace. It's a dead-end relationship."

"What happened?"

"First of all, he's no minister. I met him at the food ministry program."

"Oh, my gosh, that's so sweet," Junell said between bites of her sandwich. "He likes to help out."

"No. He was there for the help. I served him dinner the night we met. I must be getting desperate." Grace shook her head in disbelief at her own words. She was attracted to a man who could not afford to feed himself.

"So, what's the problem?" Junell asked, smiling innocently.

"What's the problem? Those hormones must be in flux already and messing with your good sense. He came on to me while I was serving him food. He can't afford to feed himself. Where would our first date be? The pantry?"

Junell gasped and covered her mouth. "Oh . . . this is so cool. It's a role reversal. You absolutely have to go out with him. You two are like Ruth and Boaz. Only you're Boaz. You have the ability to provide for him. To take care of him, encourage him, make sure he gets what he needs."

"Are you telling me to be a sugar mama?"

"No, just go home and read the Book of Ruth. And you'll see. Maybe God will work this thing out for you sooner than you think."

"Why can't I just get a man who has it together already and is established? A man like . . ."

"Like Ethan," Junell said, finishing Grace's sentence. "Honey, I think that ship may have sailed already. Why don't you give Horace a chance to dock his boat? You've been with worse."

Chapter 10

The bobbing treetops and wind-driven leaves helped Grace relax into her stance. Yoga was her first line of defense when she felt like things were getting out of control. Unfortunately, this time it had taken her too long to recognize that things were out of control. After lunch with Junell, Grace had opted for a yoga session, instead of the Bible study Junell had recommended.

"I shall not be moved. I shall not be moved," she repeated, standing in a warrior pose in front of her floor-to-ceiling living-room windows.

Grace shook her head. *No thee, thou, or shall.* It had taken only two days at Mount Carmel Community Church for her to revert to what she knew—the Bible. When she was a young girl, her mother would wake her up by singing "Bless the Lord, O My Soul." She placed her in every religious class, from vacation Bible school to the various youth ministries that convened at her church. *Honour thy mother and thy father . . . that it may go well with thee,* was how her mother had chastised her. It seemed as though the only words ever spoken in the King household were from the Bible, until Grace found herself two months pregnant. The blessings stopped, and the cursing began.

Braking the warrior pose to clutch her belly, where her baby once lived, Grace sighed. Filling the emptiness of her womb had once been her only goal in life, but as the pool of men who were not neurotic or narcissistic and were not on narcotics had grown slimmer than Kate Moss in her heyday, Grace had given up on finding Mr. Right. That longing had been replaced with the need for retribution, which burned in her like a wildfire.

"I've heard you're not in the getting business, so you probably won't ever answer this prayer, but I want those a—" Grace paused, staring up at the ceiling. "I don't have to tell you what they are, because you know what they are and where they are, and I pray that the same emptiness that haunts my life consumes them. I pray that they come to know loss and suffering the same way I know them—like the back of my hand. Amen." Having concluded her prayer, Grace returned to the warrior pose. With her arms outstretched toward the ceiling, she chanted, "I am a warrior. I am a warrior."

Her new therapist, Dr. Sternberg, had said that she internalized everything, especially the things that were negative about her, and then reproduced them in the form of rage-driven outbursts. Today Grace tried to internalize the warrior chant. "If I put in positivity, then positivity will flow right out of me." She elongated her arms and stiffened her neck, taking deep breaths between each chant and awaiting her metamorphosis.

Ethan stood in front of the cranberry-tinged metal door to Grace's unit. He fished through his pocket for the spare keys the firm had coerced Grace into giving him after her third arrest, in case of an emergency. Initially, he had resisted the idea as much as she had, since an emergency to the firm consisted of hiding any drug paraphernalia and pills before the cops came and fetching her makeup bag so that she could paint on remorse during her arraignment and sentencing. She had never gone to trial, thanks to Ethan. He was an expert when it came to poking holes in the defense's argument, and he was cunning enough to get witnesses to recant or incriminate themselves before even taking the stand.

A smile swept across his face once he finally discovered her keys. This visit was set to be a more cordial and delightful one. He was beyond elated to finally add some sunshine to what seemed like a case of torrential rainstorms in Grace's life.

Grace's plumb, arched backside greeted him. His eyes took on a life of their own and traced her silhouette, from the big toe that her left leg rested on, up her muscular calf, and to her meaty thigh. Blinking hard to fight back his former desires, Ethan tried to conjure up the image of Candace's round face. He swallowed hard and loosened the knot on his navy blue– and white-striped tie.

"Grace," he called out, his voice cracking under the pressure of desire.

He got no response.

"Grace," he called out again, noticeably breaking her concentration the second time around.

She lowered her arms to her sides and peered over her shoulder to see who it was that had breached every level of security she trusted in. The voice sounded like it had the distinct baroque quality that Ethan's voice contained. Since she'd seen so little of him in the past week, she really didn't believe that it was him.

Her eyes lit up upon making contact with his smooth brown eyes. It seemed as if she floated across the eighty square feet that stood between them.

"What did I do to have this honor bestowed on me?" Grace asked, placing her hand on her chest to add a bit of dramatic flair to her question.

"I came to check on you and—"

"Check on me? What happened? Is Candace busy today?"

"What does Candace have to do with this?" Ethan asked, slightly perturbed by Grace's line of questioning. "Do you think that I'd allow my relationship with Candace to interfere with my relationship with you?"

Grace took one more step, completely demolishing the imaginary line that existed between them. Her chest grazed Ethan's, arousing a feeling that he thought he'd laid to rest after the last bar fight Grace had gotten into.

"My hope is that nothing could come between us, Ethan." The tips of her fingers grazed the buttons on his indigo plaid J.Crew button-down. "But the reality of the situation is that I can't reach you when I need you, and I know it's because this woman has been monopolizing your time."

Ethan knew what she was fishing for and wishing for— the days when his entire life revolved around her, the days when he didn't offer just legal advice, the days when he assumed a more personal role in her unpredictable life.

Ethan took a step back, trying to ignore the pleading look in her eyes and her near nakedness, which would make this an opportune moment for him to get what every man in America fantasized about.

"Here." He dangled her spare set of keys in her direction. "We've both crossed boundaries we shouldn't have, and I apologize for that. I will not apologize for having a girlfriend or not being at your bedside the moment you wake up. You've been living for a long time, Grace, and now it's time for me to do my thing. I'd like to see my career grow, and I'd definitely like to have a friend of the opposite sex."

Instead of extending her hand to retrieve her keys, Grace stood there, her mouth agape, in shock. Ethan flung her keys to the right, aiming for the island in her kitchen. The keys skidded off the granite surface and hit the floor at the same time as her wounded heart.

"Ethan." She grabbed at his arm, preventing a quick departure. "You never told me why you really came here."

In silence Ethan flipped the flap of his leather, satchel and withdrew a script. "This came for you by courier today." He tossed it onto the kitchen counter to avoid having any physical contact with her. As much as he valued the companionship, comfort, and solace Candace offered him, his flesh was still weak when it came to Grace King.

Chapter 11

Grace picked up the script Ethan had precariously thrown onto the counter and hugged it to her chest. She ran her fingers along the edges of the paper and rejoiced over her second chance to do a film. She might not have the guy, but at least she got a gig.

Grace read the title page out loud, using her fingers to trace the letters. *"Pressure,* a screenplay by . . ."* She gasped for breath. She could not read the screenwriters name out loud. The script tumbled out of her hand as she choked on the name.

Javier Roberts.

The last time she saw him, she had hoped that would in fact be the last time that she saw him. Apparently, God had something else in mind. Her legs buckled at the mere sight of his name. Somehow he'd managed with this script to breach the fortress she had created around herself.

Nope. I refuse to get sucked in again. I refuse to give up my sanity for a movie.

Taking small strides, she walked to the steps that led to the second floor of her duplex apartment, then swiftly backed up and picked up the script from the floor. A peek into Javier's mind couldn't possibly be that bad.

She took in shallow breaths and turned the pages, studying the character description. Ria, an ingenue, was the female lead. Grace's name was scribbled next to it. Grace flipped the pages. The story seemed simple enough.

Ria moved to the Big Apple to make it big, landed a huge role in a Broadway show, and found herself alone in the theater with the show's producer, Derek, the night before the show was set to open.

Grace flipped back to the cast list to see who would be playing the role of Derek. The name she couldn't utter met her again.

Javier Roberts.

She let the script fall to the floor again and stomped on it repeatedly. The sick bum was trying to force her to relive the lowest point in her life. Grace had had to take Zoloft and attend some therapeutic hypnosis sessions to get over what had happened between them, and her nightmare was being brought to life again now.

"I am a warrior," Grace chanted, trying to reach for something higher than the valley she felt herself being sucked into as one of the worst days of her life played out in her memory. The chanting didn't work; she couldn't master her stance and crumbled into a ball on the floor. In her mind she found herself on the set of her first photo shoot with the award-winning Javier Roberts, getting her hair and makeup touched up.

When I stepped from behind the bright lights of the hair and makeup chair and onto the set of the photo shoot, I noticed it was eerily quiet. My eyes roved the set as I searched for a face I recognized, but even the lighting guy was off the set. I twisted my feet into an about-face and headed back to hair and makeup.

"Ahem . . . Where do you think you're going?" Javier called out to me from behind his tripod. "Get your tail back on this set. I don't have any time or memory to waste."

I shuffled back to the set and stood before him in a long-sleeve button-down men's shirt in orange. My dark skin glowed against the fabric.

"*Where is everyone else?*" *I asked.*

Javier stepped from behind his camera and slowly walked closer to me. He raised his spindly fingers and stuck them into my jet-black hair, which stopped midshoulder. I flinched.

"*Relax. I want to get that 'morning-after tousled hair' look. Hmm . . . no tracks,*" *Javier noted between scalp rubs.*

"*Javier, every black girl in the industry does not wear a weave,*" *I replied, smiling at his ignorance and his willingness to demonstrate it.* "*Where is everyone?*"

"*After I looked at your proofs, I recognized that you have some real talent. . . . Just look at this bone structure,*" *he said while stroking my high cheekbones with the back of his hands.* "*The way I see it, you are the next superstar, and when I work with supermodels, I only shoot on a closed set. Thus I dismissed everyone,*" *he casually explained over his shoulder on his way back to his tripod.*

I felt uneasy being on a closed set with Javier. The last time I was alone with a man, I wound up pregnant, and that was the last thing I wanted right now. I shook myself. Buck up. Be professional. Javier is a world-renowned international photographer with a wife, and the last thing he wants is an inexperienced model, *I told myself. I coached myself into trusting him.*

"*Lie down on the sofa,*" *he instructed, pointing to a modern, minimalist gray sofa in the middle of the set.*

"*How would you like me?*"

"*Sexy. Sex sells. Tell the story of that shirt.*"

I shifted into different positions, curving my foot and playing coy with the collar of the shirt. Javier complimented me and demanded more. He removed his camera from the tripod and came closer to me, calling out poses. "*Arch your back. Now cross your legs. Now open them.*"

When he said, "Now open them," I closed my legs.

"Come on. Open your legs, Grace." Javier placed his camera back on the tripod. "These photos are going to be great," he assured me. "Let me help you."

Javier walked over to the sofa, where I sat with my legs stuck together. He grabbed me by the ankles and placed my legs on top of the sofa. There was something in his eyes I had never seen before. It wasn't lust. It was something more salacious. His well-defined widow's peak made him look even more treacherous. No photographer had ever looked at me like that. His hands roved up my legs to my kneecaps.

"Open up," he said, trying to pry my legs open.

"No!" I screamed.

"Come on, Grace. Just open up a little." The more he begged, the tighter I squeezed my legs closed. The strength of my seventeen-year-old glutes were no match for the depravity of Javier Roberts. Forcing my legs open, he positioned himself between them before I could clamp them shut again. It felt as though he was trying to stuff all six feet of himself inside of me. He tore through my shirt and kissed my chest and neck over and over again.

I stiffened my body underneath Javier, thinking that he would stop. Instead, the more I resisted, the more excited and belligerent he became. Javier slapped me relentlessly until my head crashed against the wooden arm of the gray sofa.

"You're mine now," he whispered in my ear, pressing his fingers so deeply into my thighs, impressions of his fingertips were left behind.

I looked up into his demonic eyes and felt my stomach turn. I could hear my mother's constant warnings that my loose behavior was going to land me right in the hands of the enemy.

"Please, let me go. I won't tell anyone. . . . I promise. . . ." I swallowed hard, trying to keep back the Greek salad I had had for lunch, which was threatening to escape from my stomach and burst out of my mouth. My lips trembled as I tried to reason with Javier. *"No one has to know what happened. . . . I—I swear to God, I will never tell anyone. You can keep living your life with your wife—"*

Javier squeezed my cheeks together, causing my lips to form a perfect pout. He kissed me, then spit on me. *"You belong to me now. You won't ever speak of this. Do you understand?"*

Even though I didn't understand, and I didn't want to belong to Javier, I nodded my head. My body gave up its protest, and Javier Roberts usurped what little sense of self, power, and autonomy I had. When it was over, he carried me to the dressing room, then instructed me to clean myself up and go home.

"I'm going to need you on the set bright and early tomorrow for a Calvin Klein, and I'm shooting."

"I'm booked already."

"I'll unbook you. You belong to me now, and Javier Roberts always gets the model he wants." He sneered before closing the door.

I stood still for a long time, waiting for him to return, and when he didn't, I acquiesced to the weakness I felt in my bones. I collapsed to the floor, hugged my knees to my chest, and cried in the fetal position. The tears were supposed to be enough to wash away the pain.

They were not. When I was finally able to get up, I strolled to the liquor store a few blocks away from the shoot. I begged, pleaded, and then spent my entire day's pay in an effort to get one of the guys in front of the store to purchase some liquid therapy for me.

Today the tears that came down were as hot and heavy as those in the picture playing in high definition in her mind. Pulling herself up from the floor, Grace decided she could not handle this alone—she was going to need some therapy.

Chapter 12

Pushing the papers around on his desk halfheartedly, Ethan reviewed the documents before him. Grace was almost broke. Not *broke*, like she was going to be homeless, but broke enough that she might have to get rid of a property or two or auction off some of the designer duds she owned. Ethan sighed as his mind roamed to where his heart was—Candace. He wondered what kind of case she was working on today. It had to be a serious one. She usually called him when she took a break or had time between cases. He glanced at the clock; it was three, and Candace had not even sent him a text.

Avoiding the appearance of being thirsty, Ethan hadn't called her, but as the clock on his desk continued to tick, it became more difficult for him to resist calling her. Ethan reclined in his chair and reached for his phone on the Bose dock he had nestled behind his desk. As he reached for it, his phone began to chime. He looked at the number and smiled. It was some strange 212 number. Assuming it was Candace calling from the judge's chambers, Ethan whispered into the phone, "Hey, Candy. You know how to make a man feel good by sneaking a call in."

"Brother Ethan, if I had known you'd be this delighted to hear from me, I would've called you sooner," Horace said, laughing into the receiver.

Ethan brought his voice up an octave to sound as macho as possible and replied, "Ah, man, I thought you were someone else. What can I do for you, Brother Horace?"

"I was wondering if you had heard from Grace."

"Why? What did she do now?" Ethan loosened his tie and prepared for an onslaught of fresh accusations, which generally followed when someone asked if he'd heard from Grace.

"She didn't do anything, man. It's . . . it's just . . ."

"What happened, Horace? It's best if you tell me so I can take care of it," Ethan said, trying to dispel the slight sense of worry he'd picked up in Horace's tone.

"It's just that she hasn't been by the church in a few days, and I was kind of worried about her. When was the last time you heard from her?"

Ethan thought about the last time he'd spoken to Grace or seen her. While he was trying to enjoy his dinner at Serafina with Candace, Grace had called from the church and had ranted about a man. He'd dismissed her. Then he'd had to deliver the script for Javier Roberts's debut film to her. She had still had a little attitude then.

Horace cleared his throat and asked once more, "When was the last time you heard from her?"

"It's been a few days, Brother Horace. Do you need something from her?" Ethan asked, wondering what had aroused his concern. Was he the guy driving Grace crazy?

"No, just a little concerned."

"Are you sure there isn't something else troubling you?" Ethan asked, pressing, trying to squeeze the juice of the matter out of Horace. Ethan needed to know if this was a real concern, a nosy inquiry, or a call from one of Grace's potential suitors. Somehow he'd become the guardian of all things Grace, and even when he didn't want to be concerned, he couldn't help himself.

"Naw, man, it's all good," Horace replied. "I was just checking on her. I wanted to make sure she wasn't skipping out on us. You know what I mean?" He laughed.

"All right, brother. I'll look into it."

After he got off the phone, Ethan wondered if he really should look into the matter. Grace's disappearing acts weren't a new thing, but it had been a while since she'd pulled one. Ethan strummed his fingers on the desk and tried to convince himself that it wasn't necessary for him to check on Grace. After all, she was a grown woman. When was she going to take responsibility for her own actions? What would Grace learn if Ethan didn't allow her to work certain issues out on her own? He hated feeling conflicted. He needed a resolution, and he needed one now. Bowing his head and folding his hands on top of the table, Ethan called on the God of wisdom and asked for some direction in this matter.

No sooner had he said amen than Alice was half knocking as she walked halfway through his office door.

"Mr. Summerville, Javier Roberts is on the phone for you. He sounded pretty pissed off because of a certain model," Alice said, raising her eyebrows up and down. "I don't have to tell you which one, do I?" Alice folded her arms across her chest, as if she was the one who had been running to and fro for Grace all this time.

Ethan sucked up as much air as he possibly could, then exhaled through his nose to purge himself of all the negativity he could feel piling up inside of him. He picked up the phone and smiled. "Hello, Mr. Roberts. How is everything?"

"Please call me Javier. Everyone calls me Javier. Mr. Roberts is my mean and less handsome father," Javier said, laughing. "I need to know what is going on with Grace. The producers want to see her do a screen test, and I cannot reach her."

"A screen test?" Ethan shook his head from side to side. With his free hand, he signaled to Alice to call Grace. "I thought you said the part was hers," he said as calmly as possible, trying to conceal his anger. If there was one thing that bothered Ethan about this business, it was the pretentious people who pretended to have more sway than they actually had.

"Of course the part is hers, but the producers want to see her on film. They want to know if she's still got it, so to speak, in light of her recent run-ins with the law," Javier said, reassuring Ethan. "That's why I contacted her instead of your office when they asked to see her. I've been calling her for three days now, and I haven't received a reply to a single message. I know it's been a while since we spoke, but I thought that our history together meant something to her. Do you know what I did for her career?" Javier spat.

Ethan rolled his eyes and entertained Javier's delusions of grandeur. "Yes, yes, I know how instrumental you've been in her success."

"I photographed her exclusively for—"

"Five years," Ethan said. "You took her on several exclusive shoots and made her a household name." Grace was beyond beautiful, with her rounded apple face and soft doe eyes. She was every photographer's dream, with the physique of what the industry called an amazon—five feet nine, wide shoulders, and pronounced hips and breasts. And somehow she could contort that body into editorial poses. If it hadn't been Javier, another photographer would have figured out what to do with her.

"Then you understand that this type of behavior is unacceptable. She owes me at least a response. If I don't hear from her personally within the next forty-eight hours, she's going to be dropped from the film, and I'm coming after you for holding up production."

Ethan didn't know how to respond, and he didn't have to, either. Javier hung up on him after making that statement. Massaging his head with both his hands, Ethan summoned Alice into the office.

"Did you get her on the phone?" he asked when she appeared in the doorway.

"No answer. Do you want me to try her again, Mr. Summerville?"

"Don't worry about it, Alice," he said, rising to his feet. "Forward any messages to my cell. I'm going to find out what Grace King is up to now."

He grabbed his coat from the rack near the door and stormed out of the office.

Chapter 13

Ethan pounded on Grace's door, pausing between each knock, patiently waiting for Grace to respond. "This is ridiculous," he fumed, and then he proceeded to bang on the door again, his bangs coming in rapid procession.

Ethan's hope was that if he increased the fervency of his knocking, Grace would be motivated to open the door. He knew she was probably still angry with him, so she'd make him wait. After five minutes of knocking on her door, Ethan recognized that something might be tragically wrong.

Droplets of sweat began to stream down his face as he went through several possible scenarios. *She's not coming to the door, because she overdosed on pills.* He combed his mind, trying to remember what current prescriptions she had and if he'd seen any pill bottles in her condo the last time he was there. He couldn't recall any, nor could he recall a time when not having a prescription had stopped Grace from getting Oxycontin or any other pill she felt the need to pop. Maybe she fell and hit her head. *That's not dramatic enough for Grace King,* he thought. She did it; she committed suicide. The pressure of attempting to meet everyone's unrealistic standards of perfection with regard to her looks and her behavior and failing at it repeatedly had finally caught up with her, he thought. Maybe Javier's demand for a screen test had made her question her ability to transition from modeling to acting. Failure was frightening, and recently, failing was all she'd done.

His chest tightened; the rhythm of his heartbeat went staccato. Ethan began to wheeze at the thought of Grace hanging from one of the exposed pipes on the second floor of her condo or lying naked in a pool of blood after slitting her wrists.

Wiping the thick film of sweat that had collected on his forehead, Ethan removed his navy blue blazer, backed up, and tried to bust the door open with his shoulder blade. The door didn't budge, but he heard several bones crack. After the third unsuccessful attempt, he phoned the doorman.

"New Millennium Condominiums," Arnie said.

"I need you to come up here ASAP with the key, or send someone to bust this door down."

"Who is this?" Arnie inquired.

"This is Ethan Sum—"

"Oh . . . Summerville, right, Ms. King's lawyer."

"Do you want to know my sign as well?" Ethan snapped. He didn't mean to be flippant, but he didn't want to be held responsible for this tragedy, either. "This is an emergency. I need this door unlocked or busted down."

"Mr. Summerville, I'm afraid I can't do that. Technically, I shouldn't have allowed you upstairs without a key or approval from Ms. King, but I figured I'd use my discretion and allow you to go upstairs, but now—"

"Now you need to use your discretion and throw caution to the wind. Just think about it. When was the last time you saw her?" Ethan repeated nearly the same question Brother Horace had asked him on the phone.

Arnie paused to think about it. Ethan hoped he'd quickly conclude that he needed to take action, but Arnie remained silent.

"Well, man, are you going to open this door or what?"

"I don't have the key. Only the super of management can open the door. I'd have to call one of them up."

"Well, do something," Ethan growled. "Do you want Grace King's blood on your hands?" Ethan asked, trying to shift the blame for this mishap onto someone other than himself.

Ethan's prompting was enough to move Arnie to action. In less than two minutes the doorman was standing next to Ethan with his foot raised in midair, preparing to execute one of those door-busting kicks he'd seen Derek Morgan do on *Criminal Minds.*

"I could lose my job for this," Arnie said before one of his size twelve, black wingtip Rockports crashed through her door.

"I could lose Grace if you don't do this," Ethan murmured in a low whisper that only he and God could hear. "Please don't let me be too late."

Arnie was able to knock the door off its hinges, and the acrid odor that greeted them threatened to knock them off their feet. A mixture of dry heat, whiskey, and body odor welcomed them. Ethan covered his mouth and swallowed the bile that the stench in Grace's condo had elicited.

Ethan ran to the couch, where Grace was sprawled out. Careful not to step in the dry chunks of vomit, Ethan kneeled down beside her. He racked his brain, trying to figure out what could have sent her this far off the map. Pages of Javier Roberts's script were strewn all over the living room floor. Some pages had been rolled into little balls, some pages were covered in vomit, and some of them had been ripped up.

"Summerville, is she alive or what?" the doorman shouted from the hallway. "Do you want me to call an ambulance or the police?"

"No ambulance and no police," Ethan commanded, rising to his feet. He did a quick assessment of the situation. Grace was semiconscious and in the same teal racerback shirt and gray yoga pants he'd seen her in three days ago. Her skin looked like cracked wood, there was a bottle of whiskey tucked in the side of the couch, and bottles of gin that varied in size decorated the floor.

I can't call the police or the ambulance until this place gets straightened up, Ethan thought. *This will be all over the scanners, the news stations will be here, and my days as a lawyer will be long gone.*

First, Ethan tried to wake her. He shook her, he yelled, and then he banged on pots and pans.

"Water. Summerville, throw some cold water on her," Arnie stated.

Ethan darted into the kitchen. He snatched a paper towel off the silver spinning dispenser, held it under cold water, and dashed back to the couch. Ethan swiped the wet paper towel across her face. Grace jumped up, coughing and cringing, and then collapsed back on the couch.

"What's going on?" she moaned.

"I don't know, Grace. You tell me."

She lay there, unresponsive.

"Grace? Grace, you have to get up," Ethan said, shaking her languid arm.

"I can't." She rubbed her tongue across her top lip. "I can't feel my legs. You got any coke?"

"What?"

"Coke, dopamine, or anything in that family," Arnie explained. "She needs an upper. She crashed, and she wants something to help get her pumped up again."

The urge to smash Arnie's head in overtook Ethan as Arnie rattled off the kinds of narcotics that would be helpful in this situation. His ambivalent attitude was just enough to send Ethan over the edge. Ethan charged toward the doorman.

"That's why she's messed up, man!" Ethan grabbed Arnie by the collar and slammed him against the door. "You know way too much about this, man."

"Mr. Summerville, of course I know about this. Do you think she's special? A doped-up model is nothing special and nothing worth either of us losing our composure over."

The rational, logical, and legalistic side of Ethan agreed. There was nothing novel about a celebrity drowning his or her sorrows in alcohol or abusing drugs to dim the pain when the camera lights were turned off, but Grace wasn't a stranger or just a name to Ethan or to God.

As Grace leaned over the side of the couch, hacking, with spittle slowly dripping out of the corner of her mouth, he could hear the words ringing clearly in his heart. *For the Son of man is come to seek and to save that which was lost.* Suddenly, he remembered why he was there.

Ethan released Arnie, realigned the collar of Arnie's shirt, and smoothed out the wrinkles. "You're absolutely right. There's no need for either of us to lose our composure. Why don't you return to your post? I'll handle things up here."

"You sure, man?"

"One hundred percent." Ethan held his thumb up. "I've got this."

Arnie bowed and walked to the elevator bank.

Now finding himself alone with the mess that lay on the couch and the floor, Ethan paced back and forth parallel to the couch. Sunlight beamed through the windows, filling him with the warmth that this situation had zapped out of him. His first thought was to call Junell, who almost always knew what to do to get Grace out of a jam, but she was on the set, filming her show. Everyone at the firm had had enough of Grace's antics, so he decided that they would be the last people he called. With no other help available, Ethan called the one friend he had who was always there for him when his back was pressed against the wall.

Kneeling down in his two-thousand-dollar suit amid the vomit and the tattered pages of the script, he poured out the contents of his heart. "Father God, I come before you as humbly as I know how right now. Please, Lord, look upon Grace right now and have mercy on her. Lord, bring her back from the dark place that she traveled to in her mind with her body and spirit. Lord, you died so that she could be saved, and I beg you, Lord, to save her even now. I pray that you will forgive me for the harsh words that I have spoken to her, and if I caused this, have your way with me, Lord. Please deliver her from this oppression. In Jesus's name. Amen."

After Ethan finished praying, he remained on his knees, waiting for the Lord's guidance. The few minutes that Ethan spent on his knees felt like hours to him, but they were not unfruitful. He arose with a name in mind.

Candace.

The spirit urged him to call her. She was the last person he had had in mind. Actually, he hadn't thought of her at all. Ethan did not associate Candace's large brown eyes, anointed words, and faith that did not falter with alcohol-induced blackouts. Nevertheless, he decided to be obedient and call her. Candace picked up on the first ring, and when Ethan explained what had happened and asked for her help, she assured him that she would drop everything and rush over.

Upon her arrival, Ethan praised God for his omniscience. Candace took over like a surgeon who'd been called to operate in an emergency room.

"Get her into the bathroom. She needs a bath," she commanded, dropping her purse and coat on a bar stool at the island in the kitchen.

Ethan carried Grace to the upstairs bathroom, and Candace followed them up the steps. Candace ordered Ethan to go back downstairs, and then she entered the walk-in marble shower with Grace. She turned on luke-warm water and scrubbed her down. Grace's body shook in Candace's hands. Her speech improved from moaning and groaning to a few intelligible words.

"Thank you, Mom," she repeated over and over again, reclining on Candace's bosom.

"Grace, it's me, Candace," she said each time, but Grace still repeated the same thing, until Candace stepped out of the shower and then made the water colder in order to shock Grace's system.

Grace began to writhe like a fish out of water, flop-ping all over and sputtering curse words. She regained full consciousness and control of her body after a few moments. Peering through the glass door of her shower, she asked, "Who are you?"

"Grace, it's me, Candace."

"Candace? The court reporter?" Grace forcefully slid the shower door open and yanked a towel off the rack. "Why are you in my condo?"

"You blacked out, so Ethan called me over to help get you cleaned up before he takes you to the hospital."

Clutching her forehead, Grace winced. From the expres-sion on her face, it looked like her head was pounding like a djembe drum. She took a few short breaths and tumbled backward. Candace swooped down and caught Grace.

"What happened to you?" Candace asked, her words dripping with love and care.

"I don't want to go to the hospital." Grace moaned. Her brown eyes looked glassy.

Candace exhaled, relieved that she had not fumbled and dropped Grace. "I'll tell Ethan no hospitals," she said, leading Grace into the master bedroom. "I'm going to make you something that will help you out. Okay?"

Grace nodded, then looked down at the floor, avoiding eye contact with Candace. Maybe Grace was afraid of seeing herself, or maybe she was expecting Candace to spew fire and brimstone and condemn her to the pit. Yet those were the last things that Candace felt Grace deserved.

Sorry was the feeling that pulsed through Candace's veins. She was sorry that Grace's life was so messed up and was so intertwined with the life of her new beau. This much drama could lead only to destruction. But she refused to let the devil have his way in either of their lives. She stood in the doorway of Grace's bedroom, determined to prevent Grace from sabotaging her own. "Lord, I don't know why or how I wound up in this place, but, nevertheless, I am here. Please use me to demonstrate your grace."

After her prayer, she marched downstairs. Ethan was busy on his hands and knees, attempting to peel the pages of the script off the floor. Apparently, vomit and liquor were excellent adhesives when dry.

"It would help if you wet the floor first to loosen all that stuff up," Candace suggested, wrinkling her nose at the gunk all over the floor.

"How is she?" he asked, looking at Candace from over his shoulder. Just the fraction of his face that she could see sped up her heart rate.

"She's all right."

Candace opened every cabinet, looking for the ingredients her father used in his hangover soup. Most of her life, Candace had cursed God for sticking her with two alcoholic parents, but now, as she lit a burner on the sleek black electric stove, she recognized that everything in her life had a purpose.

"I didn't go to law school for this," Ethan complained, with his arms locked stiffly under the pressure of his weight.

"Gird up your loins," Candace sputtered from the kitchen.

Ethan's eyes were full of disgust, and his jaw was clenched tight.

"It sure smells good over there," he said in a polished tone, his voice brimming with appreciation, which contrasted with his jaded look.

This must be his courtroom voice, she thought while she minced garlic. "Ethan, can you get me a pot cover from the cupboard, please?"

Hopping to his feet, Ethan shuffled into the kitchen. After vigorously scrubbing his hands like he was an extra on *Grey's Anatomy,* he rummaged through the cabinets and pulled out a lid.

He lingered by the cabinets for a moment. Candace could feel him appraising her body with his eyes. His observation and silent admiration began at the nape of her neck, then twisted and turned with every dip and curve. Candace felt slightly awkward and aroused at the same time. She wanted to turn around and accost him with kisses, but she was still a little nervous about touching and kissing him.

Even though they had seen each other every day since they'd met, and had confirmed that they were officially dating during brunch on Sunday, they had not discussed how to handle physical affection. Candace didn't want to come off as one of those counterfeit Christians who were decked out in modest apparel and toted a Bible, but were willing to strip out of those clothes as quickly as they quoted scripture. Twisting her head slightly, she peered at Ethan over her shoulder. This moment was a slippery slope they were about to slide down.

She could tell by the way that Ethan's shoulders slouched that his spirits were down and that he could use a little physical comfort right now, as he was possibly thinking about all the negative publicity this situation with Grace was going to bring. Then he'd have to deal with the impact it would have on Grace's current probation violation. Even a small touch seemed like it would help make this situation positive. Getting physical under distress could also lead to some spiritual unrest, and Candace was done dancing with the devil when it came to lust in her flesh.

As she contemplated the spiritual ramifications that could come from being in such close quarters, Ethan groaned behind her.

"It smells good, right?" she asked purposefully to snap him out of his trance. Not only had his desires carried his mind and eyes away, but they had also somehow transported him to a spot only a few inches away from her. "It smells good, right?" she repeated.

Ethan inhaled deeply. Candace smiled. Her mom was right, as usual. The scent of jasmine and wild berries was a delicate and powerful combination that could bring any man to his knees.

"I don't think that's the soup. I think that's you," he said softly.

"Mr. Summerville, I do believe you're being a little fresh."

"I believe you're correct." He wrapped his arms around her waist and pulled her away from the stove. "Are there any objections?"

Candace giggled and leaned back just enough so that their bodies collided.

Chapter 14

The aroma of bacon, potatoes, and tomatoes demanded that Grace come downstairs. She applied some BB cream to cover up the cracks on her splotchy skin and dabbed on a cranberry lip stain. *How sweet of Ethan to send someone to cook for me.*

Grace dashed from her bedroom to the staircase just in time to catch what had to be by far the most passionate kiss Candace and Ethan had exchanged yet. Their bodies curved into each other, and Candace's back was pressed against the granite countertop. The ladle for the soup dangled from the tips of her fingers. She clutched Ethan as if he were the last man on earth. The heat that emanated from their kiss was greater than the crackle and hiss of the burner beneath the soup, which was now boiling over. Grace's stomach filled with a churning sensation. The contents of her stomach had already been emptied twice, so all that came out was a hacking sound, coupled by a dry heave. It was still dramatic enough to produce the effect that she wanted.

Out of either embarrassment or shame—Grace couldn't tell from her position on the steps—Candace broke from Ethan's firm grip and went back to stirring the soup. Ethan met Grace at the bottom of the stairs.

"Are you okay?" Ethan asked softly as his eyes scanned her face, assessing her well-being.

Grace turned her lips down to form a sultry pout. "No. I think I need to rest," she whimpered, shifting her gaze toward the kitchen.

"Candace, can I speak to you for a moment?" Ethan calmly requested, walking toward Candace. He'd picked up on the hint that Grace had dropped with her eyes. Ethan whispered into Candace's ear, offering her praise and thanks and promises of alone time soon to come before dismissing her.

"Thank you for everything," Grace called out, waving at Candace from the steps as she prepared to leave. A tinge of remorse plucked at Grace's heart as Candace exited, but she refused to give up the one good thing she had going in her life.

Ethan made his way back to Grace and sat down beside her at the foot of the staircase. She rested her head on his shoulder. Voluminous clouds floated past her window. Grace wished she could just jump out her window and ride the wave of clouds until the end of time.

"I know you told Candace that you didn't want to go to the hospital, but I think you should," Ethan insisted, breaching the calm that was slowly taking over Grace.

She shook her head sheepishly, like a coy little girl. "Ethan, do you know how many times I've had alcohol poisoning or ingested too many pills?"

Ethan shrugged his shoulders. "I lost count after my first two years of working with you."

"All they're going to do is pump my stomach, hook me up to an IV, and get on my nerves. I've already thrown up multiple times. I'm good."

Ethan brushed one of her stray strands of hair out her eyes and turned Grace's face toward his by gently nudging her chin.

Staring directly into his eyes, Grace felt naked. She squirmed on the edge of the step, prepping herself for the sermon that was bound to follow his direct stare and his gentle stroking of her hair.

"What in the world happened here?" Ethan asked in an accusatory tone, pointing to the mess that was still on her living room floor.

"I've got a little history with Javier Roberts—"

"I know that story already, Grace. He discovered you and photographed you exclusively for about five years, more or less."

"There are things about our relationship that neither you nor anyone else in this world knows about."

Ethan sighed and clutched his forehead. "Is this going to be a problem when it comes to filming? I hope not. I can call Javier and smooth things over, hopefully." Ethan walked to the window and planted his feet shoulder width apart and continued speaking to Grace with his back to her. "This is a big deal, Grace. Javier fought for you to have this role. Right now he's the only person in the western hemisphere who is willing to take a risk on you. He said that only you could portray the soul of this character. Do you think you can do it?"

Grace rocked back and forth on the steps. Of course she could bring this character to life—this character was her—but she didn't want to. She'd lived enough of her pain in the public's eye on Front Street, Broad Street, and Main Street. This film was where she drew the line.

"Did you hear me?"

"No. I cannot do this role. I can't." She rose to her feet, using the banister to support her still weak legs.

"You can." Ethan turned to face her. "You can." He repeated these words until they were face-to-face again. "Javier believes in you, and so do I. Let me get back to the office and try to smooth things out, since you missed an important preproduction meeting and screen test."

Grace grabbed Ethan's arms. "Please don't leave me here alone, Ethan."

"One of us has to do damage control. Stay here. Get yourself together, and I'll see you in the morning." He kissed her on the cheek and patted her hand softly before departing, leaving Grace alone with her guts on the floor.

Chapter 15

"Arnie, I did not call for a doctor. Don't let him up here," Grace said, holding her forehead.

"He says his name is Dr. Sternberg, and Mr. Summerville sent him here."

Grace rolled her eyes. "You know, I'm not in the mood for this," she grumbled half to herself.

"Listen, Ms. King," Arnie said in a whisper as he leaned in close to the intercom's camera. His forehead glistened like a full moon in the camera shot, and his earnest emerald-green eyes demanded Grace's full attention. "I don't know what the deal is with this doctor, but he's on his cell, telling his secretary to get Summerville on the phone, because he's getting paid regardless. Just let him up. What's the worst that could happen?"

"Go ahead and send him up."

Grace changed out of her pink cotton nightgown and into a pair of turquoise yoga pants and a black racerback tank in an attempt to make it look like she was returning to normalcy. Her fridge was still pretty naked, except for the leftovers of the magical soup Candace had whipped up the night before. Grace was pretty sure it was a home-made hangover cure, but she put it on top of the burner, anyway. By the time Dr. Sternberg reached Grace's unit, the air was filled with the robust aroma of bacon and potato soup, and Grace had managed to paint a little happiness on her face. She jerked the door open and drew it back until the hinges halted her.

"Hello," Dr. Sternberg said. "I heard that you had an episode."

"You've got some good sources, Doc. However, I'd rather not make it public knowledge. You can come inside if you'd like."

Doctor Sternberg took small, measured steps through Grace's doorway and into her condo. He looked at the couch, the stools in the kitchen, and then back at Grace.

"Doc, what were you expecting? The presidential welcome? This is my home. When I worked, I was barely here between gigs, and after each gig I went to the party to celebrate the gig, and then to the party after the party. I told you I need to redecorate." Grace smiled, recalling their first meeting. *It's not that bad*, she thought. Still, she wasn't about to divulge all her business to some stranger. "You've got two choices, the couch or the stools. What's it going to be?" she asked, walking to the kitchen to check on the soup, which was now bubbling on the burner.

Doctor Sternberg chose the stool. He arranged himself on top, removed his tablet from his satchel, and unbuttoned his moss-colored topcoat. "Is there some place I can hang this?"

"Give it here." Grace extended her arm across the top of the island. "You want some soup, Doc?"

"Sure. Why not?" Dr. Sternberg handed her his coat. "This story will be great to tell my grandkids. Supermodel Grace King served me soup in her condo."

Grace tossed Dr. Sternberg's coat in the skinny closet near her front door and returned to the kitchen. She scooped up a serving of soup for herself and Dr. Sternberg into two Aztec-themed bowls. Grace slid the doctor's bowl and a spoon over to him and then left the kitchen and trekked across the expansive living room floor. She took a seat on the couch and folded her legs beneath her. She blew into the bowl and peered up and down at

Dr. Sternberg. They both ate their soup in silence for a few minutes.

"Are these red potatoes or russet? They really hold the flavor well."

Grace shrugged. "I don't know. I don't cook. Let's cut to the chase, Doc. Ethan called you and told you what happened, and now you're here to give me something to keep me calm. I'm not a fan of antidepressants, but I could really go for a little Prozac right about now."

"I'm not that kind of doctor," he said and took another spoonful of soup. "I don't medicate my patients. I use psychotherapy to treat my patients."

"Psychotherapy? I ain't crazy."

Grace stood up and walked over to the island. She placed her bowl on the counter, stood beside him, and stared at him. This might have been only their second meeting, but she hoped that he could tell that she wasn't crazy. *Injured. Bruised. Disgruntled.* Those were a few of the adjectives that Grace would openly admit were applicable to her, but she didn't believe she was psycho. His silence made Grace tremble a little.

"Can you really label me as crazy after meeting with me formally only once and having a bowl of soup?"

Dr. Sternberg's eyes traveled from his soup bowl to Grace's face. His eggshell-colored skin warmed up a bit as his lips formed a smile. "Grace, undergoing psychotherapy doesn't mean you're crazy. I think you should start cooking. It is said to be very relaxing."

"So is Prozac." She chuckled.

"I don't believe in slapping a fresh coat of paint on a dirty wall to hide the dirt. That's what medication does. It masks the wound and clouds the mind. I try to treat the mind by getting to the root of the problem and providing you with techniques to deal with the issue."

"What would you like to drink? Coffee, water, or wine?"

The doctor's eyebrows met in the center of his forehead.

"I know there's not a lot of variety there, but I'm all out of whiskey," she added.

"Water is fine," the doctor replied, swiping the screen of his tablet.

Grace filled a wine goblet to the brim with purified water and handed it to the doctor. She remained on the opposite side of the island. "What kind of treatment are we talking about? I'm not checking into any facility or rehab center. I'm telling you that now, and you can tell Ethan I said that. He thinks he's pretty smart, sending you here, but I'm not going to allow you all to manipulate me and control my life."

"You'd rather alcohol and drugs control your life."

Grace bent over and rested her elbows on the island. "They don't control me. When I need a break from things, then I have a drink or two. They don't control me," she said, pointing at Dr. Sternberg. "Whoever your source is got that part screwed up."

"Close your eyes."

"I'm not in the mood for your little games."

"Close your eyes."

Grace gave in to the doctor's command. She closed her eyes and tilted her head back.

"I'm going to tell you what I heard, and I want you to tell me what the controlling agent was in each situation. A model slugged a reality television star in a nightclub. It was reported that at the time of her arrest, the model's blood alcohol level was point-forty-nine, and the legal limit is point-zero-eight. Who was in control?"

"Doc, I was angry. She was in my date's face, and I had just finished working a photo shoot where all the shoes were a full size too small. When was the last time you posed for six hours in six-inch heels that were too small?"

"A model was found semiconscious in her condo, lying in a pile of her vomit and surrounded by empty bottles of liquor."

The stiffness Grace felt in her backbone and the remnants of her recollection of those events gathered together and propelled Grace's head forward. With her eyes wide open, she said, "You think you know so much just because of those two little letters in front of your name." She covered her mouth and nose with one of her hands and inhaled and exhaled into her palm. "But you don't know me, and you don't know my story. Yeah, I get a little upset from time to time and like to deal with it by getting inebriated. Sometimes my plan doesn't work and people get hurt, and sometimes my plan works and I am able to forget what happened."

"Temporary amnesia induced by alcohol is not the answer for anger and whatever else you are holding on to." Dr. Sternberg took a sip of water from his goblet. "Forgetting your problems is not the solution to your problems."

"What do you propose?" Grace stood up straight, with her hands on her hips. "Ethan wants me to pray about everything, but I know Jesus ain't checking for me, and I'm not all that interested in Him, either. Haven't you ever been so angry that you just wanted to forget it all?"

"Yes, I have." Dr. Sternberg took a long gulp from his goblet. "After I published my first book, *What the You Inside of You Wants to Do,* my wife left me. She took everything. My money, my children, and my Rolling Stones record collection."

Grace stomped her feet. "Not the Rolling Stones. You sure you don't want any wine to go with this story? I know I have a little Moscato around here somewhere," she said, smiling.

Dr. Sternberg wiped the tip of his nose a couple of times and looked around the room before answering Grace. "No thank you. I once lived there in that fight, drink, forget zone. I fought everyone and everything I knew, including my home. At the end of my first month without her, every wall in my apartment had a hole in it, and I couldn't even recall how that had happened. At that point I began to meditate. I fasted for an entire week. By the end of the week I was able to see my role in the situation. I didn't want to forget anymore. I needed to remember so that it would never happen again."

Grace could feel her fine features drawing together to form a fierce scowl. "Fasting is a part of psychotherapy? I can't." She waved her hands in the air. "I can't do it."

Dr. Sternberg rose to his feet and walked over to Grace's side of the island. "I am going to touch you, Grace. Do I have your permission to do so?"

"Yes."

Dr. Sternberg gathered Grace's hands and pressed her palms together. "You don't have to fast. That was a part of my personal process. The process toward healing and wholeness is different for each one of us, but let's start with something simple that you can do with or without me."

"The last time you said we were going to do a simple exercise, I was dang near ready to jump out the window, Doc."

"I promise this is going to be simple. I want you to look down at your hands and explain to me how you feel physically when you get angry."

Grace followed Dr. Sternberg's instructions and shifted her gaze from his stark blue eyes to her hands. "My chest begins to tighten." Grace began to separate her palms. Dr. Sternberg pressed them back together.

"Continue," he said.

"My chest begins to tighten. I begin to sweat, and it becomes very difficult for me to hear. It's like I'm not . . ." She attempted to separate her hands again, and Dr. Sternberg held them together. "I am not a part of myself. I am a whole other entity when I get angry."

"I want you to focus on not allowing the anger to separate Grace from Grace. If it's possible at that moment to change your environment, do so immediately, and return when you come back to yourself."

"I'm supposed to just up and walk away while I'm arguing with someone?" Grace asked, attempting to separate her hands again.

"Your hands are getting warm and moist," Dr. Sternberg said. "That means you're beginning to get angry or frustrated, because you can't do what you want right now. Right now that loss of power is frustrating you, and you're ready to reclaim your power. Walking away is how you reclaim it. Every question doesn't have to be answered, and every point doesn't have to be countered, and when it's impossible for you to walk away, I want you to bring your hands together just like this." Dr. Sternberg held her hands up. "Your palms are you. When you feel that separation process beginning, I want you to force your hands to remain joined together, even if you have to interlock your fingers. Take deep cleansing breaths in through your nostrils and out through your mouth, and expel the anger. Refocus your energy on maintaining Grace, not lashing out."

"Do you know what you're asking me to do?"

"Yes, I know what I'm asking you to do. Do you?"

Chapter 16

"You know, you really put Mr. Summerville in a bind with your antics last week," Alice said between each pop of her gum as she stood behind her desk.

Grace just looked at her out of the corner of her eye, with one of her freshly arched brows raised. *Here I am, recovering from alcohol poisoning, and she wants to reprimand me.*

"Alice, my mama been dead for a few years now." Grace waved her hand to the side, dismissing Alice's comment.

"She must be glad she's in a grave and not stuck following behind yo' ig'nant self," Alice said, shaking her head like she pitied Grace.

Grace sat back in her chair, closed her eyes, and let her head roll back. An argument was brewing, and Grace was still on the mend from her little episode last week. She took a deep breath in through her nostrils, like Dr. Sternberg had taught her, and expelled the negative thoughts that had congregated in her head out through her mouth. Her hope was that the silence would motivate Alice to back down. When Grace looked up, Alice was still standing there, popping her gum, with her hand on her hip, like Grace owed her an explanation.

"Alice, don't you have work to do?"

"I sure do. I have to take out the trash, but I don't have any industrial-size bags to fit you into."

Grace rose to her feet. She was done conversing with Alice. All that "holding your palms together" business that she'd rehearsed with Dr. Sternberg went up the chimney. The only response she had left was a backhand slap. The kind that had to be administered up close and personal, the kind that would cause Alice to whip out her little vanity mirror that she kept tucked in the back of her top drawer and check to see if she was bleeding. Just as Grace pulled back her right hand, Ethan grabbed it with his left.

"When are you going back to anger management?" he asked, still holding Grace by the wrist.

"You know, I've been meaning to discuss that with you, Ethan. How could you let that doctor just pop up at my condo like that?"

"Let's have this conversation in my office." He pointed at the door. "Go on inside." He released Grace's wrist, then swiveled around to face Alice.

Grace shuffled past Alice, delighted to know that Ethan was about to reprimand her for heckling her.

"Alice." Ethan cupped her hands as she clicked away with the mouse. "I know you mean well, but you can't antagonize the girl. Why don't you take a break? Go and read a scripture, meditate, or do something calming."

"I heard that Boris Kodjoe was going to be in the office today. I'm going to patrol the office for him."

"He is married. You know that, right?" he asked, letting go of her hands.

"Yeah, but he hasn't seen me yet." She chuckled while pushing back her swivel chair. "In case I do bump into him, I'm giving you fair warning. Don't expect me back anytime soon."

Ethan winked at her before opening the door to his office.

Grace was seething on the other side. She had left the door cracked and had stood as close to it as she could in order to listen in on their exchange. The fact that

Alice's smart comments had somehow entitled her to a fifteen-minute break infuriated her. As soon as Ethan entered his office, Grace lit into him.

"That's it? Take a break? Go meditate? That's the punishment she gets for insulting your star client?"

"Star client, eh . . ." Ethan scoffed, leaving the door slightly ajar behind him. "I've got a few choice words for you, but I'm walking on the King's Highway." He walked to his desk in silence, with his head down, like a disappointed parent about to punish his teenage daughter. "So, you think you're my star client? Grace, you are my *only* client," he added.

"All the more reason for you to protect me from people like that." She contorted her lips into a frown and crossed her legs. The toe of one of her neon orange pumps grazed the front of Ethan's desk, creating a noise similar to a cat scratching at the door. She sat there, shaking her leg, which was usually indicative of an angry stew brewing inside of her.

"Are you serious?" Ethan asked, taking on a tone he had never used on Grace before. "You're my only client because I have to follow behind you, cleaning up everything in the path of Storm Grace. From behind this desk, you look pitiful with that bottom lip of yours sticking out." He pointed at her mouth with an arm of his glasses. "But if my memory serves me correctly, Grace King, you can be destructive as well. You don't need protection from Alice or anyone else. You're doing just fine damning yourself."

She interjected, "Don't get all Sunday morning on me, Brother Summerville."

"I don't have to get Sunday morning on you. All I have to do is go to last week, when I had to break your door down and when I found you semiconscious in a pool of your own vomit, which is why I asked Dr. Sternberg to do a house visit. While you were toasting the good life, I had to explain to Javier Roberts why you were not available for a screen test and why he can't begin filming this week. Your private party is holding up production of a film, which means that I have to run around begging the studio and the producers not to sue you blind."

"Sue moi?" she asked as reservedly as she possibly could. "Ethan, I did not sign on to do the film. Why would anyone want to do that?"

"Oh, but you did sign on," Ethan said, stepping from behind his desk. "I signed you on. Thus you're the lead."

"I didn't ask you to do that."

"Grace, when do you ever ask me to do anything? You make the demands, and I hop to it." He stuffed his fists into the pockets of his orange merino wool–blend pants. "Let me jog your memory." He strolled back and forth in the space between her and his desk. "You stormed in here on a balmy summer afternoon four months ago and demanded that I accept the first film, television, or commercial job that came through this office. I landed you the audition with Tim Story, and you wrecked it with that Soriah Sommers incident. It was either the Javier Roberts film or nothing."

The memory of that afternoon Ethan was referring to collapsed on her chest. She could recall how heavy her chest had felt under the pressure of desperation. The maintenance fee on the condo had been due, her quarterly statement from the firm had just come in the mail, she still had to pay off one of the people hurt in her club brawl at the start of the summer, and she'd just been hit with the criminal charges for her little tiff with Soriah. It was so clear that the old adage her mother had sputtered at her every time something went wrong was true. *When the devil comes at you, he comes at you like a flood.* The bills had been mounting, and modeling jobs had been dwindling. She'd been in an awkward space in her career.

By industry standards, she was too old to be young, and too young to be old. So she had tried to be realistic about her career: she needed to work.

Grace had had visions of receiving Oscars and Emmys for her work in film and television when she began planning her transition into acting a year ago, but by the time her reality caught up with her, all that had mattered was a check rolling in, since her party lifestyle and her lawsuits had begun eating away at her savings. She wouldn't have cared if they'd asked her to do *Snakes on a Plane 3*.

She folded her arms in resignation. It was true that she had been desperate then. "So now what?" she asked.

"Are you waiting for me to tell you that I have a plan to get us out of this?"

"No," she replied quickly. She didn't know what she was expecting him to do. She knew he had no idea what had transpired between her and Javier. She didn't expect sympathy, nor did she expect to be met with bitterness and hostility. "Maybe we should discuss this when you're feeling a little better," she suggested.

Ethan exploded into a round of uncontrollable laughter. "When I'm feeling better?" He slapped the shiny varnished top of his desk and continued to laugh. "I'll be feeling better when you're on the set of *Pressure* and I hear Javier Roberts say, 'Action.'"

Grace sucked in as much air as she could to inflate her chest before speaking to what appeared to be Mr. Hyde. "I am not going to star in this film."

"You are."

"I. Am. Not. And you can't force me to," she said defiantly.

"Well, your creditors can, this agency being one of them. You're near bankruptcy."

"Creditors," she whispered. Grace sank in the chair.

"Yes, creditors. It's time to pay the piper, Grace King. Let's just take this gig and roll with the punches. One check is all we need to start making some good faith payments. Of course, after you deliver an excellent performance, the endorsements, guest appearances on television shows, and more movie offers will start rolling in." Ethan moved his index finger in a circular motion a few times.

Grace tried to imagine filming that rape scene over and over again. Next to that, bankruptcy didn't seem like such a bad deal. Burying her head in the palms of her hands, Grace breathed in and out, trying to calm herself.

Once again she found herself having to choose between doing the unscrupulous thing that appeared to be right and going completely to the left.

Ethan continued speaking, rattling off his master plan and spewing words of encouragement, while Grace buried her head between her legs like an ostrich with its head in the sand. All his words became unintelligible. Not because Grace didn't believe him—he had plucked her out of a jam more than once—but because she found herself right back in the place she'd fought so hard not to be in again.

"Maybe we should pray on it," Ethan said, cutting into her thinking time.

"Pray?" Grace looked around the room. "You want *me* to pray? To who? To what God? A God that would allow this to happen to me again?" Her face began to wrinkle, and her voice cracked between each word. "I can't pray to that God. I can't, Ethan. Just can't." And then the dam broke. Whatever it was inside of Grace that had restrained the tears, it popped, and the tears were no longer obstructed. For the first time in as long as Grace could remember, she was able to cry.

Chapter 17

Ethan held his breath, searching for the next move to make. Consolation was not on the menu today. All he planned on serving her was a tally of all her bad debt and what she had to do to get out of it—the movie.

Her crying startled him and made the spot in his heart for Grace tender again.

While Ethan wrestled with himself, Grace continued to pour all of herself out. "I can't. I can't," she wailed.

Shoving all his logistical thinking aside, Ethan reached out to her. First, he placed his arm around her, and then he crouched down to her level to cut the distance between them. With his other hand, he cocked her chin upward until their eyes met.

"Grace, you can get through this."

She sucked up the remainder of her tears. "No, I can't."

"You can, and we will get through this."

"How?"

"Together," he said before being swept away in the moment.

Her vulnerability exposed his emotions, and his emotions exposed the desire he'd been masking for so long. Ethan was sure she could see it in his eyes, and he could see she needed comfort. Gradually, they leaned into each other, hoping to ease the frustration they were feeling.

Candace made a sharp left turn when she got off the elevator. She evaluated herself in the mirror before walking to Ethan's office. Her red lipstick made her skin beam, and her teeth seemed whiter. She smoothed out the wrinkles in the color-block white-and-black Vince Camuto dress she'd picked up at Burlington Coat Factory. She was out of her element when it came to high fashion.

Her ankles wobbled as she strode down the hall in red suede platform pumps. All this felt so unnatural, but during a talk with her mom, they had both agreed it was time to ramp up the wow factor in her relationship with Ethan if he was willing to dismiss her at the flicker of Grace King's eyelashes.

Coaching herself as she walked down the hall to Ethan's office, she reviewed the tips she'd heard the judges give contestants on *America's Next Top Model*—suck in your stomach, straighten your shoulders, and remember to smile with your eyes.

Candace had a hard time smiling with her eyes while gritting her teeth. Sharp pains shot up her calves with every step she took. She could already hear Alice making smart remarks about her sudden change in appearance, but to her relief, Alice wasn't seated at her desk.

Candace took a breath and waited a beat before making her way into Ethan's office. Even though the door was open a crack, she extended her fist to rap on it. When she did so, the door slid open, and Candace's jaw dropped. The burning sting of shock paralyzed her. In her head she was screaming, *Stop! Get your hands off him!* However, in actuality, not a single word came out of her mouth. All Candace could do was watch Ethan cradle Grace in his arms and comfort her with his supple lips. *Her* lips.

She eased the door open some more and stepped into the office. Her black clutch fell to the floor. The clatter that the clutch made when it struck the floor disrupted Ethan and Grace's makeout session. The glare that Candace directed at Grace caused her to freeze.

Ethan struggled to get his explanation out. "C-C-Candace, it's . . . it's . . . not what it looks like," he stammered.

Flashing the palm of her hand at Ethan, Candace walked directly up to Grace and slapped both of her cheeks.

Grace cupped her stinging cheeks in disbelief. She couldn't recall the last time anyone had pimp slapped her, because no one had. *Ever.*

Candace's hands shook like those of someone with Parkinson's. *What are you doing, Candace? What if she presses charges?* she thought. None of that mattered. Candace chalked up her newfound brashness to her red lipstick. Kicking butt was permissible if you wore red lipstick. She chuckled at the thought.

"Candace," Grace cried.

"Don't you dare. Don't you dare." Candace shook her finger at Grace. "You ungrateful wretch. Don't you dare call my name."

"Candace, I'm sorry," Grace said.

"You're not sorry. You're ungrateful. You're blind. You're too blind to see that your life has been seasoned with grace, too blind to see that God has blessed you and caused you to flourish in life, too blind to be satisfied with all that you have, and so you have to steal the little bone that I've been thrown," she said, pointing at Ethan. "And now I know why God suffered Naaman to be killed, because this type of betrayal is unbearable."

The fire of Candace's wrath caused Grace to break down in tears. Candace sighed, frustrated at the sight. Usually, those tears quashed any problem Grace had; however, those were not going to be enough to quench Candace's wrath. Those tears only aggravated Candace more. She was stretching forth her hand once more to slap Grace when Ethan decided to intervene.

"All right, Candace. That's enough," he said sternly while pulling her hand back.

"What's enough? Are you sure she's reaped everything she deserves when she walks around slapping people in the face all the time?" Candace spat.

"But, Candace, you are not the judge," Grace said.

"You're right. I'm the victim." Candace folded her hands across her chest. "Which one of us will you defend, Counselor?"

Ethan's eyes darted back and forth between Grace and Candace, as if the question Candace had just posed was a difficult one.

Instead of waiting to find out where Ethan's allegiance lay, Candace turned around and walked out the door just as quietly as she'd entered.

"Ethan, I'm sorry," Grace said softly. She tried to downplay the delight in her heart that he'd chosen her—at least that was how she'd interpreted his silence.

Ethan raised his tortoiseshell glasses and pinched the bridge of his nose. "Grace, let's not do this now. Let's work on getting things back on track. When do you plan on returning to Mount Carmel?"

Grace rolled her eyes. Community service was the last of her worries. Her future plans did not include returning to the church. "Do I have to go back?" she asked, pouting.

The trauma of revisiting her rape through Javier's script, compounded by Candace's slap, was enough pain for the whole month. Grace couldn't stomach spending any more time with those hypocrites at church, who, like Candace, spouted off verses of love and still criticized her life, as if they knew what was going on, as if they could endure all that she had. How could Candace even think Grace's life had been "seasoned with grace"?

There was a time when the church was a great place to her but after being ridiculed, rejected, first by her own parents and then the whole congregation because of a mistake, the church was no longer a refuge; it was more like a place of torture.

"You can purse your lips all you want." Ethan stepped behind his desk, creating distance between the two of them. "But you're going back to the church, you're going to do the darn movie, and you're going back to anger management. As a matter of fact, we're going to set that up for you right now." He picked up the phone and began dialing. With his hand over the receiver, he dismissed her. "You know where the church is, right?"

Grace nodded.

"Then get going."

Alone in his office, Ethan tried to figure out how he would get back into Candace's good graces. He called her twenty-six times and left her at least ten messages. The first ten times the phone went straight to voice mail, and the other sixteen calls were acts of desperation. He didn't want to walk out of his office after what had taken place that afternoon without getting a chance to share his side of the story. He wasn't the smooth and cunning type when it came to the ladies. Unfortunately for Ethan, he knew how to turn on the charm only in the courtroom. There he could be spontaneous, assertive, and comedic—whatever it took to win the jury was what he delivered. Yet when it came to the opposite sex, he was as inept as a toddler learning to feed himself.

After narrowing his apology strategy down to two methods—the Spike Lee, *She's Gotta Have It* "Please, baby" plea or the "Forgive me, as Christ forgave you" Christian guilt trip—he practiced each one in the mirror, weighing their effectiveness, the entire afternoon.

"How many times are you going to do that this afternoon?" Alice shouted over the intercom, daring to set him straight. "These walls aren't as thick as you think. I can hear you. You do know that, right?"

"Alice, don't you have work to do?"

"I suppose I could ask you the same question," Alice retorted. "But I'm not. What I will do, though, is make a recommendation. I don't know what you did while I was gone to wind up all alone and begging, but this is not the time to rehearse an opening statement or devise some tactical plan to divert attention and shift the blame. Now is the time to bare it all."

Ethan scooted his chair up closer to the desk, listening intently to Alice's advice.

"Tell her how you feel, admit that you did wrong, tell her why you did wrong, and apologize. If she doesn't accept your apology, you know what you do?"

"What?"

"Move on," she yelled. "I know you're looking for the one. I know you want Ms. Bible Belt to be the one, but if she's not able to deal with the truth, accept your flaws, and iron out the wrinkles in your relationship, she's not the one, and I recommend that you cut your losses now."

"Cut my losses," Ethan muttered, mostly to himself. "How am I supposed to do that?"

"It won't be easy. This will either make or break your relationship, boss."

"Thank you, Alice, for that 'facts of life' moment. Now get back to work. Please get Javier Roberts on the phone for me."

Chapter 18

"Who ran over your puppy?" Horace asked, nudging Grace's elbow.

Cracking half a smile, Grace eked out a sparse hello. She wasn't up for any chitchat this afternoon. It was Friday, and she was spending it in a church, which made her even more determined to hold on to the anger and sadness that had seized her.

"Where have you been?" Horace snatched a chair from the table to the left of Grace and sat down beside her. "This place hasn't been the same without you, Grace."

"I'm sure it hasn't," she said listlessly, without looking at him.

"You know something? I am so tired of you looking like a sad sack of potatoes, when God made you a lily. If you don't get anything else out of this experience, you're going to get some deliverance. Let's go," he said, snatching her hand so hard, she nearly flew out of her seat.

"Where are you taking me?" she demanded to know.

"To the sanctuary. The pastor is up there, and I want him to lay hands on you."

"Oh, no," she said in protest, digging her heels into the floor, to no avail. That only made it easier for Horace to drag her across the linoleum tiles. "I have to help Sister Bryce clean this mess up."

"I'm sure she'll figure something out." Horace came to a halt at the doorway. "Sister Bryce," he shouted across the dining room, "I'm taking Ms. King to the sanctuary to get Pastor to pray for her. Is that all right with you?"

Sister Bryce clapped her hands together in delight. "Praise God. Prayer changes everything, Ms. Grace. You gon' be all right now," Sister Bryce said, waving her cleaning rag in the air at them.

Grace cursed Horace and the rest of the gang of Holy Rollers, who were determined to get her, as they marched in single file up the steps that led to the sanctuary. They mounted the last step and entered the vast sanctuary.

The scent of the old wooden pews resting on top of the burgundy carpet and the sight of the hymnals strewn about reminded her of her first and only church home—Mount Moriah. Tears lined her eyes as she looked upon the scraggly pieces of wood that made up the altar.

"Hey, Pastor." Horace waved at a man who was hunched over between two pews, scraping gum off the back of the one in front of him. "When you're done over there, can you please pray for this sister over here?"

"Sure. Give me one minute to get the rest of this gum up," the pastor said, without looking up.

The smooth copper tone of the pastor's voice resonated in Grace's ears. There was something familial and intriguing about it. Deciding that his rich and welcoming voice was evidence that he was probably a good orator, Grace stepped forward to receive her healing.

The pastor stood up straight and dusted off his pants before turning to greet Horace. "Fill me, O Lord, with your words to say to bring about change and deliverance in the life being presented before me," he said, then pivoted around to face Horace and Grace.

"This here is Gr—"

"Grace King," Pastor David said, completing Horace's introduction.

"I didn't know you were a fan, Pastor David," Horace remarked.

Grace raised her eyes toward Pastor David and then backed up into Horace's chest. Pinned against him, she whispered to him through clenched teeth, "Is this really your pastor?"

"Yeah. Why?" Horace whispered back.

"I don't need him to lay hands on me. He already has."

Choking on his spit, Horace backed up and doubled over.

"Grace King," Pastor David repeated as he made his way across the sanctuary to get closer to her. By the time he reached her, tears were rolling down her cheeks in what seemed like two small brooks. "Where have you been?" he asked, reaching for her hand.

"Trying to stay far away from you," she said, snatching her hand back. "Isn't that what you wanted? Me far away from here so you could concentrate on your ministry?" She made air quotes around the word *ministry,* then awaited a response.

"Never once did I say anything like that."

"You didn't have to. Your henchmen did the dirty work and the heavy lifting."

"Henchmen?"

"I'm confused," Horace interjected, scratching the center of his head.

"Me too," Pastor David said, grimacing.

Grace wiped the tears from her eyes and began to chant, *I am a warrior,* in her head, trying to amp herself up to handle Pastor David's denial. First, he'd denied their baby, forcing her to get an abortion, and now here he was, denying that this had taken place. Denying the fact that on more than one occasion his parents and her parents had surrounded her like vultures flying over carrion and had stoned her with proverbs about adulteress women who destroy good young men. She hadn't wanted to be that. The last thing she had wanted to do was hurt

David, she thought when she gazed into his eyes, which he was still squinting in confusion.

"Get me out of here," she said to Horace.

"No, Grace, you are not going anywhere," Pastor David said, raising his voice. "You will not walk out of my life again without explaining yourself."

Grace laughed, and then an evil sort of chortle escaped from her throat. She could feel her blood pressure rising. "I am not one of your puppets. You cannot tell me what to do."

Pastor David reached for her hand again, and she backed up into Horace's arms. Grace was afraid that if Pastor David touched her even slightly it would all come back—the love, the desire, the longing for her child, who had been snatched out of her womb. Her drama with Javier Roberts and the kiss she'd shared with Ethan had been enough to keep her thoughts about the child she'd gotten rid of at bay. Now just looking at David made her wonder if it was a boy and if he would have had the same smooth birch wood complexion as his father. Batting back those thoughts, she looked up at Horace and tried to plead with her eyes for him to get her out of there.

Horace rubbed her shoulders and whispered in her ear, "I told you that you were going to get some deliverance. Your past is preventing you from reaching your future."

Grace looked up at him again. Not only was he fine, but he sure was deeper than she had him pegged for. Pastor David stared at her intently, as if that would bring the words out of her. Then he placed his palms together in front of his chest in an act of supplication. That was how he'd asked her out on their first date after church. Grace had rejected him the first time he asked her out during the break between the morning and afternoon services. He was thinner then and less muscular, she thought, taking note of the way the sleeves of his hunter green polo shirt hugged his biceps. She'd said no mostly out of obligation to her parents. They were raising her to be an elect lady, and elect ladies didn't date casually. They married. When she was fifteen, marriage wasn't something she was interested in, so she'd humbly declined.

Then David had cornered her after choir rehearsal in the kitchen of Mount Moriah. She was leaning on the soft gray granite countertop, waiting for some water to boil. Her throat was sore from belting out "I'm Going Up Yonder," and her mother had insisted she drink some tea so she'd be ready for the evening service. When he crept into the kitchen, Grace had pretended not to notice him.

He must have been thinking of that moment too, because a wide grin spread across his face, just as it had that day when her eyes softened and she agreed in a gentle whisper to go on a date with him.

"Grace," he said hesitantly.

Grace raised her head high enough for their eyes to meet.

"Please," he said, his hands still folded in front of his chest.

Rubbing her head, Grace realized that if she said yes to Pastor David this time, it wouldn't be as pleasurable for either one of them as their first date had been. Her chest tightened, and she heaved out a hard, "Yes, but can we sit down?"

Pastor David nodded and slid into a pew to the left of him. Horace supported Grace as she wobbled to the pew, and then he held her elbow as she lowered herself onto it. "I'm going to leave you two alone," Horace said tepidly, turning away from Grace.

Extending her long arm, Grace reached for Horace and caught his pinkie. "Don't leave me alone," she mouthed to him. There was no guarantee that after hearing her confession, Horace would remain a Grace King supporter, but that didn't matter to Grace. For now, at least, she had a supporter.

Horace stepped back, the floorboards creaking ever so slightly under him, and sat next to Grace. Both men looked around the sanctuary, avoiding eye contact with each other and with Grace. Horace looked straight ahead to the pulpit, and Pastor David fixed his eyes on a black spot on the carpet.

"You were being groomed for the ministry is what they told me," Grace said, breaking the awkward silence.

"Who said?" Pastor David asked eagerly.

Holding her hand up, Grace said as calmly as possible, "Please don't interrupt me. I've been carrying this pain for fifteen years." She turned to Horace, whose gaze was still fixed in front of him. He placed his hand on her knee and squeezed it gently, encouraging her to continue.

Grace went on. "I was sick for about a week straight, vomiting, fainting, and whatnot. My father declared that Jesus was going to heal me about three days in, and by the end of the week my mother was in my room, sniffing me like a bloodhound. She said I smelled like copulation, and dragged me to the doctor while my daddy was at work." Grace's heart rate sped up, just as it had when she'd sat with her mother in the waiting room of the doctor's office. She could feel the tears forming ranks around her eyeballs. The front line was ready to begin marching down her face.

"Grace," Pastor David cooed.

"I'm fine." She swallowed her hardness and bitterness. "I was two months pregnant. My mother didn't speak to me on the way home, except to tell me not to say a thing to you. She assured me that she and my father would talk to you and your family and the whole thing would be resolved," Grace said, spreading her hands out like she was clearing the air.

After a short pause, Grace crossed her legs and leaned back on the pew. "For most of the week my mother was silent, and my father kept calling me a jezebel and saying I'd put a curse on my own child by having a fornication baby." The tears began to fall. Grace swiped them from her high cheekbones. A montage of all the sights, conversations, and accusations flashed before her. The woman at the clinic who explained that abortions were safe, private, and the best option, because if you gave your child up for adoption, there was no way of knowing where the child would end up. Then there was the multitude of Bible verses that damned her, which were served as appetizers during dinner, with another round for dessert.

Horace must have sensed that she was coming apart at the seams with each word. He took her right hand and tucked it into his and began massaging it.

Grace shook her head and cleared her throat as she turned to face Pastor David. "At the end of the week your parents and my parents sat me down in the conference room and explained to me that I could not have this baby. It would ruin your career in the ministry before it even started. I . . . I . . . couldn't believe it."

Pastor David snapped his head up from the floor and directed his piercing gaze at Grace. "Then why did you?" he asked, his voice full of indictment. Once again Grace was the guilty one.

"They said you didn't want the baby." Her top lip quivered. "They said you wanted only to focus on the ministry." She sobbed loudly.

"Grace, why didn't you come to me?" he demanded, standing up. "I would have never agreed to that." His eyebrows were bunched together, and one eye rolled up, as if he was searching the card catalog of Bible verses in his head to support his stance. "Proverbs six clearly tells us that God hates the shedding of innocent blood," Pastor David spat at Grace. "I would have never authorized you murdering my baby," he shouted at her.

"Pastor, why don't you just take it easy?" Horace stood and reached out to pat Pastor David on the shoulder.

Pastor David batted Horace's hand away from him. "Don't tell me to take it easy. You don't have anything to do with this." His countenance had turned from a delightful warm brown to a darkened hue. He'd been betrayed, and it infuriated him to the bone.

"But I know who does," Ethan declared as he ran down the aisle of the sanctuary toward them.

Grace stood up at the sound of Ethan's voice. She felt like she'd just got caught stomping around the house in her father's work boots. She was in trouble.

Wagging his index finger at Grace, Ethan began his tongue-lashing. "Grace King, once again you've found a way to disrupt the atmosphere. I didn't think you could do that much damage in a church."

Grace was stunned by Ethan's accusation and froze for a moment. This time she was the injured party, and he still felt the need to come down on her. When she regained control of her faculties, she drew her hands to her mouth, trying to keep the obscenities inside of her tucked away. She knew some of Ethan's anger stemmed from the rupture that the kiss they'd exchanged had caused in his relationship with Candace, but this was not the place to hash that out.

Horace wrapped his arm around Grace and pulled her close to him, shielding her from this attack. "Gentlemen, the time has expired on this discussion," he said with a straight face.

Ethan's smooth lips curved into a scowl, and Pastor David's eyebrows folded together. They were bemused, and Grace was amused. For once it seemed that God was on her side. Smiling, Grace recalled what Junell had said. *Horace means timekeeper.*

Wrapping her arm around his waist, she cooed, "Horace, please take me home."

Chapter 19

Pastor David plopped in the pew beside Ethan and slid down. He looked like a helium balloon running out of air. Ethan was at a loss for words. Generally, he sought out counsel from Pastor David in the confines of the upper room—a conference room on the second floor of the church that Pastor David used for his counseling sessions. Now Pastor David looked like he could use someone to speak comforting words to him.

Ethan walked around the bench and sat next to his pastor. He tried to direct his gaze in the same direction as Pastor David's but could not. Pastor David's eyes were glossy, like cat eyes, and filled to the brim with tears, and though he was staring straight ahead, his gaze was fixed within. Usually, Grace didn't do this much damage that rapidly.

Ethan was out of his comfort zone when it came to dealing with matters of the heart. He was used to preparing contrived speeches that tugged on the heartstrings of an audience or a judge whom he'd handpicked, and wherever possible he had avoided emotional exchanges. He had become a legal shark and could smell any defense attorney's weakness before he or she even entered the room, which meant most of his cases hardly ever went to trial. What could he say now? There really wasn't any legal jargon he knew that would serve as a salve for a broken heart. And there was no eloquent way to say, "Pastor, you really picked the wrong girl."

Looking away from the pastor, stroking his goatee, Ethan stared out the window and tried to figure out what the next move would be now that Grace had run out of the church with Horace and had left the pastor slumped on the pew. Through the window, he watched a bulldozer move up and down, lifting up loads of earth and discarding them. Wishing that he was a building under construction, the words "I want to be gutted" slipped from his mouth.

"I have been gutted," Pastor David said, still staring straight ahead. He squeezed the bridge of his nose and sighed. "She's gotten away from me again."

"Again?" Ethan said quizzically. "What do you mean, again?" he asked, hoping there was a good explanation for what he had just heard. Ethan wished he had minded his own business, but when he had peered into the sanctuary minutes ago, he had felt good. He'd thought Grace was finally going to get the sermon she needed to set herself on the road to the straight and narrow. Instead, Ethan had discovered that she had been impregnated by the pastor and had had an abortion. He still wasn't sure how Horace factored into the equation.

"Brother Summerville," he put his hand over his chest. "I wanted to marry her."

"Marry Grace!" Ethan laughed heartily at the thought. "Grace a first lady? I don't know about that," he said, shaking his finger. "Your church would definitely be packed, even during football season, if she was sitting on the pulpit." Ethan bit his top lip as an image of Grace flashed through his mind. Her beauty was unexplainable, and most likely, that was what had brought the pastor to his knees, he thought. "Pastor, in only a matter of two weeks, Grace wound up pregnant and had an abortion, which isn't possible, unless this affair had been going on prior to her placement here. Can you explain what's going on?" Ethan wished he could call the words back. After all, just a few days ago he was all tied up in a kiss that was dripping with desire, when all he wanted to do was comfort Grace.

Pastor David sat up straight in the pew. He cocked his legs open and rested his forearms on his thighs and began his exposition. "I knew Grace King before she was Grace King—when she was just a stick. She was smaller than this when we met." He held up his pinkie finger. "She was a beauty then and sweet," he said, inhaling and exhaling deeply. What you caught was the tail end of our conversation. Grace aborted the baby about fifteen years ago. We hadn't seen each other since then. We used to attend the same church, Mount Moriah, over on a hundred twelfth. She was in the choir, and I was being groomed for the ministry. Apparently, our parents got together and bullied her into having an abortion. This is the first time I've seen her since then because . . ."

"Because she ran away from home," Ethan said, finishing Pastor David's sentence. Now it was his turn to slump down on the hardwood of the pew. If he could, Ethan would have pulled up the burgundy carpet and the creaky floorboards beneath the carpet and hid. He'd been wrong about everything.

"No, she ran away from me. I was supposed to rescue her from her father and his perverse interpretation of the gospel. Instead, they convinced her that I wanted her to have the abortion, and she ran for her life." Pastor David shook his head, fighting off the tears, and made a hiccuping noise, which he usually made when he didn't want to get too emotional while preaching.

"Now, how are we going to get her back?" Ethan asked, mostly to himself.

"I was hoping you knew the answer to that," Pastor David said, looking over his shoulder at Ethan.

***

Grace's hand shook while she twisted the key to the top lock of her condo. She felt like she was sneaking a boy into her parents' house. She looked back at Horace's statuesque frame and licked the corner of her mouth. It had been a long time since she'd had a sip of anything as sweet as him. *Pull it together, Grace.*

"You know, I don't have to come in." Horace wrapped his hand around hers as she struggled to pull the key out.

"Please, Horace, it's no trouble at all," she replied, pushing the door open. Grace held the door open and let Horace in. "Welcome to my humble abode." She smiled.

Horace looked around the condo with one raised eyebrow. Grace couldn't tell whether or not he liked the place. For some reason, she wanted to please him desperately. He walked cautiously through the kitchen, running his fingers along the top of the granite island, looking back at Grace for permission to enter the living room.

Grace nodded and hit the button on the remote sensors so that as Horace walked into the living room, the window treatments slid open. Horace shook his fingers rapidly before snapping them.

"Dang, Ms. King, you really got it going on."

Horace stood, his legs spread apart, in front of the floor-to-ceiling windows with his hands crossed in front of his chest, observing the Harlem night. Grace tossed her keys and purse onto the island and strode to Horace's side. She slipped her arm through the gap made by his arm and clasped his bicep. It was curved and pronounced, just like the half-moon that hung over the park, illuminating the entrance and pond. Cars and bikes whirred through the intersection below them.

"I'm sorry," he whispered, still staring out the window.

"For what?"

"I'm sorry about what happened back at the church." He didn't flinch, and he didn't blink. He just stared. "I didn't mean for things to go that way."

"Horace, it's not your fault. How could you have known what was going to happen?" Grace shrugged her shoulders and rested her head on his solid bicep. She felt his eyes on her now. "What you did was actually helpful. I've been carrying that pain for fifteen years, and now that's one less thing I have to be angry about."

"Angry?" he puffed, as if she had just cussed. "What do you have to be angry about? You're sitting on top of the world." He pointed to the crowd below.

There were police cars and ambulances parked on the corner, and had it not been for the view, Grace would have never known. They were so high up in the air, she could barely hear any of the sounds traditionally associated with city living—sirens, loud music, and street fights.

"No, *you're* on top of the world, church boy," she retorted. "You've got Jesus and the rest of that Kool-Aid y'all be sipping after the service to make you feel good." She withdrew her arm and backed away from him a bit.

Horace turned to face her. His glare scorched her skin like sun on a summer day. Grace spotted a hint of displeasure; however, he was too poised to let that trickle out. He licked his lips and asked, "What do you do when you want to feel good?"

He stepped closer to her. Even through his sweatshirt Grace could make out the ripples in his chest. If she stared any harder, she was sure she'd be able to determine whether he had an eight-pack or a six-pack. Grace inched forward so that their bodies collided. Her smooth, soft flesh juxtaposed against his warm, hot chocolate body sent a rippling sensation through her body. Her thigh trembled slightly against his as she inhaled fragments of his day—a crisp, clean linen scent mingled with the scent of plaster, no doubt from a job he'd worked on earlier.

Horace looked down at her and stroked her cheek-bones slowly. Grace curved her body slightly, giving him permission to take her. Horace pecked at her lips gently, then rolled his tongue along the line of her neck.

"Uhhh," she moaned into his ear.

"Grace. What are we doing?" Horace asked. Her moan had broken the trance she'd put him in.

She flung her arms around his neck and nibbled at the bottom of his earlobe. "What I do when I want to feel good."

Wedging his arms between hers, Horace broke her grip like a kung fu master. He wiped his lips and cleared his throat into his hand. "As much as I want you, Grace, I don't want you like this."

"How *do* you want me?" She pressed her chest against his and wrapped her slender arms around his waist, biting down on her bottom lip, awaiting his reply.

"I want you whole," he said, slowly resting his arms around her neck. "Grace King . . . I want you whole."

Chapter 20

"Whole?" Grace guffawed, slamming her kombucha on the table. "Junie, what type of Holy Ghost rap was that?"

Grace stared intently at her best friend, hoping she had a better understanding of Horace's last words to her before he walked out of her condo last night. She'd spent most of the night on her iPad, combing through commentary on BibleStudyTools.com, trying to find a biblical reference that matched Horace's statement. All her clicking had only led Grace back to the same statement. *Thy faith hath made thee whole.*

Junell remained silent.

"Well?" Grace nudged Junell, whose gaze was fixed on the amalgamation of dry leaves that had gathered in the gutter across the street from the Chelsea coffee shop they were sitting in.

"I'm sorry." Junell shook her freshly colored chestnut-brown bangs out of her eyes. "I totally spaced out on you. Blame it on the baby." Junell rubbed her stomach and smiled widely, reminding Grace of the announcement she'd made just a few weeks ago. "He said he wants you whole?" Junell asked, making sure she understood the matter being examined.

Grace bobbed her head up and down.

"Have you read Ruth yet?"

Grace turned down her lips and arched her eyebrows. The Bible had become like kryptonite to Grace over the years.

"I'll take that as a no." Junell raised her finger and pointed at Grace's face. She leaned back in her chair, took a deep breath as she raised her leg to cross it, and exhaled once, positioning herself comfortably. "Grace, he wants a whole woman, a woman who is not broken. I love you, but until you let Jesus in, you're not whole. You gotta surrender."

"I like your bangs," Grace stated effortlessly, diverting the conversation away from her conversion. "Who cut your bangs? Maybe I should get some. What do you think?" Grace ran her fingers through the front of her hair, which was now parted to the side.

Junell looked at the people seated beside them, leaned in, and whispered, "It's a wig. My hair is starting to fall out, and my mother says I can't cut it while I'm pregnant, or the baby will be bald, or some nonsense like that." She chuckled. "Now back to the subject matter at hand." Junell clapped her hands together and drew her closed palms to her face. "Any good Christian man worth his weight in salt would not accept you in your condition. Grace, you're like a half-baked potato. Serving a few meals in a church doesn't make you Mother Theresa, and the man wants substance."

Substance. Whole. Salt. The words sucked Grace's power from her. Everyone around her was speaking in metaphors and measurements, and she could not match those words. She rested her cheek on the palm of her hand and gazed out the window of the Chelsea coffee shop.

"When are you going to begin filming with Javier?" Junell asked.

Grace raised one eyebrow and glared at Junell.

"It's no secret that you're holding up production, Grace. You've got to give me something. Everyone is asking me questions, and I have no idea what to tell them."

Grace smacked the ceramic countertop. "Why don't you tell them to mind their f—"

"Grace! Have you taken to cursing again?"

"I need a drink." Grace swiveled around on the metal stool and hopped off it. She was grateful for this new coffee spot. Only in Chelsea could you find a place that served coffee, kombucha, and wine. For this conversation, Grace would have preferred a glass of whiskey; however, wine was enough to take some of the edge off. "You want something?" she asked Junell dryly.

Junell pointed down at her baby bump. It was barely noticeable now. It looked more like Junell had skipped some of her SoulCycle classes and was bloated rather than pregnant.

"Well, I'll drink yours," Grace said, strolling toward the wine counter behind them. Cracking half a smile at the guy behind the counter, Grace ordered two glasses of red wine and biscotti. Grace slid her credit card across the counter and watched intently as he prepared her order.

Slowly, he drew the biscotti out of the white ceramic canisters that cradled them, but poured her wine quickly. Grace took a sip out of one glass and cradled the second glass and the biscotti in her other hand as she took long, pointed steps back to their window seats, channeling her early runway-walking lessons to maintain her balance.

She set the glasses on the countertop and caught Junell staring at them and then at her. Grace shrugged her shoulders. "What? I told you I'd drink yours for you." She reclaimed her seat in the window of the coffee shop and bit into a biscotto, letting the crumbs gather at the sides of her mouth. Between bites, she grumbled, "You want to know why I'm not filming with Javier?"

"If you're going to get crazy and all worked up about it, then no." Junell folded her hands over her slight belly. "I have to be back on the set in another hour, and I don't need you freaking me out."

Grace blinked her eyes multiple times and looked her friend up and down. She'd never once cared more about filming a scene than what Grace was going through. Grace wondered if that was because of the baby or because Junell had just simply grown tired of the multitude of issues that seemed to follow Grace everywhere she went.

"Must be a difficult scene," Grace said offhandedly. She looked into her glass of wine, trying to hide her disappointment in the burgundy liquid in her glass.

"It's beyond difficult." Junell rubbed the center of her forehead, as if thinking about it was exhausting. "You know, getting pregnant while filming is difficult, and the writers have decided to write my pregnancy into the story, rather than write me off or have me go on a hiatus. So, I'm going to sleep with the captain of the squad this evening."

"Oh, yeah!" Grace perked up a bit. "Isn't the captain married?"

"Yes. Apparently, my character has been secretly in love with him since he was her teacher at the academy, and they finally have the opportunity to do the deed."

"All the Christian sisters that support you are going to be up in arms."

"I know." Junell tsk-tsked. "I had to repent so many times while reading the script. I don't think I'm going to make it through this scene."

Grace looked up from her wineglass and stared at Junell. A wet film covered her eyes. Junell was so worked up about this scene, she was oblivious to Grace's pain. She let the tears run down her cheeks. They rolled slowly over her cheekbones, creating streaks on her flawless face. Grace bent over and rested her head on the countertop they were seated at.

Junell rubbed Grace's back. "G, are you all right?" she whispered, bending over Grace.

Raising her head slightly, Grace turned in the opposite direction of Junell's coos of comfort. She let the sobs and nose sniffing flow freely.

"Come on. Talk to me, Grace. People are starting to look at us."

"Let them look," Grace spat. She sat up, picked up a napkin, and blew her nose. Her chest tightened so much, she could feel her heart rattling around inside of her. She wanted to jump through the picture window they were seated in front of to escape Junell. She'd expected more from her than this. Closing her eyes, Grace let her head fall to her chest and buried her chin in the layers of her gray wraparound scarf.

"People have been looking at us for a long time," Grace said. "Isn't that the business we're in? You're a model turned actress. Aren't you used to being looked at already? Or are you suddenly bothered because this is your real life that people are looking at?" Her voice dropped. "This is your friend breaking down, not some character on one of your little episodes."

Grace slid off the stool and turned toward the door. Junell reached for Grace's arm and caught the elbow of her oversize tribal-print cardigan. Grace had meant to move faster than that, but the heaviness of her wounded heart had slowed her down.

"Grace, what's going on?"

Their eyes met. Junell's large brown eyes zigzagged from side to side, as if she possessed the power to scan Grace's brain.

Breaking eye contact, Grace looked down at the raw, untiled floor of the coffee shop. She cupped her own arm and slowly pulled her cardigan out of Junell's grasp. "Now's not a good time to discuss it. People are looking," she whispered, backing out of the coffee shop.

Chapter 21

Grace scurried out of the coffee shop and across Eighth Avenue as quickly as she could in her wedges. She never looked back. She knew Junell well enough to know she would follow her out of the restaurant and would go to extreme lengths to right every wrong. Grace didn't want any of her apologies right now; she wanted to slap the mess out of her best friend for being more concerned about who was around them than what was going on with Grace. *She done got all Hollywood on me*, Grace thought. She slapped her hand against her thigh at the realization that she might be in danger of losing her friend to her newfound success on television, and then there was the baby on the way.

As she waited for the light to change at the next corner, Grace felt the soft vibration of her cell phone against her thigh. Her heart contracted a bit with the hope that it was Horace calling or texting to check on her. Ignoring the traffic light, Grace broke one of the cardinal sins in New York—do not block traffic. She tuned out the insults flung at her from those who had to walk around her and withdrew her phone from her pocket.

My office. ASAP.

Grace's heart plummeted. Two things were wrong. Ethan was in the office on a Saturday, and he was texting. It was never a good sign when Ethan wanted to see her

ASAP or resorted to texting. Ethan was a little old school and still relied on having actual conversations with people to get his point across. One hundred forty characters was just not enough for him to say anything meaningful. Secretly, Grace loved that about him. She dangled her long arm in the air, trying to summon a cab, as she tallied up her recent offenses—kissed Ethan, got into a minor tiff with the pastor of Ethan's church, and ran off with Horace, a member of that church. She left getting slapped by Candace off the list. After all, for once, she hadn't been the antagonist. Grace preferred not to recall that moment and thanked God no one had recorded it.

After several minutes of arm waving and shouting at the cabs that passed her by despite appearing empty, a cab pulled up in front of her. It was one of the more spacious ones for families and the handicapped. As Grace leaned in to open the door, the window in the rear rolled down and Horace poked his head out and warmly asked, "Are you going my way?"

Blushing, Grace pulled back her hand. "That depends on where you're going," she said flirtatiously. She never flirted; she simply said, "I want you," and sealed the deal. She looked at Horace's plump lips and his crooked front tooth and wondered what had happened. Grace couldn't believe how flirtatious Horace made her feel.

"Well, hop in, Grace King. I'll take you wherever you want to go." He flung the door open and scooted over so that Grace could get inside. "Where to, my lady?" Horace asked as soon as she had climbed in and pulled the door shut.

"Fiftieth and Eighth Avenue," Grace replied.

"Did you hear that, driver?" Horace tapped on the back of the seat in front of him. "Drop the lady off at Fiftieth and Eighth." Horace reclined in the seat and extended his arms across the back, slightly grazing Grace's arm with his fingertips. "Where are you off to, Ms. Grace?"

"Me? Where are you going in a cab?"

"Listen, us po' folks got to get around too, you know," he said sarcastically, looking away from her.

"I—I didn't mean it like that."

"I'm not really sure what you meant, and I don't know if I care to know. What I do know is that you don't know me, so you should think twice before you judge me," he replied, staring out the window.

"Horace."

Horace turned to face Grace. His pronounced nose was slightly wrinkled, his mouth was curled into a frown, and yet the exquisiteness of his face took her aback. She wanted to plant kisses all over his warm brown face until a smile resurfaced. Reaching for him, Grace rested her hand on his thigh and began again.

"Horace, I'm sorry, but—"

"There are no buts when you're sorry. Either you are or you aren't," he said firmly, folding his hands across his chest and cocking his legs open a little wider, knocking her hand from its position on his thigh. "I think this is your stop."

The cab pulled to a full stop at the corner of Eighth Avenue and Fiftieth Street. Horace opened the door and exited the cab, allowing Grace to exit on his side.

Grace took that to mean she still had a chance —however slim—considering the fact that he hadn't allowed her to open the door and step into oncoming traffic.

"Horace." She breathed his name slowly, staring into his eyes. She wanted to see what happened when she said his name. Then she would know where she stood with him.

His eyes flickered, and his eyebrows arched at the sound of her voice. Yet he did not respond to her. Then, reclaiming his spot in the cab, he called to her through the cracked window. "Top model, meet me at Chocolat at nine."

Grace headed to Ethan's office and was all smiles as she pushed Ethan's door open. "What's up, Ethan? You said you needed to see me ASAP."

Ethan looked up from the papers on his desk. Another crease surfaced on his forehead, adding to the other two on his brow. He stuck the cap of his pen in his mouth and sucked on it for a moment.

"Just spit it out, man," Grace commanded as she approached his desk. She casually rested her bowling bag tote on his desk, taking over his space. Based on the look on his face, nothing good was going to come from this meeting, and she didn't want to waste her time on dramatics. Ethan had a flair for them.

Ethan removed the pen cap from his mouth and held up two fingers. "Two things," he said, then took a dramatic pause. "One, your time at Mount Carmel is up." He lowered one of his fingers. "Two, if you don't get your butt on the set of that film, Javier is going to sue you blind."

"For what?" Grace flung her hands in the air.

"We went over this already. Breach of contract, loss of profits, and some other crap." Ethan sat up and waited for Grace to concede.

Twisting her mouth to the side, Grace said, "I don't know how we're going to work that out." Grace did not want to be sued. She couldn't afford any more negative press, nor could she afford any of the checks she'd have to write to the firm and to Javier if he won the lawsuit. She tapped her foot lightly as she moved on to the other issue Ethan had laid out—Mount Carmel. "The last time I checked, I am nowhere near the hours mandated by the judge. One year is three hundred and sixty-five days."

"You let me worry about the judge. I'll have you at a new placement before the week is out."

Grace swallowed hard and chewed on a small slice of regret. She had dived headfirst into the industry, and not only had she neglected to finish high school, but she'd also granted the firm power of attorney, and that allowed Ethan to make every decision for her, including where she would do her time. Grace tried to conceive an eloquent speech that would make Ethan aware that she was no longer willing to allow people who didn't clean the toilet after she sat on it to make decisions for her.

"I don't want to go anywhere else. Are you trying to protect David too?" she asked, a rough grimace emerging as she recalled how Ethan had flown down the aisle, prepped to accuse her of bringing about the downfall of the church.

"This isn't about Pastor David. Why do you care, anyway? The last time I checked, you were protesting about setting foot in a church." He tapped his pen lightly against the desk, shifted his gaze from Grace, and stared at the papers on his desk. A look of fierce concentration consumed his face.

Sensing that an argument was brewing in his head, Grace grabbed the handles of her bag and scooped it up. She was trying to flee the scene while Ethan categorized his thoughts to determine whether there was evidence that this was about Pastor David or an assumption. "I want to stay there, and that's it," she said matter-of-factly, pivoting on her heels to leave. Her hope was to clear the doorway before Ethan launched into his attack.

Ethan lurched forward before she made it to the door. "This is about your knight in shining armor, isn't it?" he asked loudly.

Grace did an about-face and zoomed back to Ethan's desk. "Are you serious?" she asked, leaning in over the desk. "I don't need anybody to protect me. I know how to put my foot up someone's behind and how to put it down when necessary." She snickered, looking Ethan up and down. "I know what this is about. This is about that kiss, isn't it?"

Ethan rose from behind his desk, walked around to the front of it, and stood next to Grace. He grabbed her hand and rubbed the back of it while staring deeply into her eyes. "I don't blame you for that, Grace. We crossed all kinds of lines that we shouldn't have a long time ago, and things really just got out of control. I'm sorry," he said, still caressing her hand. "I shouldn't have let that happen."

His apology seemed genuine, and the worry painted on his eyes gave away how conflicted he felt. He'd given in to his flesh and lost both Grace and Candace. The thought made even Grace feel sorry for him. For the first time since she'd met Ethan, he had broken from the script and had decided to ad-lib, and it had resulted in disaster. She wished they had acted on the desire and chemistry between them before falling in love with other people.

"I'm sorry too, Ethan." She withdrew her hand from his palms and straightened the knot on his lavender and gray silk blend tie. Grace was sorry she wasn't the simple client who just booked jobs and didn't start bar fights. She wanted to be better but didn't know where to begin. "I'm going to fix this—for you." She laid the tie back down against Ethan's chest and stroked it softly, then looked up at him. "For us."

Chapter 22

Showing up early wasn't typical behavior for Grace, but she wanted to make a great impression on Horace. Grace asked the hostess to seat her while she waited for Horace to arrive. After slathering on a dollop of matte fuchsia lipstick, Grace used the camera on her iPhone to check her face. She dabbed some stray mascara away with her finger and covered the spot with a pinch of concealer. She tousled the front of her spiked-up hair a bit. Her face was beat, her hair was laid, and thanks to the courtesy waist trainer she'd received in the mail, her body was looking snatched in the formfitting orange body-con dress she was wearing.

She adjusted the neckline a bit to obscure some of her cleavage, which was popping out. Grace bit her lip and stared at her image on the camera screen for a moment as worry set in. *Maybe this is a bit much for an evening with Horace,* she thought. *After all, he is a church boy and he hasn't said this is a date. On the other hand, it is Saturday.* According to Grace's fashion philosophy, stepping out on a Saturday evening was a prescription for wearing anything that fit like a glove. She ran her finger along the rim of her teeth to remove a stray lipstick mark.

"Leave the lipstick there. That'll level the playing field for the average women in here," Horace whispered into her ear, leaning over her shoulder.

Grace turned around and stood up to greet him. She was going to ask for a drink, but his clear cognac skin quenched her thirst. Breathing deeply, she inhaled the scent of sandalwood about him and was ready to collapse as he drew her close to him for an embrace.

"I thought you were angry with me," she whispered.

Horace held Grace by her waist and stepped back, taking in her whole frame. His eyes softened, and his lips curled into a smile.

Body-con does it every time, Grace thought. Returning the flirtatious smile, she placed her hand on his chest.

"Offended, yes, but angry? How could I be angry with you, Grace King?" he said, releasing her waist to pull out her chair. He walked around the table and took a seat directly across from her. "Have you thought about what you want to order?" Horace opened his menu and began to scan it.

She cleared her throat, thinking about the most diplomatic way to broach the topic of the cost of the food at Chocolat. It wasn't for the ultrarich, but the menu certainly wasn't for someone who ate meals at the church pantry. Grace considered herself to be a modern woman. She didn't mind paying for a meal or two, as long as that was established before the date, but since she still didn't know if they were on a date or not, Grace had no idea what to say.

"Ummm . . . I was thinking I'd order two appetizers instead of an entrée. What do you think?"

"I think I need more light to make a decision." He laid the menu on the table, picked up the candle, and used it to illuminate the menu. "I didn't think that whole 'not eating' thing was true, but if you're not going to get a full meal at Chocolat, something is wrong with you. If you're worried about the price, don't be. I have a job, *remember?"*

Grace wanted to rebut his response with the facts of the matter. If his job was so good, why was he eating at the church? It didn't make an ounce of sense for him to be this fine and foolish enough to blow his whole check on wining and dining Grace. Heck, she'd slept with many a strange man for less than a meal at Chocolat. When she considered it, she had never got much in return out of the deal except for dirty linens.

"Grace," Horace called out to her gently, snagging her out of her surmising. "Does it bother you that I work construction?"

"No," she replied, smiling.

Horace put his menu down, folded his arms on the table, and leaned in closer. "Then what is the problem?" he asked, licking his ripe lips.

Giving him the once-over again, Grace couldn't find a fault. He looked pretty relaxed in a forest-green plaid button-down shirt. His freshly shaved bald head was glowing, despite the muted lighting, and the small triangular tuft of hair beneath his bottom lip was neatly trimmed. "I don't have a problem."

"Yes, you do," he insisted.

"Hi. I'm Juliana, and I'll be your server this evening. Would you care for an appetizer or drinks to start out your night?" the waitress offered, switching her gaze from Grace to Horace.

Grace was relieved by the diversion from the present conversation that the waitress's presence created, and smiled at her. Biting her tongue was like swallowing stones for Grace—unnatural and unhealthy. The truth was, it did bother her that Horace was a construction worker who was eating meals at the church. It bothered her that he looked like Prince Charming and had the pockets of a pauper. It bothered her that she couldn't discern whether the glint she saw in his eyes came from him searching for her name on CelebrityNetWorth.com or from him being genuinely captivated by her. Shifting her focus from Horace's pockets back to the waitress, Grace began her order.

"I'll take a lime-infused water and . . ." Grace paused, trying to think of something conservative to pair with her glass of water. By now she ordinarily would have asked the waitress for two scotches and inquired if she knew where she could get any good weed, but Grace was trying to play the reserved role to impress Horace. It was still not really clear why the opinion of a man who most likely had taken one of those purity vows and wouldn't be giving up the goods anytime soon mattered. But it did. "May I have the grilled Caesar salad with French dressing?" she finally said.

"A Caesar salad?" Horace questioned. "We did not come all this way for you to order no Caesar salad. Juliana, she can have the salad as an appetizer and give her this." He pointed at the menu, then looked Grace squarely in the eye with a raised eyebrow, muting any protest that was stirring inside of her. "And I'll have the shrimp quesadilla and the grilled Scottish salmon with a glass of rosé." He folded his menu, scooped up Grace's menu, and handed them both to the waitress. "Thank you, Juliana."

"Rosé, huh? You don't have to try to impress me, Horace," Grace said after the waitress had disappeared. She delicately stroked the spot on the small of his arm that was exposed by the eyelet on the sleeve of his shirt.

"I suppose the same could be said of you, or have you started attending AA meetings? Lime-infused water, my foot." Horace stomped his foot. "You want to drink that about as much as I want a colonoscopy right now."

Breaking out into a small fit of laughter, Grace clutched her side and slapped the table. His deadpan was good, and she was thrown completely off the mark. She didn't know where to take the conversation now.

"Seriously, I want to get to know you." Horace pointed at her. "I want to know Grace King."

"You want to get to know me or my money, Horace?" she asked, questioning his motives. "Since you want to talk, let's talk about why you seem to be so fond of me without actually knowing anything about me besides what's on MediaTakeout.com." Grace leaned back in her chair, crossed her legs, and folded her arms across her chest.

Horace pinched his nostrils together before speaking, as if he was preparing to give a dissertation. "Grace, I am not fond of you," he announced.

Grace's eyebrows met in the center of her forehead, creating a scowl on her face, at that proclamation.

"I am not fond of *you*. I am fond of who you have the potential to be. I can see why your parents named you Grace, because you are seasoned with a great measure of it, and when you tap into it and figure out how to be victorious in your trials, instead of the victim"—he clapped his hands together—"that grace is going to shine right through. I am not fond of you." He leaned in close to the table and whispered, "I want you, but I want you whole. Trust and believe me, every man is searching for his rib, and at the bare minimum, for a woman who can make ribs like his mama, but I need a whole woman to stand by my side."

Unsure of how to respond to that statement, Grace turned her eyes to the silverware lined up in front of her, hoping that the fervor going on inside of her wasn't evident to Horace. *Is something wrong with me? Allusions to the Bible shouldn't arouse me this much.* Grace had never known that a man who served God could be so sexy. She thought back to her early romance with David. Was that love or some strange preacher man fetish? Whatever it was, she was hoping it wouldn't be reenacted between her and Horace. If they were going to have something, then it had to be real and honorable. She had to know what his intentions were before she proceeded any further.

She cleared her throat, ready to respond to Horace's remarks. "Horace, obviously, you've been given the gift of oration, and I thank you for the compliments, but it appears as though you're evading my question. Are you digging me or digging for gold?"

Horace took his time responding to Grace. The waitress arrived with his rosé. He sipped it casually and even offered Grace a sip. Finally, he wiped the corners of his mouth and said, "Money ain't a thing to me, Grace. At one point in my life I threw it out like rice at a wedding. I used to run these streets." He laughed. "Man, I had at least twenty blocks of Harlem on lock, and I was pushing those designer drugs to people just like you on the weekends at spots like Lunar, Greenhouse, and Limelight, before it got shut down."

Grace's eyes widened as she took in his testimony. Maybe that was why he felt so familiar with her. He had probably sold her some drugs and was trying to make amends now. "Are you serious, Horace?" she asked, squeezing a lime into her water.

"I was running drugs heavy up until about five years ago, when I met Pastor David at a funeral. His words really changed me."

"How did his words change you?" Her question slipped off her tongue rapidly. Her wondering was really meant for her and her alone. She'd always been fascinated by people who converted to Christianity and declared that they'd been liberated, when all that she had experienced was how restrictive Christianity was.

"Really, they weren't *his* words. They were the Lord's words." He tapped the back of his hand against hers, summoning her full attention. "You see, the funeral was for a friend of mine who'd been shot during a robbery gone way wrong. Near the end of Pastor David's sermon, he began telling the story of a rich young ruler who'd been asked to give everything he had to the poor and follow Jesus. The rich young ruler walked away, full of sadness, and Jesus declared to his disciples that it was harder for a rich man to get into heaven than it was for a camel to get through the eye of a needle."

"And that changed your heart?" Grace balked. She'd heard some sappy stories about deliverance before—people trapped by the fangs of death, unsure of their next move, and then they surrendered everything—but one little Bible verse melting Horace's heart was incomprehensible to her and hardly worth sharing.

"Then he went on to give an excerpt from the scripture. He asked us if we knew what happened to that rich young ruler. Some of the boys laughed and shouted, 'He kept getting that money,' and Pastor David said, 'No, he's in the coffin lying before your eyes. Rather than give up his riches, the young ruler tried to hoard everything he had and let the devil rob him of eternal life.'" Horace wiped the corners of his mouth, as if he'd just bitten into a succulent piece of steak. "From there I was open. I ran to Pastor David and begged him to tell me what I had to do to inherit eternal life. He turned to me and said, 'Rich young ruler, sell all that you have, give it to the poor, and follow Jesus.' And I did. I don't buy more than I need, and I live modestly, all to His honor and glory," he said, pointing his index finger at the ceiling.

After Horace finished telling Grace the story of his conversion, the waitress arrived with their appetizers. "Bon appétit," she said, setting their plates before them.

Grace pushed her food around, trying to avoid how foolish Horace's story had made her look. Here she was, obsessing over money, when in fact he'd given all his money away. There weren't many Christians who could make that their boast. It seemed that the gospel being preached today was all about greed and gain to Grace.

"So, are you no longer speaking to me?"

"I . . . I feel kind of like an idiot," Grace confessed.

"That's fine. We all make mistakes. Now, stop thinking evil thoughts, and think good thoughts."

"Is that possible?" she asked, scrunching her face up.

"With God all things are possible."

I need to see something good first to believe that's possible. Stirring her ice, Grace recalled some of her encounters with men. Every single one of them had melted like the ice in the water right before her eyes. They had all appeared to have a solid frame that she could rest on, but when the heat was on, they were long gone. The only love she'd felt was between her and David, and it had felt like this—electric.

Horace signaled for the waitress to pour him another glass of rosé and then stroked the back of Grace's hand. "Where are you?"

Waving her hand, she replied, "I was lost for a moment, but I'm back, and I want to be wherever you are." She arched her back and let all the sensuality in her drip onto the table.

"You know, Adam never knew Eve was naked."

"What?" She scrunched her nose up, disapproving of his biblical commentary at the moment.

"Adam didn't know he was in a garden, buck naked, with that woman. All he knew was that she was for him and he loved her. That's what I want. Actually, that's all I want."

His morality and unwillingness to compromise only made her desire for him more palpable. She wanted to feel all the goodness that was wrapped up in the drop of chocolate seated before her. *This ain't right. I don't know what it is, but this ain't right.* Grace reprimanded herself for being focused on the flesh while Horace was trying to commune with her spirit.

"How do I become Eve?"

"Get right, Grace. Get right in the sight of God. Seek forgiveness from those that you have offended."

Grace groaned. "That's a long list."

"Listen, in Matthew, chapter five, the Word tells us that if we've offended our brother, then we must first go to our brother and 'be reconciled' and then offer our gift. The only real gift we have to give to God is ourselves. Apologize to those you know you've done wrong, and then ask God for His forgiveness."

"What if they won't forgive me?" Grace couldn't believe she was sharing her fears with Horace after only a few sips of water. Usually, it took some coke and a few shots before she did that. But Horace made her feel protected. Safe. "What do I do if they won't forgive me?"

"Then you go to your Father. Leave them and yourself at His feet for a cleansing. They'll have to deal with God after that."

Grace liked the sound of that—having the Lord as her father had to be better than having her biological one.

Chapter 23

Cautiously, Grace planted her pointy-toe pumps on each marble step of 60 Centre Street. This wasn't the first time that she had walked up the steps of the courthouse, so she wasn't sure why buckets of fear filled her belly. She came in peace and had nothing to worry about, based on what Horace had explained to her over dinner Saturday evening. If Candace didn't accept her apology, then Candace would now have to carry that weight, and Grace would be absolved of her guilt.

Using all her weight, Grace forced the brass revolving doors to turn. She slid her purse through the scanner and maneuvered around the metal detectors, greeting every guard who manned the lobby by first name and stopping in front of one guard who had to be a descendant of Goliath.

"Hey, Paterson. I could use your help today," Grace said, patting him on the shoulder.

"My help?" he said, sounding surprised. "What can I do for you, Ms. King?" he asked, tipping his hat without taking his eyes off the metal detectors.

"I'm looking for a court reporter by the name of Candace. I can't remember her last name. She's kind of petite, with great caramel skin—"

"Real conservative, though," he interjected. "She's always wearing pearls and sweaters." He tapped Grace's elbow with his elbow.

"That sounds like her."

"She's working with Judge Toomer today. If she's not in chambers with the judge, she's on lunch now," he said, staring at the round clock that hung above the entrance.

"Thank you, Paterson," Grace replied, looking up at him. "What do I owe you?"

Placing his hand on his heart, he said, "This one is on the house."

Grace dashed to the elevators and up to Judge Toomer's chambers on the fifth floor. She'd appeared before Judge Toomer a couple of times. He was definitely a fan, so she knew it would be easy to get in and see Candace. After knocking on the door of his chambers once, she heard his commanding voice boom on the other side of the oak door. "Enter."

After smoothing her A-line skirt, Grace pushed open the door and began speaking right away. She talked quickly to ensure the judge didn't have a chance to ask one question and to make sure he heard only one thing, "I need Candace." Without hesitation Judge Toomer gave in to Grace's seemingly desperate plea for a moment with her girlfriend.

Judge Toomer came from behind his grand desk, escorted Grace to the door, and told her exactly where Candace could be found. "She's in the pavilion, feeding the pigeons and praising God."

Grace looked back at the judge in disbelief. *Who the heck spends their lunch like that?*

Pointing toward the window at the end of the hall, Judge Toomer said, "Come see for yourself." Linking arms with Grace, he led her to the window. Grace looked down at Candace, then back up at Judge Toomer. The pity that had entered her heart the moment he told her where to find Candace had been doubled now that she'd seen it for herself. The chiming of Grace's phone broke the state of quiet contemplation that she and Judge Toomer had entered.

Raising one finger, Grace excused herself and turned her back on the judge to read the text from Junell.

Sorry about the other day, G. Where are you? Want to do lunch?

I forgive you. Can't do lunch. I'm at the courthouse now.

Court?

Grace cracked up at the series of emojis that followed the word *Court*. I'm attempting to be a whole woman for Horace.

G, you have to become a whole woman for you. Ciao. The cameras are about to start rolling. Call me later.

Sucking her teeth, Grace turned around to face Judge Toomer, who was still watching Candace toss shreds of bread at the pigeons that surrounded her.

"Is everything all right, Ms. King?"

"Absolutely," Grace lied, conjuring up a smile to support her lie. She wasn't going to be spilling her guts twice this week, and she wasn't even in anger management. "Judge, do you think you would be willing to excuse Candace for the day?"

Judge Toomer raised an eyebrow and drummed his fingers on the ledge. "Grace, feeding pigeons in the park alone is a sad state to be in, but don't bring me back a drunk court reporter who likes to get into bar fights." He wagged his finger at her. "Is that clear?"

"Yes, Your Honor." Grace placed one hand in the air, as if she was being sworn in. "I will not get her involved in any of my shenanigans. I promise."

Grace used the emergency exit staircase that led right into the courtyard. She flew down the steps as fast as her pumps could carry her. Clearly, she'd spent way too much time in the courthouse if she knew where each staircase let out. This was definitely something that needed to be amended on her journey toward wholeness. *Maybe only one trip a year*, she thought, until she completely got breaking the law out of her system.

"If you feed them too much, they'll explode," Grace said over Candace's shoulder.

"That's rice. If you feed them rice, they'll explode. A little roll won't kill them. Are you the bird police?" Candace asked, looking over her shoulder at Grace. She jumped to her feet, swiping her purse and the remainder of her lunch in preparation to take flight. "Grace, if you attack me in public, you'll be locked up on the spot."

Grace smiled. Candace's fear was amusing to her. Stepping over the pigeons, Grace moved closer to Candace. "Worried about retaliation, huh?" Grace hiked up the sleeves on her jacket. "You should have thought about that before you raised your hand to me."

"I don't know what came over me." Candace waved her hands in surrender.

Grace grabbed her wrist. "I know what came over you. . . . You're in love with a man. That has been known to cause many women to do some utterly ridiculous things that no one in their right state of mind would do."

Candace's arm stiffened in Grace's hand.

"Relax. I came to make peace with you. Did you have lunch yet?"

Candace held up a plastic bag containing some Tupperware. "I was about to get started. I always feed them first"—she pointed at the pigeons—"so they won't bother me while I'm eating."

Grace interlocked her arm with Candace's and pulled her close. "Come on. Let's have lunch." Grace ripped the plastic bag from Candace's hand and tossed it into a nearby garbage can. "You won't be needing this." Grace looked Candace up and down. The various shades of brown adorning her slender body made Grace's stomach feel queasy. "First, let's make a stop at Bergdorf, because I can't be seen in public with you looking like . . ." Grace waved her hand up and down, searching for an accurate term to describe Candace's muddy brown outfit.

"Like what?" Candace asked, breaking out of Grace's armlock.

Candace looked like a pot of beef stew that had been left out overnight, but Grace had to find a more appropriate way to say that. "Like a librarian. Now, come on. We'll settle our score later." Grace wrapped her arm around Candace's again and began walking out of the courtyard.

Candace didn't budge, causing Grace to snap back like a rubber band.

"Grace, I'm on lunch. I can't go traipsing around the city with you."

"Don't worry. You've been excused." Grace looked up at the window where she and Judge Toomer had been watching Candace feed the birds. "Just smile and wave at the judge," Grace said through her already smiling lips.

The brilliant lights of Bergdorf welcomed them, along with the doorman, who swung the door open for Grace with his lips cut into a simple smile. He let go of the door immediately after Grace passed by, and Candace had to scurry through on Grace's heels or get clipped by the door. Grace kept looking over her shoulder, like she was escorting kindergarteners on a school field trip. Candace paused at every item that shined and walked over to every sales clerk who leaned on the counter and summoned them.

"Get your tail over here," Grace said, yanking Candace away from some new European collagen cream. "You don't need that crap, and stop looking around like this is some sort of amusement park."

Bowing her head, Candace said, "I'm sorry."

They rode the escalator upstairs in silence. When they stepped off the escalator, a gentleman in a beige tailored suit greeted them.

"Ms. King, welcome back." He reached out and double-cheek kissed her.

Grace leaned in, returning the pleasantry and gagging on the inside. This boy didn't know her from a hole in cement, yet he felt the need to impose himself on her, because he thought he might get rich off her this afternoon.

"Would you like me to call Sercee and let him know that you're here?"

"No." Grace waved her hand, shooing the man away. If this trip were about her, Grace would have demanded that her personal shopper, Sercee, be summoned immediately. However, this shopping excursion wouldn't require his special touch.

Grace scanned the floor for Candace, who'd taken a wrong turn somewhere. Grace rolled her eyes when she found her tucked in a corner with a flat white sheath pressed against her. "On second thought," Grace said over her shoulder, "call Sercee and tell him we're doing a fashion intervention." Grace marched across the sales floor and snatched the sheath from Candace's hands. "No way."

"Don't worry." Candace squeezed her lips together and flicked one of the tags at Grace. "All this stuff is way too expensive."

Grace looked at the tag and smiled. A grand on a dress from Bergdorf was a steal.

"The price is irrelevant. A boxy sheath on your pear shape . . ." Grace stuck her finger down her throat like she was gagging. "Here are the ground rules for this little excursion. No knee-length, free-flowing skirts, Baptist convention suits, or cardigans, and no worrying about the price. Today is about fashion. Let's just get you hooked up."

"Grace, I think you should be careful with how you spend your money. Ethan told me—"

"I don't care what Ethan told you about me," Grace said through clenched teeth. "Let me worry about me, okay?" Grace put the dress back on the rack in front of them. "Thank you for your concern, but now is not the time."

"Ms. King, room four is ready for you. Would you like me to escort you up there?"

"No, I know my way around." Grace waved good-bye and grabbed Candace's hand. "Follow me," she said over her shoulder.

"Where are we going now?"

"You'll see."

"Welcome to room four," Grace said slowly when they arrived at their destination.

Candace inhaled and let out a little squeal when Grace pulled open the door to room four. "Grace, what is this?" she asked, scanning the room.

Grace strolled across the camel carpet and plopped into a large, cushy chair. "This is one of the perks of being rich and famous in the city of dreams." Grace crossed her legs and took a sip of the champagne on the black end table beside her chair.

Candace ran her fingers along the edges of the clothing that hung from silver bars along one wall of the room—a beaded, embellished blush-colored dress, a sleeveless black pantsuit, and a long-sleeve gray lace gown. She fixed her eyes on the shoes that neatly lined the floor like soldiers. She'd never been one to follow trends, but she recognized the Louboutins. They were in colors she'd never seen—a rich navy, canary yellow, and some kind of animal skin dyed electric blue. Perching herself on top of a maroon ottoman in the corner, Candace continued her survey of the room. There were more outfits hanging on the opposite wall and a three-rowed mirror in the center of the room.

"You should check out the clothes on that rack. You'd look great in Valentino," Grace suggested.

"Valentino?" Discomfiture marked Candace's voice, and her wrinkled eyebrows demonstrated her confusion. "I don't speak fashion."

"Clearly." Grace rose from her seat and plucked a long-sleeve, multicolored butterfly-print dress from the rack. "This is Valentino."

Candace's eyes softened. Grace walked over to her with the dress in her hand. "Try this one on first."

Rising to her feet, Candace asked, "Grace, what is this all about?"

Before Grace could respond, Sercee bounded through the door. Grateful for the interruption, Grace skipped into Sercee's arms, greeting him with a hug, and then mounted her tippy toes to deliver the customary double kiss to his cadaverous cheeks. Sercee's fashion taste and timing were impeccable. Grace really hadn't thought about how she was going to win Candace over. She'd grown accustomed to the PR department at the firm or Ethan drafting her apologies. She had no clue what she would say. Sercee would most certainly be enough of a distraction for Grace to hunt for the words she needed to smooth things over.

"Dahling, you said we were doing a fashion inter-vention." He peeled his glasses off his face and looked down at Candace. "But she needs a total overhaul. Is she barefaced?" He gasped, slapping his cheeks.

"Relax, relax," Grace said, fanning both hands in Sercee's direction. Grace wrapped an arm around Candace, whose tawny skin was turning a cinnamon color under the distress of Sercee's criticism. "Let's do the wardrobe first, hair, and then makeup."

"Grace?" Candace said.

"Don't worry. We're not doing anything too drastic, but it will be better than that 'fashion on a budget' makeover you tried." Turning to Sercee, Grace began to pour out the praise for the magnificent collection he'd pulled together. "These looks are so awesome. I love how you think. She is going to look great in Valentino. I think Lanvin would be good too, something with a little ruching or a tapered waistline. Do you have any menus from BG available?"

"Has it been so long that you need a menu, Grace?"

"No, but Candace could use one."

Sercee reached inside his blazer and withdrew two menu cards for BG, the restaurant nestled discreetly on one of the upper floors of Bergdorf Goodman. "You better order a salad. You're wide around the sides, and I don't think you'll fit into the special treat I've been holding on to for you," he said, tapping her nose. "Let me go and fetch it. Feel free to place your order while I'm gone."

Grace handed one of the menu cards to Candace. "Order whatever you like."

"Grace, you still have not answered me. What is this sudden bout of generosity about? I hope this isn't about Ethan."

"Kind of, sort of." Grace shook her hand from side to side.

"Listen, I don't want any gifts to look the other way. If you all think you can buy me off—"

"Buy you off?" Grace laughed at the notion. *This chile watches too much TV.* There was no way on earth Grace would waste a dime paying off a court reporter. You paid off only people with juice or with a story to tell. What could Candace say? That she had walked in on Grace kissing Ethan, as if the world didn't already know she had a voracious appetite when it came to the opposite sex? "Please, it's nothing like that. Actually, I was hoping we could be . . ."

Candace jumped into the gap before the *f* in "friends" could even roll off of Grace's tongue. "I hope y'all don't think I'm going to join you in some ménage à trois or something." Candace rolled her eyes in disgust and continued. "You're crazier than what I thought. Imagine me breaking my covenant with the Lord to experiment with a washed-up model." Candace stood up and flung the menu card on the floor. "Do me a favor while you're being generous. Please tell your little boy toy that I have lost all respect for him. However, I will keep him in prayer."

"Ménage à what? With who? Not you, boo." Grace chuckled. *Reality television has everyone thinking someone wants to get with them.* "I might be washed up in your eyes, but I'm still a hot commodity to some." Grace looked in the mirror and ran her fingers through her raven-colored hair, which was now coifed in thick waves. She adjusted a few strands and added a dash of gloss to her lips before turning to face Candace again.

"I just wanted to apologize to you, Candace. I brought you here to apologize to you." She sighed. "I mean, I meant to take you to lunch, but then I saw you feeding pigeons, wearing a cardigan, with a tight bun in your hair. I mean, I couldn't . . . Ah, never mind. I'm getting ready to start rambling, and that's not going to be good for either of us. Have a sip of champagne, relax, and enjoy a dose of retail therapy."

"Do you think shopping solves everything?"

Smiling, Grace replied, "It solves most of my problems." She reached for a glass and the bottle of champagne.

"That won't be necessary."

"A glass of champagne ain't going to get you into hell, Ms. Holy Roller."

"If this is how you apologize, it's no wonder you don't have friends," Candace shot back.

Shaking her head, Grace absorbed the blow. She wanted to be strategic about how she responded to Candace in this situation; she was supposed to be putting out this fire, not pouring gasoline on it. Candace was still hurt, and this was her chance to lash out. *Swallow it, Grace, and make peace.*

"I haven't eaten all morning. Let's order lunch and then discuss this."

"I don't have anything to say to you."

Grace locked eyes with Candace. A residue of hurt lined Candace's eyes, and it looked like forgiveness was definitely on vacation for an undisclosed amount of time. Grace refilled her glass and then filled the other one for Candace. "A sip is not going to kill you."

"This may be a foreign concept to you, but I try to glorify God in everything that I do, and consuming alcoholic beverages doesn't fit into that equation for me."

"To each his own." Grace downed her glass and followed it up with Candace's. "You know, you Christians crack me up. You claim you serve a loving and forgiving God, but when it comes time for you to love and forgive, those concepts are alien to all of y'all."

Chapter 24

"You know you miss him," Grace said, chomping down on a scallop.

Candace shrugged her shoulders and turned down the corners of her mouth. "I'm satisfied."

"With what?" Grace asked, leaning across the table.

"With my Savior," Candace sang lightly, as if she was leading the Sunday morning devotion at her church.

"Look here . . ." Grace raised her fork and pointed it at Candace. "You might be fooling some people with your 'Long as I got Jesus' routine, but I know when the nights are cold and that rain is beating against your windowpane, you want a man that's there in the flesh, not in the spirit."

Grace already knew the church rhetoric that went along with the single life. Her mother had fed it to her when she was a teen and to many of the women at the church who came to see her mother after service to discuss itches that they just couldn't resist scratching.

It was always about waiting, abstaining, and being content with the things that they had, and maybe one day the Lord would invite someone into a relationship. There was no help for the woman who wanted to invite a man into a relationship herself. She was the jezebel and the adulterous woman that Proverbs warned about. Nobody wanted to be her, and Candace was trying to dodge that bullet by running away from Ethan and rejecting his love.

"I hear you, Grace, but I'm not about to chase a man that I caught all invested in you." Candace took a sip of her water and raised her eyebrows, soliciting a response from Grace.

"Candace, how many times do you want me to say I'm sorry? I'm sorry. I'm sorry. I'm sorry. That was an accident."

"Didn't look accidental to me. It looked like the woman whom I had admired for a long time was kissing the man whose rib I thought God had plucked me from."

Grace inhaled deeply and clutched her chest at Candace's revelation. She knew the two of them cared for each other, but she had had no idea that their relationship had gotten all biblical already. Scratching her temple, Grace recalled the time she'd thought she was a rib. The one time in her life when she'd thought that she had been made for a purpose, and when nothing but love had coursed through her veins and into her heart. In her mind she'd been made for Pastor David, and she had actually envisioned herself seated behind him while he preached. She'd rehearsed responding to the title of first lady, and she'd compiled a file full of all his favorite foods, which she would prepare every Sunday. But those dreams had been snatched away from her before they were even close to coming to fruition, and now she was responsible for robbing another woman of her chance to be with her Adam.

"Listen, I'm sorry, and I'm not just saying that. I've been where you are right now," Grace revealed, rocking from side to side. She hadn't told this story to anyone else besides Junell, and she didn't know if she'd be able to share it now. Swallowing hard, she braced herself and prepared to spill out as much of the story as she could. "I once loved a man, a good man, a man like Ethan. Gentle and upstanding. He was full of God, and all that jazz, and I lost him because of people meddling in our relationship. I don't want to be responsible for coming between you two. Please allow me to help put this puzzle back together."

Candace flung her freshly streaked honey blond tresses out of her eyes and replied, "Grace, I can go on without him. I have a replacement."

"A replacement—" Grace choked on a scallop while getting the words out. There was no way Candace was going to dump Ethan after all Grace had just done to get them back together. Between the new Valentino dress that was hugging every inch of Candace's body, including the petite waistline she'd been hiding, the pantsuit in the bag, the new pumps, and the hair and makeup, this transformation would have Grace in the red for months. She'd charged seven thousand dollars to her shopping account at Bergdorf today, and then there was the price she was paying not only to swallow her pride, but also to have some for dessert.

"I know you believe that every woman needs a man, but I'm not going to wind up like you, wandering to and fro, trying to fill some empty space or burning desire. That hole in my heart belongs to the Lord, and if you would allow Him to reign in you, the life that you now live wouldn't be so painful." Candace paused and sopped up some sauce with her roasted cauliflower and took a bite. "On another note, while I appreciate your little 'what not to wear' party and lunch, that's not enough to get me to run back to Ethan. So, whichever one of you came up with this idea, it is my prayer that you have a backup plan in case you have to abort the mission."

Oh God, I really messed this up. Help me fix this, Lord, Grace prayed in her heart and then looked around a bit, wondering where that voice had come from. *I have got to stop hanging out with all these saints. They're really messing me up.* She was completely shocked that she was now praying to God, whom she didn't even want to claim as her own. That was when her help came.

"You know, you need to stop acting like you are so tough and to just lie at his feet."

Candace's eyes widened. She seemed to be just as shocked as Grace was that she was ministering.

"Don't look at me like that," Grace told her. "Just accept the Word. As my mother would say when she was alive, 'God will use a jackass to preach to you if necessary.'"

Grace's self-deprecating remark was enough to change the tone of their heated conversation. Both Grace and Candace doubled over in laughter.

"No, seriously, Candace. If you think that's the man for you, just cut the nonsense and lie at his feet, like Ruth did to Boaz, and see what the result is."

"Don't take this the wrong way, but when did you become a Bible scholar?"

"My best friend, Junell, encouraged me to read the book of Ruth to figure out how to deal with my relationship with Horace, this guy I met while doing community service. I finally got around to reading it this weekend, so I guess it's still fresh in my mind." Grace shrugged and signaled the waiter for a refill of the champagne she was drinking.

"You know, Grace, that story is not just a story, and it is not just about the love between a woman and a man. What Boaz does for Ruth is what Christ has done for us. Out of love, he willingly received a woman who was not his own, and paid the dowry that was necessary to have her. That was exactly what Christ has done for us."

Grace sat up straight as goose pimples rose up and down her arms. Their waiter began fiddling with the empty plates. Frustrated by the distraction, Grace scooped up the plates and shoved them into the waiter's hands. "Go on," Grace said to Candace, folding her dainty fingers into a coaster for her chin.

"Jesus's blood speaks for us, and He paid the price for our lives, just as Boaz spoke for Ruth. So . . . the one who really needs to lie at someone's feet is you." Candace pointed at Grace.

Grace didn't think she liked the new, saucy version of Candace. "Whose feet am I supposed to be lying at? Shoot." Contorting her peachy lips into an exaggerated pout, Grace folded her arms over her chest, crossed her legs, and bounced her long leg up and down in tune with the smooth jazz filtering through the restaurant.

"You're supposed to lie down at Jesus's feet, just like Ruth did with Boaz. That is, if you accept what He's offering."

What is it with these people? Grace wondered. *Why does every single conversation turn into an attempt at conversion?*

Switching the subject, Grace reminded Candace of the reason they'd met. "I'm supposed to be helping you get your man back, not planning my baptism."

As Candace rattled off more reasons for Grace to give in to the higher power, Grace watched a woman seated at the bar, her back bent like the branches of a weeping willow. She drummed her fingers and shook her empty glass of alcohol in the air like a maraca, summoning the bow-tied bartender back to her. Either she sensed Grace's gaze or had great peripheral vision, because she twisted slightly and sent a smirk in Grace's direction. Her dark eyes were heavy and laden with dissipated desires, and they were surrounded by a gathering of crow's-feet. She was once someone important, Grace gathered, but as beauty fled, so did the crowd.

"Grace, you don't want that to be you, alone and hunched over somewhere."

"She looks fabulous, though," Grace mused, admiring how the black Givenchy one-piece framed the woman's aged silhouette. But then she noticed how the draped neckline revealed a few rivers of blue spider veins. Old age scared Grace; she'd never seen anyone grow old gracefully, as the adage went. She'd watched the few women in her family become bitter and dreadfully unfashionable as they entered their senior years. Especially her mother, who'd allowed her constant bouts of anemia to suck the life out of her before she passed away.

"Fabulous and alone, nonetheless," Candace noted.

Gulping the last bit of champagne that remained in her glass, Grace retorted, "Well, you don't want to wind up like that, either, so let's go get your man back."

Chapter 25

"Are you sure this is going to work?" Candace asked, her fingers shaking as she ran them through her new tresses.

"Just as sure as I was that you'd look snatched in Valentino." Grace snapped her fingers and then ran one of them across her teeth after getting a glimpse of herself in the elevator. "Listen, between that waistline, those hips, and those smoky eyes, Ethan is going to die. He'll be asking for your hand in marriage by this evening."

The elevator opened on the fifth floor, where Ethan's office was located. The floor was unusually empty. The clacking of their heels was the only sound that filled the air.

"Grace, are you really sure this is going to work?"

"This is going to work. You and those heels, however, I'm not that sure about." Grace looked over her shoulder at Candace, whose ankles were rolling like dice in a craps game as she attempted to match Grace's effortless stride in her six-inch sling-back, peep-toe Giuseppes. "Just follow and let me lead. I'm going to go in first, and you wait outside the door until I tell you to come in." That was about all the planning Grace had done. With her relationship with Ethan still in shambles, Grace hadn't put much thought into what she'd say to him, either. Counting on charm and Ethan's loneliness, she hoped that she wouldn't have to say more than "I'm sorry" and "I've brought your beloved to you, so please accept her as a peace offering." It was slightly selfish, but it was good selfish, since everyone would benefit.

Grace opened the doors of the vestibule that led directly to Ethan's office, and focused her mind on the benefits of her master plan rather than on the screwed-up expression painted on Alice's face. One good slug would've shut her up a long time ago, but out of respect for Ethan, Grace restrained herself by stuffing her fists in her pockets whenever possible. That didn't stop her from throwing any verbal daggers, but this situation was too good for Grace to allow Alice's foolishness and funky attitude to hinder her. Gaining Candace's forgiveness would get Grace in good with God, which in turn would get her in good with Horace. *Real good,* she thought, imagining herself swaddled in his arms, feeling safe and protected by those sculpted biceps and triceps. And her attempt at matchmaker would get Ethan off her back. He'd let her stay at Mount Carmel, and maybe he'd let her off the hook about this Javier Roberts movie thing.

"You cannot walk in there unannounced." Alice held up her hand. "He's busy."

"Doing what?" Grace asked, without breaking her stride or taking her eyes off her destination. "His premier client is out here. He can't be that busy in there."

Before Alice could skirt her desk, Grace opened Ethan's door, shut it behind her, and leaned on it to suppress any attempt at entry Alice might make. Just as she'd thought, Ethan wasn't busy doing a thing except preparing to take a swing at a golf ball. He was so deep in concentration, her presence went undetected. From what she could tell, Ethan wasn't any good. His knees were bent too much, and his feet were too far apart—his stance was awkward and amateurish. Steadying the club in his hands, Ethan twisted to the side and set up a shot that would crack the window to the left of his desk at best but wouldn't make it into the hole in the green felt square in the center of his office.

"What is this? The ninth hole at the Masters?" Her words cracked the air.

Ethan lowered his driver, pivoting slightly in the direction of the voice.

"Alice told me that you were busy. Is this what I have to pay a retainer fee for?" Grace said lightheartedly. It was as she had expected: if she wasn't in some stuff, then Ethan had absolutely nothing to do.

"I am busy, for your information. I'm trying to figure out how to straighten things out with Javier and resuscitate two careers that are about to flatline. If you go down, I'm going down as well. Do you know what he said about you this morning on the *Today Show?* Never mind." Ethan waved his hand in the air, dismissing his own remarks. "I'm just trying to clear my head."

"I thought you were supposed to pray when you needed to do that," Grace returned, stabbing Ethan with his own knife.

"Well, now that you're here, I don't need a miracle from God," he said, raising the driver and pointing it at Grace. "I just need you to take your butt down to Javier's office and tell him you're ready to begin filming. That's all that I need." He lowered his club and prepared to swing again. The slim fit of his trousers was stifling his stance.

"Your knees are bent too low, and your feet are too far apart."

Ethan made the adjustments and took a swing, and the ball rolled into the fake hole.

"Thank you." He teed up again. "When should I tell Javier you're coming?" He stared up at her innocently as he set the ball on the tee.

"I didn't come here to discuss that. I already told you I'm not interested, and I don't care what that nut is going around saying about me. I don't want to do the film, and you're not going to bully me into doing the film."

After standing up straight, Ethan stared into her eyes. His brown eyes were full of the power to cut right through Grace's anger and touch her heart. Grace was sure he knew that, which was why he'd decided to begin a staring contest before responding to her statement. Ethan was using his stare like a mallet to tenderize the meat of her heart before squeezing what he wanted out of it.

"Well, what *did* you come here for?" He put the driver aside and stuffed his hands into the pockets of his forest-green slacks, awaiting her response.

"I didn't come to argue with you. I didn't even come to discuss business with you. I come bearing gifts. I got something for you. I got you something that will put you and me in a better head space, and then we can move forward."

"Move forward?" he huffed. "Grace King, you have a lot of nerve. You don't want to discuss business. I'm your lawyer and your manager. What else do we have to discuss?"

"At one point we were friends," she wanted to say, but as his countenance had become marred from the pain of what he'd lost after kissing her, she knew it was best not to remind him of what once was.

"Fine. We can talk a little business, but first may I present my gift to you?" Grace said, trying to speed things up.

Grace felt that the longer they spent rehashing their disagreements, the more opportunity Candace had to rethink why she was sitting out there. With each passing minute her newly cultivated confidence might be slowly ebbing away—especially since she was seated out there with Alice, who was probably whispering poison about Grace into Candace's ear. By now she'd probably already slipped her heels out of the backs of the pumps and begun massaging them, and she'd probably entered into a healthy gabfest with Alice that included commentary on Grace's disposition and insatiable appetite for men. Alice had once been quoted in the newspaper as saying that Nelly Furtado's song "Maneater" was inspired by Grace. Grace had to get Candace into this office—and into Ethan's arms—now.

"Business first," Ethan said, picking up his driver. "I want you at Javier's studio tomorrow morning, before the crack of dawn. I want you there apologizing profusely and claiming that he is nothing short of the next Spielberg. A visionary. Please tell him that he is a visionary and that his debut film is sure to be legendary." Ethan hit the ball. "Today I want you to set up your next appointment for anger management."

Grace sucked her teeth.

Ethan looked back at her with his eyebrows huddled together. "Court's orders, or else you can march yourself right on down to jail. Dr. Sternberg is pretty flexible. We may be able to get him to come and make another house call. And then I need you to focus on completing these community service hours."

Grace drew in both of her cheeks, displeased with Ethan's commands. She tried to conjure up a proposition that would get the movie off the table and her back at Mount Carmel. Candace might not be a big enough bargaining chip. Anger management was doable. Grace had actually experienced some benefit from attending the session the first time, and she wasn't about to give up Horace. He was harder to get into than the White House, but worth the trip.

What about me?

An electrifying voice was echoing inside of her, yet it was outside of her. Grace looked at Ethan, who had redirected his focus to his miniature green and was taking serious swipes at the ball. Maybe it was Candace who'd asked the question.

Cracking the door slightly, Grace stuck her head through the opening to check on Candace. The scene was completely as she had imagined. Candace's feet were out of those heels, and she was using the carpeting to massage her soles, and Alice was assaulting her eardrums with useless cackling about Grace. She tucked her head back into the confines of Ethan's office and rested against the door. Now more than ever, she wanted to get back to Mount Carmel, lie down on the altar, and perform an exorcism on herself. She was going crazy.

Grace, what about me?

"What about you?" she retorted aloud, hoping that Ethan would engage in a conversation with her and that the voice truly wasn't in her head.

"What?" he asked, squinting at her like she was peering through fog.

Scratching her head, Grace tried to dig her way out of this. "I can't do the movie. I'll go back to anger management, and I'll go back to Mount Carmel, tonight even."

"You're doing the movie, and you're not going back to Mount Carmel to turn Pastor David into the next preacher scandal. Is that clear?" Ethan commanded, walking over to Grace.

"I'm not doing that movie. I cannot work with Javier. He . . . he . . ." Her chest began to heave as her confession climbed its way up from the dregs of her belly and from the recesses of her mind, and she met head-on the anguish that she'd tried to camouflage with alcohol and drugs.

"He's an idiot. He's a buffoon. A self-absorbed moron whose work is highly overrated," Ethan said. "However, he has the Midas touch, and every model he works with turns to gold." He lovingly caressed her cheek. "Grace, we're running out of options, and you've already signed on. I'll be there every step of the way."

Looking up at the ceiling, avoiding Ethan's powerful gaze, Grace tried to accept his decision without breaking down. "Can I still go to Mount Carmel?"

"No, that's my church, and I won't let you ruin that for me. You already slept with the pastor."

"Has it occurred to you that he slept with me too? He's not perfect. He's just the servant of a perfect God."

"Yes, it has," he said, dropping his voice and turning his back to Grace. "That's why I can't let you go back there. You make him weak, and I can't be the intermediary in this relationship."

"It's not a relationship. We haven't seen each other in a long time, and our emotions got the best of us both. I won't start anything with him. I promise, Ethan. Let me give you my gift as evidence of my commitment to you."

"No movie, no gift," he said.

"Ethan . . . I'll do it."

He spun around quickly and looked at her.

"Call him and tell him I'll be there with bells on . . ." she said reluctantly. "However"—she stepped in front of him, blocking his path to the telephone—"I'm going back to Mount Carmel, and you have to accept my gift first."

Chapter 26

Ethan planted his driver firmly on the floor, rested his palms on top of it, and assessed the sharp look in Grace's eyes, trying to determine her level of commitment.

"If I accept this gift, you can't back out on me," he said.

She shook her head sheepishly, like a schoolgirl in front of the principal, and turned to open the door.

Ethan grabbed her by the wrist and tested her eyes again. This wasn't the first time Ethan had to convince Grace to do something that she didn't want to do. She had been antsy when it came to doing *Sports Illustrated* in a bikini the first time. Grace had agreed, and then she'd frozen up on the set. It wasn't until Ethan had shown up that they'd actually been able to unglue her from her seat in hair and makeup. He groaned inside. Did this mean that he would have to show up on the set of Javier's film as well and walk her through her lines?

Still wary of Grace's intentions, he released her wrist from his vise grip. The look in her eyes served as reassurance that Grace was committed to this film. Whatever gift awaited him on the other side of the door wasn't just another trinket to bribe him to keep his mouth shut and turn a blind eye to her irresponsibility. But there was still a hint of apprehension in her eyes. He recalled the multitude of times that anxiety had coursed through his vein like a virus and had him bent over the toilet in a stall of the men's bathroom before any negotiations or hearings. Each and every time the Lord had guided him through those situations, holding his hand and whispering the right words to say. *God has never forsaken me. Why am I forsaking her? Please help me deal with her, Father,* he prayed silently.

Now that Ethan had released her, Grace opened the door partway and stuck her head and arm out. Ethan couldn't make out who she was motioning to or what she was doing. While she got things together on her end, Ethan figured this was the perfect time for him to let Javier know that they could finally begin filming.

Javier had created a short and tight film schedule for *Pressure*. He claimed he wanted to shoot and edit the picture in under ten months and release it by next fall. Seemed like the perfect plan, and it would leave them with more than enough time for Grace's image to be rehabilitated and for Grace to earn a little Oscar buzz. The role was dark. Grace knew dark. The role was dramatic, and as Ethan simultaneously dialed the number to Javier's studio and watched Grace prep his gift by motioning and jerking her arms up and down like she was a conductor for a philharmonic, he thought that she was definitely dramatic.

Javier's assistant picked up the phone, and Ethan took a seat behind his desk. He exchanged pleasantries with her and explained that his call was of the utmost importance, only to fall silent as Candace entered his office. Ethan fumbled as he searched for the cradle for the telephone receiver, covering his mouth with his free hand to hide the fact that all the muscles in his jaw had collapsed at the sight of her.

The sunlight streaming through the windows bounced off the apples of Candace's cheeks, and with each blink, her eyes seemed to whisper his name from across the room. The hair that he'd become so used to seeing pulled tightly back in a bun now framed her face like loose feathers. He didn't know whether to stand up and greet her or let her keep walking closer to him. Her beauty touched him and filled his belly from across the room. Ethan would have continued watching her float before him if it hadn't been for Grace, who was waving at him, signaling that he should stand up and greet Candace.

He stood and tugged at his collar, trying to tease out the words lodged in his throat. His tongue clung to the roof of his mouth, scraping against the ridges. Candace's presence had awakened both the inward man of his heart and the desires of his flesh.

Clearing her throat and bobbing her head to the side, Grace unlocked the handcuffs that Candace's presence had place on his mind.

"Candace . . ."

"Ethan . . ." Candace said, bowing her head and then raising it partway and looking up at him.

He reached for her hand. She allowed him to grasp only her pinkie. "You look different."

"Do you like it?" she asked, biting the corner of her lip. Candace raised her head fully and met Ethan's eyes completely.

Oh God, I love it. This is what Adam must have felt when he saw Eve and said you are a "wo-man," Ethan thought. He realized that restraint was necessary in terms of both words and deeds. He wanted to pull her in by her waist with both hands and demolish the space between them with his lips. All of him ached for her. He tucked her hair behind her ears and cradled her face in his palms.

"Ethan, we can't—"

"Shhh . . ." he said, swallowing every word of resistance with his own lips.

Candace tried to speak again, but with each syllable she attempted to spit out, Ethan pressed his lips on hers, until she finally gave up her protest. Once their bodies had melded together, Ethan wrapped one arm around her shoulders and the other around her waist. Flicking his fingers back and forth, he dismissed Grace. Later on he would have to compliment her for her bribery tactics.

After a few moments, Candace broke out of his grasp. Breathless, flustered, and radiant.

"Ethan, we can't just go from not speaking to kissing without so much as having a conversation," she asserted, holding her fingertips to her lips.

"I never stopped speaking to you, Candace." Ethan placed his now free hands in his pockets. "I've called you every day for the past week."

"So a phone call was supposed to make up for the fact that I found you with your tongue down Grace King's throat?" She folded her hands across her chest. "How am I supposed to trust you around her?"

Ethan decided that now would be a great time to shout out, "Objection, Your Honor. She's badgering the witness." Managing his emotions and speaking plainly about them had never been Ethan's forte. Now he was going to have to figure out how to win this trial, even though the jury had reached a verdict before he had the opportunity to issue his opening statement. He'd begun working with Grace with the hope of advancing through the ranks and opening his own boutique law firm. Now she'd sucked up so much of his life, he couldn't even manage something as simple as claiming the blessing that God had clearly sent his way.

"Well?" she said, prodding, tapping his foot with hers. "How am I supposed to trust you, Ethan? Sorry isn't enough."

"If you weren't interested in working this thing out, Candace, why did you come here?"

Her tough girl facade began to crack like the exterior of a prewar brownstone. Reaching across the gulf of empty space between them, Ethan delicately scooped her hand into his, took a full step backward, and perched himself on the edge of his desk. He studied her eyes and waited for them to respond before her mouth. No words came. Only love and longing seemed to radiate from her eyes and penetrate his skin. The combination of her sultry eyes and pouty lips sent a surge of heat through his body. She couldn't bring herself to say, "I've forgiven you," but her body spoke to him. Candace dropped her hip and curved her body toward him. Her arms were no longer stiff but hung loosely at her sides. This takeover would not be hostile.

Parting his legs, Ethan pulled her in closer. He was ready to bathe in the warmth of her body. He wanted to nestle his head in the center of her chest.

"How do I know that after my hair goes back in a bun, I take off the Spanx and the lipstick, and I lose the smoky eyes, you're still going to look at me with those same goo-goo eyes?" she sputtered, halting his efforts to craft in his mind's eye a picturesque reconciliation.

"Here's the long and short of it." He looked down at his hands as he squeezed hers tightly, then began to confess. "She was vulnerable, and I was weak. My flesh was weak for her, but in that moment I learned something."

"What?" she groaned, dismissing his remarks before he'd made an admission.

"When Grace is around, my head aches." Ethan dropped Candace's hands, placed his hands on her waist, and looked up at her. "But when you're not around, my side aches. I don't feel good without my rib," he admitted, collapsing onto her chest. In her arms he felt at ease and free from the burdens that came along with managing someone like Grace.

Candace hesitantly stroked the back of his head. The first stroke was heavy handed and awkward, like she was just looking for a place to rest her hand, but as Ethan secured a position in the groove between her breasts, she continued stroking his head, eventually finding a rhythm that soothed him and reminded him of what was important in life.

With each stroke, he clung tighter to Candace's waist. His heart was beating faster than Usain Bolt could complete the two-hundred-meter dash.

"Ethan . . ." Candace spoke softly to him. "What do you want from me?"

He looked up into her soft brown eyes, which were wide with expectancy. She expected an answer. She deserved an answer. Only, he hadn't prepared for this line of questioning. "Do you think we could discuss this over dinner?"

The corners of Candace's mouth began to fold, indicating her displeasure. There hadn't even been time for him to compare the pros and cons of this relationship and think this thing through logically and systematically. He'd thrown his decision-making system out the window when the firm tossed Grace his way, and now he was deeply buried in a pile of mess.

"I still have to secure a meeting for Grace with the director of this film ASAP and . . ."

"And you don't know if you could be my Adam or I could be your Eve? Well, you better figure it out this evening, busta." She touched him on the temple playfully, then turned and headed toward the door, a smile on her face.

"I thought love is patient," Ethan replied, following behind her and extending his reach to grab her hand. He kissed the back of her hand tenderly.

"You're right. Love is patient, and God is love. However, I, Candace, have not yet been perfected. So you better come correct and come quick," she quipped before slipping her fingers out of his hand and stepping out the door.

Chapter 27

Ethan hummed "What You Won't Do for Love," filling Grace's condo with remnants of what must have been an evening well spent with Candace. The wash and glow of love had adorned him when she'd opened her front door for him at 7:00 a.m., and it had not dissipated after an hour of waiting on her. Grace wanted to be happy for him, but she couldn't bring herself to be happy under these circumstances. He'd shown up at her doorstep, chipper and ready to hand deliver her to Javier Roberts, as if she were a trinket that could be written off as damaged.

Not only had this realization stunned her, but it had also left her utterly incapable of making a single decision. She'd taken off her wig at least three times, unsure whether it made her look too youthful or too sexy. Grace didn't want to stimulate Javier's visual senses in any way. Actually, she planned on showing up there looking disheveled and lost, hoping that he'd back out and release her from her obligation. The slightest hint of disarray was a turnoff for Javier Roberts, and she planned on playing on what she knew to get out of this deal. Ethan's reunion with Candace was supposed to be enough to absolve Grace. Apparently, that aspect of it was an epic failure. Their reunion must have spurred a new focus and sense of vigor in Ethan—landing him on Grace's doorstep.

"Grace, you're not preparing for a fashion show. You know that, right? This is just a sit-down. So hurry up and come down," he shouted up the steps.

"Yes, Ethan," Grace whined into the air like a teenager talking back to her crabby father.

With the pressure on her, Grace settled for a slouchy tee under a pin-striped blazer, a pair of distressed boyfriend jeans, nude pumps, and a maroon fedora. She paused in front of her full-length mirror and smiled at her reflection. She'd managed to pull together a funky and fashion-forward look without brazenly flaunting her sex appeal. The rawness of her skin tempted her to put on a splash of makeup, but her inner voice prompted her to appear at this sit-down barefaced. *Javier won't be the least bit interested in you when he sees all your imperfections,* she thought.

Sunlight cascaded through the rectangular sunroof of the conference room of Javier Roberts's studio, causing the square, open-centered conference table to gleam like brass. The brown table and the clean white lines indicated that Javier was still in his purity phase. Grace couldn't recall how long after she'd started working with him that he transformed into this purist and wanted everything in a natural and untempered state.

Staring at Javier through slits for eyes, Grace took measured sips of the kombucha tea Javier's assistant had placed in front of her when she arrived. It was a wee bit cold, mirroring how she felt inside as soon as he entered the room with the producer and took a seat across from her and Ethan at the conference table.

"I think you're a bit underdressed for this meeting," Ethan whispered into her ear as Javier and the producer took their seats.

"Ethan, what do you want me to do now? Go home and change?"

"Don't be ridiculous. There's no time for your diva antics today. Javier and Dalton Dally didn't request a sit-down before allowing you on the set to play around."

"Well, then, let's get this over with," Grace insisted, rolling her neck and raising her voice slightly. "Make sure everything is legit, and spare the small talk," she said, pursing her lips tightly. The plan was to not utter a word. It had been a long time since she'd sat in Javier's presence, and she didn't know whether or not she'd be able to maintain her composure when she saw him. Every time Grace even thought about his name and this little stunt he was trying to pull, nothing but cuss words filled the cavities of her mind. There were a few times when she envisioned laying hands on him, and not in the biblical sense. Now she had to keep it together or forget about ever getting close to Horace.

Nothing is guaranteed. You could just walk away from this now. Walking away from the sit-down before it began seemed like the only logical thing to do, but with Ethan seated to her right and that huge vein pulsating in his temple staring at her, this was virtually impossible. Furthermore, the chance to experience even a sliver of love outweighed whatever torture was bound to be wrapped up in this film.

After shuffling through some papers, Javier clapped his hands together, signaling he was prepared to begin this meeting. Grace directed her gaze to the wing-tip shoes Javier was wearing, instead of to his face, as she listened to what he had to say.

"It really, really is an honor to have Grace make her big-screen debut in my film. I can't imagine what took so long to get you here, but I hope that you're fully prepared to star in a Javier Roberts film." His shrill voice bounced off the walls of the abandoned factory he'd converted into his photography studio and office.

No words came from her mouth. Grace had dissemi-
nated her fair share of lies and had labeled them storytell-
ing while she was growing up, but right now saying she
was fully prepared to tackle this role was a fable that not
even Mother Goose would write.

"Is everything all right, Ms. King?" Dalton Dally, the
film's producer, asked, placing his folded hands on the
table. "We're prepared to do all that we can to accom-
modate your schedule so that the filming doesn't conflict
with your other obligations. However, I cannot waste any
more money holding up production, waiting for you to
get it together," he stated, squaring up his chest like a bull
preparing to pounce on a matador.

Grace glanced at Ethan from the corner of her eye and
elbowed him, prompting him to be her voice today.

Clearing his throat and adjusting his tie, Ethan chimed
in. "Please excuse Grace's silence. She's delving into the
role right now."

"Is that what this fresh-faced look is all about?" Javier
asked, winking at Grace. "I love it." He shifted slightly
in his seat to face his partner. "I told you she would be
excellent for this role."

Grace chewed the inside of her cheek. Her plan had
backfired: her appearance had only made Javier more
excited about reenacting his violation of her temple on
the silver screen.

"We don't plan to waste any of your time. Grace is
ready to work and is prepared to be on the set as soon as
you need her to be."

Javier drummed his bony fingers on the wooden table.
"We've already begun shooting the scenes that we don't
need her in. So, here's what I'm thinking . . ." Rising
from his metallic swivel chair, Javier traveled around
the conference table and sat down beside Grace. "I'll
e-mail you a revised version of the shooting schedule this

afternoon. I think we can carve out some time for you to begin shooting next week." He rested his palm on her shoulder and massaged it gently.

Grace tightened her body under his hand. It felt like she was being stabbed with a thousand t-pins. "That sounds fine," she said quickly, trying to get out from under his grip and put an end to this meeting.

"We'll begin with the most difficult scenes first, just to get the gory stuff out of the way." Javier brushed the apple of her cheek with the back of his hand. "Let's take a look at the storyboards for the film, just so you have a visual to work with until you're on the set. How does that sound?"

"That sounds great," Ethan said, smiling while backing his chair away from the table. "I'll head back to the office and get the PR machine pumping."

Grace grabbed his arm and whispered through clenched teeth, "Don't leave me alone. Please." She dug her fingers so deeply into his flesh, she could feel some of his skin rip as her nails cut into his arm. Her arm shook as she held on to Ethan's. Leaving her alone with Javier would be disastrous. He'd greedily undressed her with his eyes the moment he sat down beside her, and his hand was now slowly traveling from her shoulder to the center of her back. If left alone with him, Grace was sure that what had happened before would happen again.

Hold on to me. I will cover you with my feathers.

Grace shook her head, trying to shut out the voice she'd heard.

Hold on to me. No man is able to pluck you out of my hand.

She studied Ethan's lips and disregarded Javier's traveling hand. His lips weren't moving, but she was sure she had heard something. "Ethan, what did you just say?"

"I didn't say anything."

"Are you sure you didn't say something about a hand?" Grace asked, still clutching his arm both for safety and for clarity.

"I'm sure. But I was about to say, 'Let go of me, Grace.' You're squeezing the life out of me." Ethan pulled his arm close to his body and investigated the scratches.

Javier cleared his throat and rested his palm on the center of her back. "You must have heard the voice of God, Grace. His hand is all over this. My dreams and my visions—I mean our dreams—will be on the big screen soon."

The devil is a liar. God's hand is not in this perversion, she thought, recalling a Sunday school lesson on how the devil had caused lightning and wind to destroy Job's children's home, but those who saw the event said that fire had fallen from heaven. Furthermore, she reasoned that even if God's hand was in this, when He spoke, it wasn't to people like Grace.

Chapter 28

"Clearly, she's still in character," Ethan said, fudging in order to fill in the gap in the conversation. "Let's have a look at the storyboards. Together," he added, eyeing Grace.

His look and words were exactly what she needed to move to the next phase of this meeting. Javier shuffled out of the room to get the storyboards, and Dally excused himself to attend another meeting.

Ethan reclaimed his seat beside her. He must have sensed her continued discomfort, because he whispered, "I got you," directly into her ear and locked hands with her while they waited on Javier to fetch the storyboards.

Javier reentered the conference room with a black stand in his hand on which to mount the storyboards. Several storyboards were under his arm, and a twinkle of delight was in his eyes. Grace wondered what made him tick, what made him think that what he was doing was fine, what made him think that he could get away with defiling her for a second time. While the flames of rage rallied within her, threatening to scorch anything in her line of vision, her memory dulled the fire. Her father's words cooled her and settled her. "You have played the harlot," and "I will laugh during the time of your calamity," he had said to her repeatedly. There was no one in this world—God or man—who was concerned with what happened to a harlot.

The Word of God confirmed the verbal beatings her father had bestowed upon her when he discovered what she'd done with David. He'd pick up the Bible she cherished, the one she'd received after her baptism. It was a teen study Bible, with her name embossed in gold on it. The youth leader, Pastor David, had given it to her. He'd said it was "God's love letter to her," but her father had shown her that like Israel, God had written her a letter of divorcement for having tainted herself.

The gasp that escaped from Ethan's mouth brought her back to the present. Grace followed his eyes to the storyboards Javier had placed on display. Javier stood in front of the storyboards, smiling and waving his arms up and down in front of them like Vanna White did before revealing a letter on *Wheel of Fortune*. The handcrafted black-and-white drawings were clearly Javier's handiwork. Each panel vividly portrayed part of a rape scene. Detailed drawings of the photographer mounting the young ingenue while ripping her shirt off sat before them. Buttons bounced all over the storyboards. The drawings seemed to be three-dimensional.

The room began to spin like a Cracker Jack prize, just as the studio set had the first time it happened. Javier's onion breath crept up Grace's nostrils, and her skin began to crawl as her eyes followed the story being played out in front of her eyes.

"Stop!" and "I don't want to do this!" tried to climb out of her throat, but her eyes landed on the storyboard in which he'd wrapped one hand around her throat and the other around her mouth. The words reneged on her. Her throat closed and seemed to cave in on her.

"This is so graphic . . . so . . . ." Ethan paused. The images on the storyboards had paralyzed him as well.

"Raw. I was striving for the same kind of grit that *Monster's Ball* had. A story that was pure and rife with . . ."

The sound of Javier's voice bounced off the walls and shook Grace up so much that the contents of her stomach—a bran muffin, blueberry-pomegranate juice, and kombucha—were suddenly all over Ethan's side, and she was barely able to sit up straight in the chair. Perspiration descended from the pits of her arms like the water in Niagara Falls.

"I'm sorry, Ethan," she gasped, using her fedora as a fan.

"Oh my God!" Ethan shrieked. Panic engulfed his face and took his deep voice hostage. "Grace . . . Grace," he repeated before turning to Javier.

At that moment Javier was standing at the open door and screaming, "I need a cleaning crew in here immediately!"

"Javier, this is not going to work. If just these images can traumatize her like this, she can't do this role," Ethan declared.

Relief swelled in Grace's chest. Maybe she wasn't going crazy. She was protected and covered by the Lord.

"She was born for this. This type of visceral reaction is necessary and will register with audiences and with the academy instantaneously." Javier snapped his fingers. "Can you imagine what's next for her, and what's next for you after helping ink the deal that got her in this film? You'll be golden, Summerville. Golden."

Grace couldn't make out the rest of the conversation the two shared. Based on Ethan's smile and the pats on the back that Javier gave him, she knew there was no turning back from here on out. This left Grace to wonder, *Lord, where are you in all this*?

Chapter 29

After their meeting with Javier, Ethan escorted Grace to the Suburban with tinted windows that was waiting outside of Javier's studio in the Meatpacking District. Grace ducked her head and took a seat inside the car. She abandoned all her model etiquette and slouched in the seat. Doing the jitterbug with her legs, she looked at Ethan, who was still standing on the curb and holding on to the car door.

"What are you waiting on, Ethan? I want to get out of here." Grace's skin was still crawling, and her stomach was still jumpy. She wanted to get far away from this place and fast.

"Just hang tight for a moment. Please allow me to go down the block and get a new pair of pants. I believe I saw a Hugo Boss shop on the way here," he said, looking away from the car. "Listen, Grace." Ethan leaned on the roof of the car and peered in at her. A trace of sympathy registered in his eyes. "You've got to pull it together. Our next stop is the church, and you can't be in there tripping. Forgive me for the lack of a better word, but you can't lose it again today. Tomorrow . . . fine. You can go to anger management tomorrow and crack up in there all you want. But today you need to keep it together until everything is settled."

Then Ethan slammed the car door and scuttled down the block as quickly as possible. He moved along awkwardly, trying to avoid bumping into anyone on the street. After a few minutes, Ethan returned and opened the passenger-side door with a smile on his face.

"Are you ready to take care of business?" he asked.

Sucking her teeth audibly and turning her head so she faced forward, Grace didn't bother responding to Ethan, who was obviously trying not to acknowledge her problem and was more worried about business than her well-being.

"What does that sound mean?" he asked, climbing in the SUV one well-tailored pants leg at a time.

"That sound meant I want to curse you out, but since we're on our way to a church and I already have enough to repent for, I figured I'd keep it to myself."

Ethan drew the door shut, reached across Grace, and tapped on the driver's seat to indicate they were ready to roll. After securing his seat belt, he turned to Grace. "What are you so angry about? I'm the one running around, doing damage control for a grown woman, not some teenager who let fame go to her head. What I wouldn't give to be Justin Bieber's lawyer or publicist right now instead of yours," he said. Then he turned his gaze to the traffic outside his window.

"Humph . . ." Grace folded her arms across her chest and sat there silently for a few moments, staring at Ethan's profile, trying to coax him with her eyes out of this frenzy he was in. When she got no response, she tapped him on the leg. "When did I stop being a person to you and become just a client?"

"When I stopped being a person to you," Ethan replied. "Driver, turn on some music please."

Just like that he'd silenced her. With her thoughts and feelings muted, Grace resorted to kicking the back of the driver's seat for the rest of the ride to release her frustration. All the while she was wondering what it was going to take to get him back on her side.

***

When the Suburban pulled up to the curb in front of Mount Carmel, shouts of praise were coming from the church.

"Ethan, I don't think they're doing community service today," Grace said as they walked to the door. "What's going on today?"

Ethan shrugged his shoulders and scratched the center of his head. Apparently, he wasn't aware of what went on in his own church.

"What do you mean, you don't know?" Grace asked, mocking him. "This is your church, isn't it?"

Ethan looked down instead of answering her question. It was valid, after all. He was the one who was supposed to be leading her to Christ, and he hadn't even set one foot in the house of the Lord enough to know what was going on.

A voice could be heard whispering in the recesses of her soul to leave him alone, but she'd been listening to the voice of destruction so long, she couldn't resist pouncing on him and highlighting his flaws.

"What happened to all your praying and the faithfulness of God, huh?" She nudged him with her shoulder. "Where are all your words and scriptures now? Got nothing of substance to say now?" Grace fumed.

The fear and shame from what Javier had done to her, and was about to do to her again, had joined forces with the anger and hurt she'd been collecting over the years like interest. Everything she'd thought about men and God was beginning to make sense. Their words were merely that—words. None of them cared about her pain or her loss, and they were quick to judge her actions and discard her when she displeased them. First, David had done so, using her parents, and her father had been God's messenger, distilling and delivering His wrath. And Ethan had to be on the cleanup crew.

"Just as I thought," she said, taking large strides toward the door. "You're just as lost as I am, but you don't want to say we're in the same boat." She rolled her eyes and continued walking toward the door. Maybe today the Lord would reveal why every man she met was so royally screwed up.

You're wrong. When my spirit is in a man, he is different. All things are made new.

Grace's neck snapped back quickly. There was that voice, invading her thoughts again. Ethan's head was down, and he was dragging his feet. All that positivity could not have come from his lips, and judging by his demeanor, he definitely hadn't heard any of those words.

Either she was losing her mind under these circumstances, all the drugs had finally caught up with her and she was day tripping, or God was speaking to her. With those possibilities looming before her, Grace hurriedly snatched the gold handle on the door to Mount Carmel, pulled open the door, and walked in. If she had a choice in the matter, her choice seemed rather clear to her. She didn't want to be saved, but she didn't want to be anybody's *E! True Hollywood Story* episode, either.

The organ music died down. The brass cymbals of the drums emitted a rattle to back up the powerful voice resonating throughout the sanctuary.

"Reclaim your life. Reclaim your life," was the chant coming from the pew and falling on the people like dew. "Today. Be whole. Today."

Narrowing her eyes on the speaker, Grace realized that it was Horace who was standing in the pulpit, running things today. She slid into a tight corner seat, next to a heavyset woman and a bunch of children who looked like they were from *Bébé's Kids*. She crossed her legs, wrapping them tightly around each other. She didn't even bother to check if Ethan had found a seat. Grace's focus was no longer on her issues or Ethan's when a different kind of man stood before her.

Horace strode across the platform, completely comfortable. Not a speck of nervousness could be found in his eyes or heard in his voice.

"When God comes into your life, He gives you a new one. The one that you lived is no good. Did you hit a roadblock? Been stuck at a pit stop for too long? Turn it over to Jesus and reclaim your life. Every hurt, every pain, every injury, every scar."

As Horace went through the list of possible troubles, a tingling sensation zipped through Grace. It collected in her wrists, compelling her to raise her hands to the Lord. Every burden Horace had named belonged to her. Suddenly their weight had caught up with her, and she no longer wanted to carry it. The Holy Ghost was using Horace's words like a scalpel to peel back years of anguish buried in the cavities of Grace's soul.

Grace swayed from side to side, rubbing against the wet flesh of the woman beside her. Perspiration was dripping from every crevice of the woman's body. The Holy Ghost must have been working on the entire bench. The children who sat beside the woman were now silent, and every hand was raised to the air.

Fighting with the spirit, Grace bit down on her bottom lip. The pressure of her maxillary incisors were no match for the power of God. Her lip trembled and quivered under her teeth until they were able to break free. Next, a cry launched from her throat. Grace didn't understand why her faculties would not obey her. The next body parts to break ranks were her legs. Grace pushed down, and her legs pushed up involuntarily, forcing her to stand. She wobbled down the aisle until she reached the front of the church.

The ushers surrounded her, and she shifted from side to side, barely escaping their white-gloved touch. Horace batted them back, then manipulated his fingers to summon someone from behind her. Straining to see through the film of tears that covered her eyes, Grace fought to keep her eyes glued to Horace. Horace continued preaching as he marched down from the pulpit.

The underarms of his mustard button-down shirt were lined with semicircles of sweat. This didn't seem to faze him. His dark eyes glittered like augite, igniting a conflagration of emotions within Grace. Faces flashed before her. Words resounded in her ears. *Mistake. Monster. Love. Grace. Grace. Grace.*

I want to find grace. I want to find grace. "I want to find grace. O Lord, I want to find your grace," she cried aloud. Amid the shadows of the people who had gathered around her and had covered her, she let go.

When Grace opened her eyes, she could see three things: the paint peeling from the ceiling of Mount Carmel, Sister Bryce's hand extended to help her up, and Sister Marva's crooked smile. It was doubtful that Sister Marva was delighted that Grace had found redemption; seeing Grace laid out was probably a joyous moment for her. Grace latched on to Sister Bryce's hand, and Sister Bryce cupped her elbow, helping Grace to a standing position. Sister Marva flicked a tissue in Grace's direction, while Sister Bryce dusted off the back of Grace's blazer and fixed her fedora back on her head. Reluctantly, Grace stretched forth her fingers to retrieve the tissue from Sister Marva.

"Come on now. Dry those eyes. There's no reason to be crying in the house of the Lord, unless it's over His goodness," Sister Bryce said to Grace.

"Humph . . . She better come on with all this falling-out business." Sister Marva sneered. "She ain't even a member of the church, and she carrying on like that."

Sister Marva was right. Grace wasn't a member of the church, and she hadn't been slain in the spirit long enough not to consider slapping Sister Marva or at least stepping on Sister Marva's shoes while she struggled to find her legs. Grace's evil intentions must have been plastered on her face. Sister Bryce locked arms with Grace and leaned into her, advising her about righteousness.

"You pray for people like that," she said. "You pray for sisters who haven't found their way yet and are in the church, still holding on to bitterness. Smile. Just like this." Sister Bryce paused to demonstrate for Grace. She leaned forward just a bit, looked in Sister Marva's direction, and cast a wide smile at her. "Then you pray, and you let the Holy Ghost do the whippin'. You understand?" she said, laying her hand on top of Grace's and patting it gently.

Sister Bryce led Grace to a seat on the front row, beside Horace. Grace crouched down slowly. She fixed her eyes on the handcrafted pulpit. A cross with Jesus hanging on it was carved into the wood. Horace whispered something to her, which she refused to hear.

Please, Lord don't let anything get in the way of this moment, she thought.

Pastor David mounted the pulpit and addressed his congregation. "Thank you all for attending our men's ministry celebration of our members. We have some real gems at Mount Carmel. In closing, remember what our very own Brother Horace said. 'It is time to reclaim your life.'" This was all Grace could hear.

Chapter 30

Grace was bombarded after the service by a bevy of boys, girls, and some adults who wanted to take photos with her. She posed for countless selfies. Social media had turned everyone into the paparazzi, and at this stage of the game she already knew how to grin and bear it. However, she wished that she had followed her gut and had at least applied some concealer this morning. If they were true fans, they'd all use the filter function on their phones before posting her photos.

Once they were done treating Grace like a museum exhibit, the churchgoers discussed whose house they would eat at if they were not staying for the meal being cooked up in the pantry, and then they slowly disassembled. The smell of chicken broth and collard greens had somehow made its way up the stairs and into Grace's nostrils. Famished, she was ready to find Ethan so she could resume her community service and get herself a plate too. Grace didn't have to look far to find Ethan. He was in the middle of the aisle, conversing with the other two men in her life—Pastor David and Horace.

Grace approached the band of men and stepped in the middle of their circle. Standing up straight, she was practically eye to eye with each man, give or take a few inches. She didn't allow those few inches to impede her. She exhaled a long breath and began speaking so rapidly that her words ran together. "This was a great service, man. I didn't know y'all got down like that on a weekday." She clapped her hands together, trying to center herself and regain the composure she'd lost moments ago, during her meeting with the Holy Ghost. "However, I'm ready to get back into the groove of things, Pastor David," she said, waving her hands from side to side like she was surfing.

"We were just discussing that issue," Pastor David said. "We're not sure that this is going—"

"Uh-uh . . . You don't get to make this call for me," Grace said, wagging her finger at each one of them. "None of you get to make this decision for Grace King. That's how my life got so messed up. Other people who thought they knew better than me meddled in my life, and now I'm all screwed up."

"Don't talk about yourself so negatively," Horace told her. "You are not screwed up. You have been broken, bruised, and mishandled, but you are not screwed up. You're reclaiming your life today." He grabbed her hand and interlocked his fingers with hers.

This simple gesture bolstered Grace's confidence and gave her the green light she needed to proceed. Someone was in this fight with her.

"That's right. I'm reclaiming my life, and I like it here," she declared while squeezing Horace's hand firmly.

Pastor David cleared his throat and fidgeted with the black band on his watch before responding. "There are a number of reasons that we"—he pointed at Ethan and then back at himself—"thought having you continue your community service here at Mount Carmel was not a good idea." He glanced down at Grace and Horace's interlocked fingers with a slightly pained look in his eyes. "However, Grace King, y-you are right," he stammered.

"What?" Grace asked, staring intently at him.

Pastor David clamped his burnished, brown, hard-knuckled hands against his chest. They seemed to glow against his toasted orange button-down. He ran his hands straight down his chest as he inhaled and exhaled deeply.

"You're right," he said. "You were manipulated into doing something that was against God to make others forget about their sins or feel ashamed. You're manipulated every single day to sell some product, and you don't get a say, but today the ears of heaven are open to your request. Where the spirit of Christ is, there is liberty. You are free to do your community service here and to worship here if you like."

"Pastor David," Ethan interjected while stepping forward to stand beside the pastor. "Are you sure that this is going to be beneficial to all the parties involved?"

"It's by faith and not by sight, Brother Ethan," Pastor David said, shaking his head. Pastor David placed one hand on Ethan's shoulder. "I know only one thing for sure. . . . Jesus would do anything to save even one lost sheep, and I can't deny my own role in what happened to Grace by pretending she isn't around or acting like I don't know something is going on." Pastor David shifted his attention from Ethan to Grace. "Grace King, I pray that you can forgive me for my role in what happened to you and our baby."

The words *our baby* reverberated inside of Grace, shaking her insides, as if someone had just banged a gong right beside her. She leaned on Horace's shoulder and placed her free hand on her abdomen. It seemed like she'd been waiting her entire life for someone to acknowledge the fact that she had been pregnant once— that there had once been someone living and breathing inside of her. The guilt associated with being responsible for the murder of her baby had eaten at the marrow of her bones. Unlike other models, Grace didn't have to resort to bulimia, anorexia, macrobiotic diets, or extreme workout regimens to maintain her weight. The guilt and the shame she'd felt over the years had done a good job of keeping her at a model's size. It took Grace a few beats to find her words.

"What are you saying, David?" she asked, dropping the title and speaking to the boy she'd once loved.

"I am saying that I am sorry. I am sorry for being complacent. I watched them usher you into back rooms for meetings with the elders of the church. I allowed them to cordon you off, as if remaining silent would help, because I was ashamed." He dropped his head and lowered his voice one octave. "I was ashamed. . . ."

Now it was Ethan's turn to play the supporting cast role. He patted his pastor and brother in Christ on the back, while Grace tapped her toes on the floor. She was growing impatient as she waited for Pastor David to reveal what he'd been ashamed of. No one had walked around calling him a jezebel, Bathsheba, or any other name. There had been no whispers when he walked by, and his parents had continued to speak to him with love in their eyes.

"Forgive me, Grace." A solitary tear slid down Pastor David's face. "My silence made it possible for me not to acknowledge my sin before God or my parents. I was ashamed . . . that I was not the man of God everyone thought I would be."

Pastor David's head remained down. A hush covered the sanctuary. Ethan and Horace seemed to be paralyzed. They barely looked at each other. Grace doubted that they'd ever seen or imagined Pastor David as a man or even as a boy. Although they were still locked tightly in Horace's, Grace's fingers trembled as all the hurt, the shame, and the names returned to her. She didn't want to say what her heart was saying. *Go on. Say it. Take the first step to reclaim your life.*

"David, you were just a boy then."

Raising his head to meet her eyes, Pastor David replied, "Now I am man seeking forgiveness on behalf of the boy who hurt the girl still chained up inside of you."

"Well, are you going to forgive him or not?" Horace called out to Grace from his favorite spot in her condo—in front of the floor-to-ceiling windows. "If you're going to be at Mount Carmel, then you've got to find a way to reach some sort of closure." He stuffed his hands into the pockets of his pressed graphite-colored khakis.

"How do you like your coffee?" Grace asked, leaning over the countertop and dangling a large white porcelain mug from one finger, ready to fulfill his caffeinated desires.

"The same way I like my women—strong and uncompromised. I like my coffee black," Horace stated, finally looking over his shoulder at Grace.

"This will be done in two shakes of a horse's mane." Grace spun around and tapped each K-Cup on the rack until she found the flavor she thought would best meet Horace's desire for strong and uncompromised coffee. *Dark Magic, extra bold, ought to suit him,* she decided, thinking the description applied more to herself than the coffee. She popped the K-Cup into her Keurig, and in less than two minutes she was traipsing across her living room with a steaming hot mug of coffee in her hand.

"Here you go, Horace," Grace said softly as the mug of coffee exchanged hands. "Be careful. It's hot," she advised him, delicately resting her hand on his arm.

"Thank you."

Horace blew on the mug a few times. Each time he puckered up, his supple lips called Grace in for a kiss. She eased a bit closer to him as he took his first sip of the coffee. She couldn't understand why all that talk about reclaiming your life and a few minutes of hand holding had her feeling like she was sitting in a hot spring. Grace removed her blazer and threw her shoulders back. She knew her breasts were still perky enough to command attention from even the most devout worshipper. Horace, however, didn't even try to sneak a peek from his periphery.

"Well, Grace, what are you going to do?"

"Is this a decision I have to make right now?"

Horace turned around and looked at her face-to-face. "What do you think?"

Grace knew what Horace wanted to hear. He wanted her to do the good Christian thing and say that she forgave Pastor David for everything that had happened. However, those words had not entirely taken root in her heart yet. She understood his position now, but that didn't mean she forgave him. Thankfully, the intercom buzzed, announcing the arrival of an unexpected guest.

"Hold that thought," she said as she sped off to the intercom.

"Who is it, Arnie?"

"Some woman in dark glasses and a ridiculous hat, claiming to be your best friend," Arnie said, rolling his eyes. In the background Junell could be heard shouting, "It's me, Gracie," and it was evident that she was trying to force her head over the counter into the camera's view.

The tip of her nose and the extra-wide two-tone brim on the fedora they had bought the last time they were in Milan were enough to let Grace know that it was, indeed, her best friend. "Arnie, let her up, and tell her she's lucky this is a video intercom."

"My best friend, Junell, is on her way up," Grace announced to Horace. "You two should get along well. She's all saved and fire baptized like you."

Grace remained by the door, waiting to greet her best friend and avoiding Horace's question. As soon Junell rapped on the door, Grace whipped it open. Removing her glasses and fedora, Junell waddled in. The little pouch of fat she had had when she first announced she was pregnant was now a pronounced mound on her belly.

"Hey, G!" She wrapped her arms around Grace and scooped her into an embrace. "I missed you so much. Where have you been? Wrapped up in the arms of that chocolate drop you told me about?"

Grace stared at Junell fiercely. If Junell wasn't pregnant, she would have popped her one time.

"I hope I'm the chocolate drop she's been telling you about," Horace said as he turned from the window to face the ladies, a wide grin on his face.

"Oh my . . ." Junell covered her mouth. "I didn't know you had company."

"I'm sorry I didn't have a chance to post it as my Facebook status," Grace said, letting out a gurgle of laughter.

"Well, don't be such a bad host. Introduce us," Junell instructed, walking to the center of the open living room.

"Horace, this is Junell. Junell, this is Horace," Grace mumbled quickly, her cheeks still glowing from embarrassment.

"Horace, you *are* the chocolate drop she told me about. When are you going to give my girl some play?"

"*Junie.*" Grace stomped her foot on the parquet floor. "Horace," she said, pleading with him with her eyes. "Don't mind her. I think it's the hormones that have her speaking like this. Usually, she sings hymns and quotes Bible scriptures to me."

Chuckling, Horace replied, "You mean when she's not chasing perps on *Bloodshed*. Grace, I had no idea you were friends with Junell Pierce." He turned to Junell. "I am so glad to meet you," he said, raising her hand to his lips.

"Oh, Grace, he's a keeper," Junell said. "What do you have to eat in here?" she asked, turning toward the kitchen.

"Have a look around, Junie."

"Grace, I'm going to head out. A pregnant woman on the hunt for food can get ugly," Horace said.

"All the more reason why you should not leave me alone with her." Grace clasped her fingers together and pouted. "Please."

"She's your best friend. You'll be fine." He placed both of his hands on her shoulders. "I'd rather keep the vision I have of her as the no-nonsense, hot cop in my mind."

"You know, I never pegged you for a groupie," Grace said, poking Horace in the chest.

Horace leaned in closer to her and whispered, "And once you give yourself over to the Lord, I'll be glad to be your biggest groupie." He rubbed his nose against hers, transforming an Eskimo kiss into foreplay for Grace.

"Don't torture her like that," Junell shouted from the kitchen.

"She's the one torturing me." Horace looked into Grace's eyes and then swiveled his head to face Junell. "All I want is a whole woman, and she keeps on withholding herself from God. I don't want to have a woman who's not on my side, like Job's wife, or a Delilah, who will do me in for a few pieces of silver, and I'm not trying to lose her, because she's looking backward." Shifting his gaze back to Grace, he said, "I want her, but I want her whole."

His deep-set dark brown eyes and the way his lips curved when he said the letter r made Grace's legs weak. Her desire to become whole was increasing, but it had not yet grown larger than the enmity that she carried for the church that had been so quick to cast her aside. Then there was the debacle of a movie that his church brother was forcing her to do. A return to the vortex of darkness that she was sucked into after her initial dealing with Javier Roberts didn't come with a return ticket, either.

"I'm working on it, Horace."

"Stop working and let Him do it," he said softly, looking up at the ceiling. "I'll see you at the church for dinner tomorrow. Just know that your chocolate drop is expecting an extra serving of mac 'n' cheese and yams."

"I'll see what I can do." Grace swiveled around and led Horace to the door.

By the time Grace escorted Horace out and locked the door, Junell had seated herself on Grace's red leather couch and was noshing on slices of provolone cheese and crackers.

"I see you made yourself at home."

"You have the strangest stuff in your cabinets, girl. If you're trying to keep Horace, you're going to need some meat in that fridge and some meat on your bones," she said, taking a sip of almond milk.

"Meat on my bones? Junie, what happened to all that 'I need to read the holy writ' if I want a man like that?"

"That was before I saw him for myself. He is a little banquet for the eyes. Of course you need to get saved. I still stand by that notion, and I don't think you should be doing it for a man. What I do know, though, is if you're going to keep a brother like that, you're going to need something for him to hold on to."

"I don't believe you. I think you just want me to walk around, waddling alongside you," Grace said, laughing as she took a seat beside her friend. "What brings you uptown?"

"We're shooting in Central Park, and I was, like, 'Forget a trailer. I'm going to crash at my girl's house between takes.' If I knew you were holed up with him, I would have waited awhile."

"It's not what you think. All he did was sip coffee. See?" Grace pointed to the mug Horace had rested on the table near the window.

Junell slapped Grace on the thigh. "Well, since we're both not getting any, we're in the same boat. Patrick won't touch me with a baby in the belly. What else has been going on?"

"My plan to get Ethan and his girlfriend back together worked out. Javier Roberts wants to sue me blind if I don't do his ridiculous film—"

"Wait. What is the deal between you two? I really don't get why you don't want to do the film. He's supposed to be the next Lee Daniels, and you know what that means. Oscar buzz."

Grace massaged her face with the palms of both hands. She'd been friends with Junell for a long time now, but it was highly unlikely that Junell would believe Javier had raped her and was now casting her in a movie that depicted said rape. It definitely sounded like a great plotline for a movie, but it didn't sound plausible, Grace reckoned.

"I've run out of good excuses for not filming. I report to the set at the end of the week." Grace used one of her hands to support her head. "Actually, I've got to read through this script a few times if I'm going to be ready by Friday."

"Want my help?"

"No, thank you, Junie. I just need some peace and quiet to get into this role."

"Chamomile tea always helps me transition from Junell Pierce to Detective Agnes Base. I'm going to waddle out of your way. Call me if you need me. I'll be shooting in the park for the next three days. Don't move. I'll let myself out, and I'll tell that doorman to stop playing with me."

Grace laughed. "Arnie is innocent. Be nice to him."

Junell let herself out, leaving Grace alone with her thoughts. She walked up the steps to her bedroom and pulled out the fresh copy of the script that Ethan promptly had delivered as soon as Grace agreed to have a sit-down with Javier. He must have done it before he headed out to dinner with Candace. After grabbing the script, Grace sat down with her legs folded on the edge of her queen-size bed. She ran her hand along the cover page a few times. She felt light-headed before she even opened the script. Her mouth began to feel prickly, and the stench of Javier's breath filled the room as she cradled the script. She vaulted off the bed, pelted down the steps, and ran into the kitchen and grabbed the one thing that always drove the bad memories away—whiskey.

Her right hand shook as she poured the first glass. After two sips, she checked her hand, which was still shaking. She refilled her glass tumbler and downed the whole thing. Her right hand was still shaking, and she could feel a twinge in her left hand. She put the bottle on the counter and grabbed her wrist to control the shaking.

Reach for me. Reach for me.

"Is that you, God?" she shouted, looking up at the ceiling. "Is it really you? Why don't you reach for me? Where were you when I needed you the most?"

Here. Here. Here.

"I suppose you would say that, but I don't have any use for a God who says He's always here but hasn't shown up." She growled at the air, then snatched the bottle of whiskey off the counter and poured it directly into her mouth. "I almost thought I could trust you again. I prayed for you to take away the pain."

Healing comes in the fight. Fight the good fight of faith.

"I don't know what you're talking about. Whiskey always dulls the pain of unanswered prayers."

Chapter 31

Grace awoke to a shadowy figure standing over her bed, clapping his hands and shouting, "Lights, Camera. Action. Let's go. Today is the day you become a star."

Raising her head slightly, Grace looked out the corner of her eye and shooed the figure away. "I don't want to be a star," she said, burying her head deeply in her pillow. She hated when her dreams were all animated and lifelike. Now was not the time for that. She needed at least three more hours of sleep to shake off her hangover.

"They don't give out stars on the Walk of Fame for sleeping or being tardy," the figure said, snatching the sheet off Grace and tossing a pair of jeans and a T-shirt at her.

Grace sat up and massaged the corners of her eyes and tried to make out the identity of the blur of brown standing before her. She saw dark brown pants. Her eyes scrolled up, and she noticed that a simple Ferragamo belt accented the waist and kept a freshly dry-cleaned navy blue button-down in place. A matching dark brown blazer covered the frame of the figure standing before her.

"Grace Terisha King, I'm going to need you to get out of bed and move. You skipped anger management yesterday, and I'm not going for your games today."

Finally it clicked. The brown blob standing before her was Ethan. "Don't ever wear this god-awful color combination again. How'd you get in here?" she said, massaging her aching temples. "I thought I took the spare key from you."

"Correction. I returned the spare key, and after the last alcohol-induced coma debacle, I took the liberty of securing another spare key once your door was repaired. It was, and clearly still is, in your best interest."

"I'm not a baby, Ethan."

"Then dress yourself and make sure you brush your teeth. I'll make you some coffee. I need you ready to roll out. I promised Javier I'd have you on the set by nine thirty."

Grace coasted through hair and makeup on autopilot. She didn't blink or speak to a single person on the set; she just stood as still as a mannequin while being prepped to be raped on-screen. It didn't make a bit of sense, but this was what she'd signed up for. It had occurred to her that she could just walk off the set. People already thought she was a basket case; she didn't have a reputation to lose. At the same time, her future and Ethan's rested on the completion of this film. Javier Roberts was promising them fortunes untold and Oscar nominations at a minimum. There was no way she could forfeit the opportunity to be in the same league as Halle, Lupita, and Jennifer Hudson. This would be her chance to show her father and all those people who said she was nothing but a whore that she was more. That line of thinking would have helped her if wounds weren't still raw.

When the stylist tapped her shoulder, the bristles of the brush collided with skin, causing her to cringe. The rough texture of the bristles reminded her of Javier's coarse, dry hands prowling her body. One of the runners handed her a steaming cup of kombucha, while others directed her to the set.

"You can't have the tea on the set with you," Javier said sternly when she got to the set.

Grace looked at her hand and then placed the cup on the floor, next to the wooden legs of the director's chair. Javier was already in position behind the camera. For this scene he was both the director and the perpetrator.

"Remove the shoes and undo a few buttons on that shirt. Your hair is shouting innocent, and I need your body to sing a siren song on camera. You have to be vulnerable and desirable in this scene."

Following his commands, Grace stepped out of the slippers she was wearing and opened the first three buttons of the oversize men's button-down shirt she was wearing. She dipped the tip of her toe onto the institutional white tiles on the floor of the set, like she was testing the temperature of the water before jumping into a pool. She snatched her foot back and looked around the set. The walls were pristine white, like they were that night. The noise embargo that Javier had issued gave them the appearance of privacy, but when she looked out the corner of her eye, she saw that the boomer was there, holding the mic, and the cameraman had one eye glued to the camera and was signaling for Grace to hurry up and get on the set.

"All right, ladies and gentlemen. Lights, camera, action," Javier Roberts commanded.

In a trancelike state Grace stepped onto the set, then took long, lethargic steps toward the couch in the center of the room. She slowly sat down. Arching her back, she rested on an elbow and let her legs, which were wrapped around each other like twisted tree branches, dangle off the couch. She rattled off her lines as quickly as she could and took short, quick breaths between lines, trying to keep her breakfast down. It worked until Javier touched her. He placed his fingertips on her wrists, and his coarse fingers scorched her skin. The pain of his touch coursed through her veins, and memories of the past mixed with the present.

Grace shouted, "Please. Please don't do this to me. Please. I don't want to go through this."

"Cut!" Javier screamed over the pleas and dribble-filled cries.

The room spun dangerously out of control for Grace. Before she could contain them, her coffee, bran muffin, and a spot of kombucha were on the floor. Javier let go of her wrists and helped her to her feet.

"I'm sorry," Grace said, wiping the corner of her mouth with the collar of the shirt.

"You need to take five?" Javier reached for her arm, and Grace stepped back on her wobbly legs.

"Don't you dare touch me," she muttered under her breath.

Grace headed back to her trailer, which was parked just outside the studio, on Tenth Avenue and Twenty-sixth Street. Once she arrived at her trailer and stepped inside, the first thing Grace saw was her reflection in the mirror over the vanity table. When she looked at herself, she saw beneath the M·A·C foundation and concealer and noticed the soft sparkle that the orange button-down created against her skin. The image in the mirror was a fractured and fatal version of herself. She was hollow and dry. The prickles of a cactus were softer than Grace right now.

Picking up the vase that decorated the table beside her, she heaved it at the mirror in an attempt to stop the hollowing-out process unfolding before her eyes. This film was sucking the life out of her. She dragged herself to the vanity and took a seat in front of the mirror. She rubbed the palms of her hands together and pushed back her face and looked in the mirror. Javier's sharp eyes met hers in one of the distorted pieces of the cracked glass in the mirror. She hadn't noticed when he walked in.

He closed the door of her trailer behind him and rested his palm on the frame of the door for a moment. He walked over to her in silence and stood behind her seat at the vanity. He placed his hands on her shoulders, and she squirmed beneath his heavy hands like a fish out of water. A sharp and vicious look clouded his eyes.

"Why are you doing this, Javier?" Grace asked.

"I came to check on you, dear. I've already told hair, makeup, and wardrobe that you'll need to be touched up and to change your clothes."

Grace twisted partially in her chair and faced Javier. "You know what I mean. Why are you making this film?"

"America loves these kinds of stories. They love the embattled hero who defeats the villain. They long for the moment when the pigs outsmart the wolf. Danger and redemption mixed together is so classic. It's a pity you were never able to outsmart the wolf or slay the dragon, but this picture will change that." Javier cupped Grace's rounded chin. "You should be grateful I threw you this bone. My work has laid the foundation for you, and now I'm setting the stage for you." Releasing her chin, he twisted Grace's body so that she faced straight ahead.

Grace's cheeks expanded as she held back another round of vomit, induced by being in close proximity with Javier.

Working from the center part of Grace's fluffy jet-black wig, Javier ran the palms of his hands down the sides of her head. "What I want you to do now is gather yourself. I knew this scene might be a tad bit difficult for you, so I've got something to take the edge off." Javier dug his fingers into the pocket of his jeans and pulled out a small key. Bending over slightly, he unlocked the cabinet in the vanity to reveal a drawer stocked with some of Grace's favorites— whiskey, Jägermeister, and marijuana. The urge to pour a drink seized her, and she reached around him and pulled out the Jägermeister.

"Now, you take a few sips and smoke a couple of joints and relax," Javier said, patting her lap before walking out.

"Grace King, open this door," Ethan commanded, jiggling the knob on the door of her trailer. "The knob is twisting, but the door isn't opening," he said over his shoulder to Javier. "Why don't you get a crowbar or something and pop this door open, instead of standing over my shoulder, yapping about lost time and money wasted?"

Ethan didn't usually snap on sets, but something about this film wasn't right. Lately Grace had been acting more erratic than she usually did. He couldn't believe he'd fallen for Javier's fortune and fame speech. Now his client and closest friend was unresponsive on the other side of a locked door. The Bible verse of the day came to mind. *For what shall it profit a man, if he shall gain the whole world, and lose his own soul?*

The events of the past few weeks unfolded before him. Each nasty word and threatening tone was magnified before his eyes one blink at a time, like he was viewing his life through a child's viewfinder. Frame by frame, he saw his own growing obsession with the successful career he envisioned for himself, which had caused him to dismantle his greatest career achievement—his work for the Kingdom. A whiny client wasn't on the other side of the door; a soul precious in the sight of God was locked in the trailer. Ignoring the commotion surrounding him, Ethan called on his Father for help.

"Father God, please forgive my absentmindedness. Please forgive me for neglecting the call and not acknowledging my true profession. As a lawyer, you have positioned me in the same place as your dear Son. I am supposed to serve as an advocate and mediator, and to help those who need to reconcile their relationship with you. Please, God, restore my faith, and focus and order my steps, Lord, in Jesus's name. Amen."

Ethan stood in front of the door with his hand on the knob, waiting for specific instructions from God. He turned the knob slightly and pushed the door.

Not so hard.

He pushed it again and could see strands of black hair caught beneath the door.

"Grace."

She moaned in response to his call. He pushed the door again, this time using his body weight. As he pushed, Grace's skin squeaked as she skidded across the tiles of her trailer. Once the opening was large enough for Ethan to wiggle through, he eased into the trailer. He checked her vitals. Her breath was flat. Then he checked the surrounding area for the culprit in this escapade. An empty bottle of Jägermeister was at her feet, and an overturned bottle of whiskey was near her right hand and quickly spilling. He detected a hint of marijuana in the air.

Ethan swallowed hard and rammed his fist into the wall of the trailer to suppress the anger welling up in him. He could feel a good lecture mounting in him, but the grace of God was greater than all the words he could speak to her right now.

"What's going on in there?" Javier asked, poking his head in the cracked door.

Protect her.

"My client is leaving this set," Ethan told Javier while swooping down to pick Grace up.

"For how long?"

"Do you see the condition she's in?" he snarled. "She's leaving this set indefinitely—until I get to the bottom of what is really going on here, Mr. Roberts."

Ethan kicked the door back with his foot and charged down the steps.

"What do you mean, indefinitely?"

"I mean I don't care more about you or all the riches in the world than I do about Grace's well-being, and I will not compromise her to fulfill your lust and my thirst for success. Believe me, Mr. Javier Roberts, I will get to the bottom of this. I'm going to find out why your film has Grace over the edge, and when I do, you better have an excellent lawyer sitting next to you when I call you on the phone."

Ethan didn't wait for Javier's response. He bumped Javier out of the way, using Grace's legs to bat him back. He dived into the car he'd rented for her, and took her back home. On the drive back uptown, he texted Candace for some more hangover soup and Junell for moral support for Grace.

"Driver, please pull into the garage. I don't want anyone to see her like this."

"Understood, Mr. Summerville."

As planned, they coasted into the garage, while the paparazzi waited in two separate huddles. One group stood near the subway station, because Grace was notorious for taking public transportation, and the other group was perched a few feet away from the glass and gold doorway of Grace's high-rise building. Just in case there was a paparazzo lurking in the garage, Ethan removed the dark chocolate brown blazer that Grace had ripped into him for wearing and used it as a shield for her face.

He carried her through the garage and took the service elevator up to her unit. Grace moaned and mumbled gibberish in Ethan's arms. He responded to the statements he understood. Ethan was at a loss for words as she mumbled over and over about the Big Bad Wolf being after her.

"There's no wolf here," he said, once they were safely inside her condo. He removed the blazer from her head. "We're in your condo, Grace." Ethan laid her on the couch. "Look, Grace, you're home. Everything is going to be fine."

Grace reached for his yellow- and navy blue–striped tie, catching the triangular tip of it between her fingers. Her fingers inched up his tie until she was able to grasp it with the palm of her hand. "You don't understand." Her cheeks tightened and fright filled her eyes as she yanked Ethan's tie and pulled him closer to her. "The Big Bad Wolf is coming for me."

"Don't worry, Grace King. I'm going to protect you from the Big Bad Wolf."

Chapter 32

With one open eye and both ears fully tuned in, Grace eavesdropped from her couch, listening in on the powwow taking place in her kitchen. Ethan was playing commander in chief as he prepared to head into the office.

"Candace, Junell, come closer," he said, wrangling them to his side. "I've been holed up here with you ladies all weekend, and now it's time for me to hit the office and do major damage control."

"Damage control? Now, Ethan, don't you think you've waited a little too long for that?" Junell said. "Since you texted me, my phone's been ringing off the hook with calls from every outlet from TMZ to *E! News*. Javier and his people are way ahead of you."

Ethan placed both of his hands on his hips like he was Superman and responded firmly to her. "Junell, I'm not going unless God sends me and tells me what to say. When Grace hires you as her publicist, you can tackle these mishaps any way that you would like. Now I've had enough time to meditate and hear from God just what it is I need to say to cover Grace."

Grace wanted to clap her hands when she heard Ethan speak. He had returned to his senses and was back on her side.

"And what is that?" Junell asked, twisting her neck in what Grace could see was a failed attempt to bully Ethan into revealing what the Lord had spoken to him.

"Junell, I understand that's your best friend in there, but we're all concerned about Grace," Ethan said.

"We're all concerned about Grace? Is that right?" Junell sucked her teeth and turned her back slightly toward Candace. "No shade, but I know you've been treating my girl funny ever since you met ole girl over here, and I don't want to see G get hurt any more. I can't take this. I need her well and ready to spoil her goddaughter rotten when she pops out," she said, rubbing her belly repeatedly.

"Believe me, Junell, Candace wouldn't be here if she didn't care," Ethan said, grabbing Candace's hand. "What I need from the two of you is for y'all to work together to coax Grace into sharing what the real problem is. Something happened to trigger all this drinking. She was ready to give her life to Christ the other day, and now she wants to be the worm in a tequila bottle. The only way her image and career can recover from this is by airing the truth, and I need y'all to get it out of her."

"Not a problem, Ethan. I know how to talk to Grace," Junell declared confidently. "Candace, you just keep on making soup."

A small burst of laughter escaped out of Grace's mouth. She muffled it with fake coughs coupled with the phony hawking of spit. Junell sounded ridiculous trying to throw shade. After all these years of friendship, unfortunately, Junell hadn't learned how to sling mud properly.

"Candace," Ethan said, looking at her, "before I leave, please cover this situation with a prayer."

Candace sweetly shook her head. "Father God, right now we pray that you would intervene on behalf of Grace. Bring every truth to the light, Lord. Search the hearts and minds of everyone gathered here, and remove every ounce of pride that is preventing us from operating on one accord, in Jesus's name. Amen."

Now, that is how you throw shade. Grace popped up in appreciation of the art of throwing shade disguised as a prayer, something that Christians did so well.

Grace cocked her legs open and rested her forearms on them. "Ethan, isn't it time for you to hit the office? I'm sure these ladies are going to take good care of me."

Ethan snatched his briefcase off the countertop and shoved his iPhone into his pocket. He squinted at her from across the room, and Grace could see the questions forming in his eyes.

"There's no time for you to examine me, Counselor. You promised to protect me," Grace said, quashing his concerns about her miraculous recovery. He didn't need to know she'd been lying there listening in on their conversation.

"I will do just what I said I would do." He pecked Candace on the forehead and waved good-bye to Junell and Grace before exiting.

The three of them stood there, looking at one another. Candace's right eye quivered a little as she looked at Junell. Junell smiled at Grace. Both women had been caught off guard by Grace's sudden awakening. She'd left them with no time to figure out how to attack her.

"You look good, Junie," Grace said, admiring the sleeveless purple and gold Donna Karan wrap dress that clung to her body. "I didn't know that dress came in maternity sizes."

"It doesn't. It came from your closet," Junell said, laughing hysterically.

Her high-pitched chuckle was contagious and spread almost instantaneously to Candace, whose rosy cheeks were on fire as she bent over in laughter.

Grace threw the pillows she'd had her head buried in for the entire weekend at them. She narrowly missed Candace, who twisted out of the way like she was an extra in *The Matrix,* and smacked Junell right in the face. Still in a fit of laughter, Junell tossed the pillow back at her best friend.

"Glad you're feeling better," Junell said.

"I'm not feeling better until I get some water on my behind," Grace said, pressing her index finger into her glutes. "And some BB cream and concealer on this face. I feel like the bride of Frankenstein."

"You look like her too," Candace said, doubling over with laughter as Grace and Junell froze and looked at her.

"It's a little bit too early for you to be telling jokes," Junell said, giving Candace a funny look.

"Calm down, killer," Grace said to Junell as she walked over to them. She hadn't expected Junell's possessive nature to pop up when she was the one who had suggested Grace fix things between Candace and Ethan. "Candace is a good girl. You'll enjoy her if you give her a chance. I'm going upstairs to shower. You two make some coffee, polish your nails, or do something normal women do to bond."

Grace recognized she was asking for a lot by trying to get Junell Pierce and the thirteenth apostle to act normally under the given circumstances. That really wasn't a possibility. Unless Jesus came down Himself and told Junell to stop acting like the first girl who got kicked out of the *Bad Girls Club.* Right now she was a little too anxious to prove how aggressive she was. Junell didn't like sharing her best friend and was always willing to whip out her claws when she thought Grace was in danger.

"Junie, why don't you see what you can find for Candace to put on? I'm going to die if I see her in another cardigan. And at least put a swab of lip gloss on that pucker of hers." Grace shifted her weight to her left leg and twisted up her mouth as she looked Candace up and down. "What happened to everything you learned during our field trip to Bergdorf?"

"At least I've been keeping up my hair," Candace said, shaking her bob from side to side like she was trying to land a spot in a shampoo commercial.

"Hair like that does not go with a knee-length black skirt and a black cardigan. Ugh! Let me shower up before I get sick." Grace turned and headed up the steps. "I'm sure you'll find something that fits you if the pregnant girl did."

When Grace returned from the shower, she was pleasantly surprised to find Candace perched on a stool at the island, dressed in a mustard-colored maxi that grazed the last rung of the stool and a scoop-neck white tee that showed off her clavicles and a trace of cleavage. Junell was seated right beside her, hugging Candace, with her hand pressed to her chest. Both of them were holding hands, staring at the screen of Junell's tablet.

"What's got you two singing 'Kumbaya' over there?" Grace said from behind. "No one made me any coffee?" She walked around the island, looking for a third cup of something freshly brewed. Neither of them responded to her; only more bated breaths and chest clutching came from each of them.

"What is going on?" Grace asked.

Junell slowly curved her fingers back and forth, the way you did when a child was in trouble. Grace stood beside her, looked down at the tablet in her hands, and watched as a camera zoomed in on Javier Roberts's gaunt, ghoulish face before he said, "I cannot believe she's still not over me. I thought that having her in this film would be therapeutic for us both. This was supposed to be an opportunity for us to make the magic we made in her early days. I really thought this was a great opportunity for her to turn the page on a new chapter in her life and revive her career. People need to see each one of us in a new light."

"Wh-who is he talking about?" Grace asked, pointing at the screen.

Junell pushed Grace's floating finger back to her side. "Hush. There's more."

"What made you come to *Access Hollywood* today, Javier?"

"If I had done this to her . . . you know . . ." He rotated his hands in front of him. "You know, if I had made sexual advances toward her while no one was around, I'd probably be receiving death threats from her legion of fans. I could not let her just be whisked off of my film set, like she was some damsel in distress, because she decided to hit the bottle after I rejected her advances."

"There you have it. An *Access Hollywood* exclusive. Supermodel Grace King returns to alcohol and storms off the set after her sexual advances are rejected by director Javier Roberts," the reporter stated before going to a commercial.

"Allegedly!" Junell shouted. "Allegedly."

"Who are they talking about?" Grace asked again, still mystified by the comments she had heard. She knew the reporter had said her name, but there was no way on earth that Javier was walking around telling people that she wanted to sleep with him, and that, after being rejected by him, she had resorted to drinking. "Who are they talking about?" she repeated, now shaking violently as she spoke.

"You." Candace said innocently, giving voice to words that Junell didn't seem to have the courage to say to Grace.

Before anyone could stop her, Grace swung wildly at the counter, knocking over Junell's mug of tea and taking out her tablet. From there she ran to one of her cabinets, ripped the dishes from the shelves, and threw them on the floor. Each ornately decorated dish crashed to the floor and shattered into hundreds of pieces, mirroring what had become of Grace's life.

Candace and Junell pleaded with Grace to stop, but she could see only their lips moving. The rage inside of her spoke louder than they did. She went from shelf to shelf, pulling out glasses, bowls, and plates of fine china. They'd been reserved for special moments in her life. Now was as good a time as any to bring them out. With each toss of a dish, she thought about the last time she'd seen Javier's face, which was in the zigzagged fragments of broken glass in the mirror on her vanity in the trailer.

Grace stooped down and picked up one long sliver of china from the mess. Then she straightened and stood as erect as a soldier. "When I see him, this is what I'm going to do to him." She swung her hand in the air haphazardly. Completely wrapped in a web of anger and shame, Grace didn't even notice that Candace had crept up behind her until she felt Candace's bicep lock around her neck. Her body stiffened like a board in Candace's arms. Candace forced Grace's body against the island in her kitchen and bent her over.

"Get that dagger of china out of her hand," Candace said to Junell.

Grace lifted her head a few inches to see Junell standing in the center of the living room, crying and shaking.

"Come on! We need to get this dagger out of her hand. She's starting to bleed," Candace shouted.

"I can't," Junell squealed.

"You can." Candace adjusted her stance and tightened her grip around Grace's neck. "Hurry up. I can't restrain her for much longer," Candace added, struggling to hold Grace's hand containing the long sliver of china steady.

"How did you do that? You've got to teach me that move to use on the show," Junell said. As Junell tiptoed

toward Grace and her little belly entered Grace's field of
vision, Grace opened the palm of her hand and let the
sliver of china fall to the floor. Slow and steady droplets of
blood followed the china and created a burgundy puddle.

"Just give me some paper towels," Grace said once
Candace released her from her death grip. Candace
complied, and Grace snatched the paper towels from
Candace's hand and wrapped them around her palm as
a makeshift bandage. Next, Grace began to massage her
sore neck. Stepping over all her broken dishes, Grace
reached for the one glass she had not smashed, and
pulled a bottle of whiskey out of a green container that
had the word *sugar* embossed on it in black script.

"What are you doing, Grace?" Candace and Junell
shouted at the same time.

"A time like this calls for a drink. *Shoot*. When did y'all
become Oprah and Gayle?"

"This is not the time for any drinks. We need you sober
if we're going to attack this thing head-on," Junell said,
stepping on the shards of dishes like there was nothing
on the floor. She wrapped her arm around Grace's and led
her to the couch.

"Javier's been on TV all morning, talking about you,
but I know that's not true. I don't know what happened
in that trailer, but I know you did not come on to him. If
you're going to win this thing, then you're going to have
to start talking and fast, Grace."

"I can't."

"You can," Junell retorted.

"I can't," Grace said, her voice cracking, signaling her
tears would soon betray her and reveal the gravity of the
situation.

"You can," Candace chimed in.

"I won't," Grace said as the tears streamed down her
face.

Chapter 33

If he could, Ethan would climb out the window to escape the influx of phone calls, e-mails, tweets, and Google alerts attacking him. The first thing he did when he entered his office was call up TMZ and issue a statement on behalf of his client.

"The graphic nature of the film struck a chord in Grace's personal life and triggered a memory from the past that she wished had remained dormant. She is sorry about the loss of time and money on the production of this film. However, she and her management team have decided it is in her best interest to walk away from this project before any further damage is done to her psyche."

The reporter asked him twice if he was sure he wanted to go with that statement. Ethan ran his tongue across his pearly white teeth and thought about his statement each time the reporter asked him. Each time he answered, "Yes, I'm sure." He felt peace on the inside and as light as a bird. Javier Roberts had had his face plastered on every media outlet that would listen, but Ethan's heart and mind hadn't gotten the chance to align fully with the spirit of God, because he didn't see this attack coming. Now he had to find a way around this mountain.

After he spoke with TMZ, he paced back and forth across the floor in front of his desk, running his fingertips along the smooth wood of his desk. "Lord, I'm waiting on you to lead me and guide me," he said into the air to reaffirm his confidence.

"Hey, Mr. Summerville," Alice said, letting herself into his office. She was carrying a cordless phone and had a Bluetooth hooked up to her ear, and the corners of her mouth were folded into an expression that was marked with a mixture of hostility and irritability. "I know you're not taking any calls, but Candace is on line two. She said it's about Grace."

Contorting his body so that he could pick up the phone and still face his secretary, Ethan grabbed the phone. "Candace?" He stared down at the rounded tops of his two-tone oxfords while Candace caught him up on the day's events.

"She what? What do you mean, she won't talk? And she hasn't left her room since then? Candace, relax. Tell Junell I'll be there soon with the heavy artillery."

"Come down, or we're coming up," Ethan shouted to Grace.

"I'm not discussing this with you, Candace, or Junell," Grace yelled back.

"Do you feel comfortable discussing this with Horace or Pastor David? They're both here. Take your pick, but you're going to talk to someone today," Ethan told her.

Grace looked at her hand. Her blood had saturated the paper towels and had turned them a deep burgundy. She fingered the layers of brittle skin that covered her bottom lip. As she took stock of her situation, she realized that she'd let Javier do it again. He had taken her power, reduced her to shreds, and had her cowering in her bedroom like a little schoolgirl.

"Grace, I thought you were reclaiming your life," Horace said coolly.

"I'm not like you, Horace. I can't just trade in my life for the life of Christ. You were weighed down by currency, and I am chained to my pain," Grace called.

"But you don't have to be, Grace. You can be free," Pastor David said, joining the conversation. She imagined his hands exploding in the air like fireworks when he said the word *free*. "Grace, the man in the Gadarenes was bound by chains and fetters, but even those weren't strong enough to hold him, and every now and then he'd bust out of those chains—like you do. Yet every time the chains came off of him, he would remain at the graveyard, crying and cutting himself."

Grace looked at her wound.

"Even though the chains were off of him, he couldn't leave, because a legion of demons dwelled within him. A *legion*. Do you hear me?"

"Yes," Grace squeaked, rocking back and forth on the edge of her bed.

Pastor David went on. "Anywhere from three thousand to six thousand soldiers could be included in a legion. Pain was there, most certainly, and shame too. They had that man living far from his family, surviving the best way he knew how, but they never, ever allowed him to step away from the lonely place in the graveyard. He was surrounded by dead things, like memories of the past, which the enemy uses to taunt us. Those demons had him twisted up inside and out.

"But when he saw Jesus, it all came stumbling out. When he encountered the truth, the thousands of lies that flooded his body, saying he wasn't worth anything, saying, 'This is where you belong, you rotten piece of trash, you filthy thing,' they all had to cease. Jesus was able to cast a legion of demons out of that man, and I say that same power is available to you right now, you hear me?"

"Yes!" rang out upstairs and downstairs in the condo.

The story of the man in the Gadarenes was faintly familiar to Grace. It was the topic of one of the last few sermons she'd heard before running away from home. Her pastor, Dr. Wyatt Kendrick Clarke, had taught a monthlong series to his congregation on riding their lives of demonic possession. His sermon from Mark, chapter five, was to be the last one in the series and the final one that Grace would attend. At that time, as he spoke about vanquishing darkness from your life, she believed she had the power to do it. In her sixteen-year-old mind, it wouldn't be actualized until she was far away from the church and her family. That time she'd heard the sermon only with her ears; this time she listened with her heart.

Rising from a corner of her unmade bed, Grace approached the full-length mirror in the corner of her room. She gripped the fourteen-karat gold borders of the mirror and stared into her empty eyes. What she saw in the mirror could not be who she was. Her apple-shaped face seemed to have sunken in since she last looked at herself. A veil of darkness had taken up permanent residence over her face; small bean-shaped bags rested under her eyes. Grace thought of her first session of anger management. "What do you see?" she asked herself.

As Pastor David rallied the group downstairs in prayer, Grace looked at herself for the first time in her life.

"I see God's creation. I see a woman. I see . . . I see . . . I see . . ." Streams of tears ran down her face, washing away all the shame, all the names, and all the pain that had held her captive for so long.

Grace ran out of her room to the foot of the stairs and stopped. The first pair of eyes to meet hers was Horace's. His eyes fastened on to hers and held her. He transmitted strength and warmth. There was no need for embarrassment; she could speak her truth.

"He raped me. Javier Roberts raped me on the first job that I did with him," Grace said.

Junell gasped.

"We were shooting a—"

"Jonathan Black ad for his fall shirt collection," Junell interrupted, finishing Grace's sentence. She sandwiched herself in the pocket of space between Ethan and Horace. "I worked that job with you. When the shoot was over, he sent everyone home."

"Except for me." Grace pressed one finger to her chest.

With each step she took toward them, she revealed the details of that night. She rocked and shook as she teetered down the steps. Collapsing on the bottom step, she exhaled. "This movie is a reenactment of that rape." The tears came back again.

Horace knelt in front of her. He wrapped his large hands, which were coated in white dust from a construction site, around Grace's hands. It had been so long since she had thought about the differences in their financial status. His job as a construction worker no longer mattered. Monetary support wasn't what she needed. Right now she needed his comfort. She gripped his hands and brought them to her face.

Grace rubbed her cheek against his knuckles like a cat. For the first time ever, she noticed the dimple in his strong chin. Leaning into him, she pecked his chin. Following her lead, he began to peck at her lips.

Pastor David cleared his throat loudly, interrupting Grace and Horace's comforting exchange of kisses. Grace covered her mouth, and her cheeks turned a burnished bronze. Junell and Candace both flashed her a thumbs-up.

"Grace," Pastor David said, stepping to the right side of her, "I am sorry this happened to you, but if you believe with your heart and confess with your mouth that Jesus Christ is Lord and that He was raised from the dead by God, as Romans, chapter nine, says, salvation and healing will be granted to you, just as they were granted to the man in the Gadarenes."

Ethan took a wide step over Horace's feet and sat beside Grace at the foot of the steps. She looked into the faces of each one of them. They were beaming with love, goodness, faith, patience, and peace. It was time to be made whole.

"I do believe that Jesus Christ is Lord and that He was raised from the dead by God, and I fully expect God to do the same for me," Grace announced.

Chapter 34

After Pastor David led everyone in prayer, Ethan asked that everyone except Junell leave. Now it was time for them to prepare Grace for the damage-control process. In the industry damage control usually meant a lot of sobbing and wailing on every talk show or news outlet that would have you, followed by several interviews and photo shoots with magazines, to reveal the dark secrets that had served as the catalyst for the celeb's trouble. Then there were the public appearances and the scheduled photo ops with the celebrity as he or she attempted to reestablish a normal life. None of that was going to work in this situation.

"Junell, Grace, pull up a seat," Ethan said, setting up his command post in Grace's kitchen. Layers of purple, lavender, and pink coated the sky. Dusk enveloped the Harlem sky and filled the room with the splendor of God.

Junell eased into her seat, cradling her belly, and Grace sat in hers with her eyes wide open and fully focused on Ethan.

"You know what comes next?" Ethan said.

"Damage control," they both replied in unison, feigning excitement, with spirit fingers in the air.

Ethan unbuttoned the cuffs of his black-and-white gingham-print shirt and rolled them over. "Now, here's what I'm thinking." Ethan paused for a few seconds and stroked his goatee. "We have to do things a little differently for this situation."

"Precisely what I was thinking," Junell said, jumping up from her chair. "We've got to get you all over prime-time television, not just daytime."

"Would you sit down and let me finish, before you try to commandeer this outfit?" Ethan barked.

With one raised eyebrow, Junell looked at Ethan and walked to the refrigerator. "What baby wants, baby gets," she said, pouring herself a glass of vanilla almond milk before returning to her seat.

"Ethan." Grace raised her hand in the air. "One moment please. Junie, thank you for the spectacular job you did cleaning the place up, and thanks for getting me some new dishes."

"Girl, this stuff came from Target. While Candace cleaned up all the glass and china, I asked one of the runners to go and pick up some dishes from Target."

"You sent a runner?" Grace squealed. "Junie, you're finally learning how to use this actor thing properly."

Ethan clapped his hands together and positioned them to make the time-out signal. He'd had enough of the girl talk; it was time to take care of business. This stuff needed to be released while he could hear the Lord speaking directions into his heart. There was no time for flamboyance and distraction. Jesus was most definitely about to turn this whole thing around.

Both ladies closed their mouths and sat at attention, with their hands folded in front of them, like class was in session and Ethan was the headmaster in charge.

"*Red Tape.*"

"With Diane Khan?" Grace asked, with her pointed nose, eyes, and flower-petal mouth scrunched together in the center of her face. She planted her hands firmly on the countertop and shouted, "Are you crazy, Summerville?"

"No, he's brilliant," Junell noted, lightly tapping her temple. "*Red Tape* is live. The audience will have a chance to see you and connect with you on a deeper level, and no one will be able to censor you."

Shaking her head rapidly from side to side, Grace said, "I can't."

"You can handle Khan. There are bloggers who are more intense than she is. You survived Perez and Wendy. You can do this."

Grace was still shaking her head.

"We're casting a wide net, right? One show, one night, and we're going to put this thing to bed." Ethan leaned on the counter and stared directly into Grace's eyes. "What do you say, Grace King?"

"Grace King says no. I can't do this," she said, banging her fist on the granite countertop.

"You're not going to be alone when you do this," Ethan said smoothly.

"You'll be surrounded." Junell pointed up. "The Father, Son, and Holy Ghost will be present, and so will we," she added, grabbing her friend's hand.

Apprehension had taken flight long ago. Now shock and awe filled Grace's heart as she took a seat on her bonded red leather couch. Glancing over her shoulder at the men in her life—Pastor David, Ethan, and Horace— she thought of everything they represented: her past, her present, and her future. Yet she thanked God that He'd represented Himself in the Father, the Son, and the Holy Ghost, assuring her she could do this.

"Gracie," Pastor David called to her in a whisper, like he used to. She turned her head and stared into his eyes. Water lined the rims of his eyes.

"Pastor, I know you've never been interviewed before, but you're not supposed to start crying until during the interview."

He placed his hand on her shoulder, smiled, and leaned in close to her ear. "Gracie, I just wanted to tell you that I'm sorry for everything and I'm proud of you. Don't tremble or shake. Your truth is more powerful than any lie of his. God is going to bless you in this."

God is going to bless me in this. God is going to bless me in this. Grace held on to that thought and adjusted herself on the couch to make sure she received the right amount of natural light while the cameras were rolling.

One of the runners brought in a high-backed black matte stool and placed it in front of them. Ethan, Horace, and Pastor David took their seats on mounted chairs that had been place behind Grace's leather couch. A soft hush covered the room as they waited for the interview to begin. A few moments later Diane Khan emerged from Grace's downstairs bathroom, which had been turned into hair and makeup for the reporter.

"I thought the stool worked with the intimate, conversational style of the interview and the condo's low-key decor," Diane Khan explained, leaning on against the stool.

"No problem, Diane. I can call you that, right?" Grace asked. She stood, smoothed down her golden-yellow, A-line, peplumed dress, and stuck out her hand.

"Absolutely," Diane replied as she extended her arm and shook Grace's hand. "I can't believe this is the first time we're sitting down to chat, considering how long you've been in this industry. Let me meet your people." She scuttled over to the chairs mounted behind the couch in her platform heels and stuck her hand out in Pastor David's direction, paused, and placed her other hand on her earpiece. "We're going live in fifteen . . . fourteen . . . seconds," she announced, shuffling to the stool to take her place.

As soon as the director said, "And we're live," Diane Khan was ready to turn it on.

"This is *Red Tape,* and I'm your host, Diane Khan, sitting down for an exclusive interview with Grace King and what looks like the Three Musketeers." Diane pointed her copper-colored arm toward the men seated behind Grace. "Who do we have here with us today, Grace?"

"This is Pastor Lawrence David of Mount Carmel Community Church. I just call him David. When I met him I decided I like the name David way more than Lawrence, and I've called him that ever since." Grace reached back and rested her hand on his knee. "Now, this brother right here is Ethan Summerville, my attorney, agent, manager, my everything. He keeps me ticking." She pointed at Horace with a smile wide enough to expose both rows of teeth. "And this guy is my Adam. A man made to love and lead me. They are all a part of my past, present, and future. If it had not been for their guidance, love, and support, I wouldn't be here to tell you my story or expose Javier Roberts for the snake that he is."

"Snake?" Diane repeated. "Are you saying that there is no truth to the rumors about you being dismissed from the set because you continually made sexual advances toward Javier Roberts?"

"Horace, please come here," Grace said, ignoring Diane momentarily.

"What do you need?" Horace stood beside the couch.

"Please, make sure you're getting all this fineness," Grace said, pointing at the cameraman.

Even Diane paused to absorb Horace's fine-tuned physique and the shine that emanated from his cocoa skin.

"Diane, you gotta get your own." Grace snapped her fingers and rolled her neck. "No shade intended," she said, sitting back and crossing her legs.

"I feel naked. Can I sit back down?" Horace asked.

Grace patted the vacant seat next to her on the couch, indicating Horace should share the spotlight with her. She waited until he sat down beside her before continuing her defense. "I'm pretty sure this speaks for itself, but let's clear the air. Why on earth would I need or want to make sexual advances at Javier Roberts when I could have this man?" Grace asked, wrapping her arm around Horace's rock-solid bicep to brace herself for the firestorm she was about to set off.

Grace went on. "It's Javier who is loony. He's a rapist. He raped me. Ten years ago on the set of a Jonathan Black photo shoot, and now he is trying to victimize me all over again." Grace's leg shook as the words tumbled out of her mouth. The floor beneath her felt like mush. "This movie isn't some unchartered territory or the efforts of a cinematic genius, as he would have others believe. What happens to my character in the film is what he did to me. He is sick," she said, with her lips turned down in disgust.

Diane placed her hand on her earpiece, waiting to receive directions from the segments producer. Grace could tell by the way she sorted through her cue cards that none of the questions she had prepared were related to the bomb that had just been detonated, and that she did not have a good segue ready.

"Grace, are you alleging that Javier Roberts raped you?" Diane finally said. "Those are serious allegations that could lead to more legal woes for you."

Clearing her throat to respond, Grace sat upright to address Diane's underhanded accusation, but she was interrupted by Ethan's protective interjection.

"In addition to being her publicist, I serve as Grace's legal counsel, and I can assure you that the only person who will have legal issues after this interview is Javier Roberts, who preyed on an innocent girl. Then, when he thought she was at her weakest point, he tried to use it to his advantage. We are fully prepared to fight this thing to the very end, if that is the route Mr. Roberts chooses to take."

Grace reclined, with a grin spread across her face. The Lord had certainly provided her with a ready defense.

"Grace, Javier Roberts's fans have taken to Twitter and Facebook and are flooding our news feed with the same question I have for you," Diane said. "Why did you wait so long to report this alleged rape?"

"Fear. That and the need for acceptance. They both held me hostage for a long time. My life hasn't been horrible, but it hasn't been bright, either. After making some mistakes as a teen, I tried to use my modeling career as a way to redeem myself. Then I discovered that redemption doesn't work that way. Only Christ can clean up the mess that we make of our lives."

"Why sign on to do a major motion picture that depicts your rape?" Diane asked.

Grace exhaled. "Again, I was afraid, and I was trying to cover up something while saving face, but then a wise man said something that broke me down and woke me up. Those words freed me from this and all the bad things that happened to me. The truth is more powerful than any lie. I am grateful for Pastor David for urging me to take the devil on."

"Is that why you invited Pastor David to sit in on this interview?" Diane asked, now motioning toward him.

"Diane, I kind of invited myself," Pastor David chirped from behind Grace. "I feel partially responsible for the things that have happened to Grace, because of the things that I did to her. Grace and I once had a romantic relationship. We were sexually active, and that relationship produced a child. Some members of the church we used to attend urged Grace to abort the baby so as not to put a blemish on my budding ministry. I don't know what I was doing or where my head was that I didn't see what was happening, but the next time I looked up, Gracie was gone."

Pastor David paused and took a deep swallow. Grace knew this had to be one of the most difficult situations in his life. The thought of his former sins being revealed to the whole world shook him way down in the city of his soul.

"Do you need a moment, Pastor?" Diane asked, passing a glass of water and a napkin to Grace to give to the pastor.

Pastor David gulped loudly and then continued. "That was the first time she was raped. In that moment people who were older and seemed wiser used their age, wisdom, and control over her to assert their own will on her—usurping the power that she had over her own body. I am here to be the first to confess that I damaged her and opened the floodgates for the devil and his demons to prey on her. I am here to apologize to her."

Pastor David swiped a few stray tears from his face. "Sunday after Sunday I beseech the congregation of Mount Carmel Community Church to dig deep within themselves to make right their errors, reconcile their affairs with men, and stop hiding behind their sin, but a leader must lead by example, not through speeches." Pastor David bent over slightly and placed his hand on Grace's shoulder.

Grace adjusted herself and faced Pastor David.

"I am here to say, Grace, I am sorry. I know that I cannot restore the things that are broken, but I am sorry that these things happened to you, and I will stand by you regardless of the outcome of this situation."

Chapter 35

The constant vibration of Grace's phone caused the steel countertop of the island in her kitchen to reverberate. Before the camera crew was done scuffing her floor on the way out, Grace had over a thousand new e-mails, direct messages from Twitter, and Facebook notifications. Just a few years ago, a day or two would go by before the lawyers or public relations team of a celebrity would reach out to him or her, and at least three days to a week would pass before a celebrity started receiving death threats for something said or done.

Grace covered her mouth in horror as she scrolled through her e-mails, just reading the subject lines: "He should have killed you too." "Waste of time." "Why would Javier need to or want to rape you?" "Liar, liar, liar."

Horace, Pastor David, and Ethan had formed a congratulatory circle near the window and were patting each other on the back for each defensive move they'd executed efficiently during the interview. None of them seemed to hear the squeals of agony Grace let out as she read through each bitter and antagonistic message. After admitting to being raped, she had expected to be embraced. Instead, she was vilified and was accused of being a monster. The three men continued to boast, complement each other, and give each other daps, one of them saying, "Yeah, man, you handled Diane that time," until a jarring cry erupted in the kitchen. They tripped over each other as they leaped toward the kitchen.

Grace tried to control it, but she couldn't stop shaking like a loose shingle on a roof during a storm. Tears streaked her copper skin as she bit down on her bottom lip. She stared at her cell phone, which now lay on the floor.

Ethan stooped down to pick up her phone, Horace massaged her shoulders, trying to soothe her, and Pastor David was the one soul in the room who was brave enough to speak.

"What happened?" he asked.

Burying her head in the slither of space between Horace's arm and chest, Grace pointed at her cell phone, then proceeded to cry..

Ethan tapped the phone's screen and entered her password. After reading the message on the screen, he passed the phone to Pastor David, who read the message and adamantly shouted, "The devil is a liar!"

"What does it say, man?" Horace demanded, slapping Pastor David on the shoulder with his free arm and still cradling Grace with the other.

Pastor David stood perfectly still, with his mouth hanging open so wide, his chin hid his Adam's apple.

"Speak, Pastor! What does it say?" Ethan asked, chiming in.

"I don't know what's more harmful—what the message says or its origin," Pastor David said.

Breaking from the safety of Horace's arms, Grace ran to the sink. She leaned over and threw cold water on her face. She arose from the sink with splotches on her face, which marked the spots where her foundation, concealer, and blush used to lie. She addressed her support crew. "I am done for the day. I can't handle any more of this. I'll be upstairs. Please let yourselves out." Pivoting on her heels, Grace turned to make her exit. Horace reached out to grab her arm, but she snatched it away so quickly, he was left clutching the air.

"Solitude isn't what's best in this situation," Horace said.

She whipped her head around and stared at Horace, hard enough to bore holes into his head. "You think you know when you have no idea," Grace cried.

"Well then, can someone please tell me what in the world just happened?" Horace said.

"Read it," Ethan said to Pastor David.

"Read what?" Horace asked, shrugging his shoulders.

"An e-mail," Pastor David said, finally breaking his silence. "An e-mail from a very disturbed person."

"Pastor, please just tell me what it says."

"The subject line of this e-mail reads 'You deserved it.' It goes, 'Dear Grace, what a shame it is to see that you have accused someone as talented as Javier Roberts of raping you. I wonder if you understand the magnitude of your accusations. Probably not, or you would not be on national television, trying to play Diane, when really you are the woman at the well, misusing the blessings of God to distract holy men of God from their calling. I was completely shocked to see Pastor David behind you, supporting you as you recited these fables. As I watched that interview, all I could do was pray that Pastor David does not fall from his steadfastness again, after all that we did to protect him. And now my prayer is that you might come to know the Savior before that spirit of Jezebel really takes ahold of you and has you carted off to hell. You should be ashamed of yourself and the acts that you participated in. Sincerely, Thomas King.'" Pastor David ground his teeth. "You know that there are a hundred more like this."

"Who cares what those kooks think?" Horace said. "If you ask me, that's what's wrong with our country today— everyone's too wrapped up in the lives of celebrities, and they don't even know what their own child is doing.

Grace, you need to forget about Thomas and his whole crew."

"She won't," Ethan said before Grace could muster up a response to Horace. She was grateful they were still in tune like that.

Horace frowned. "Why?"

"Because she can't," Pastor David added.

"Thomas King is my father," Grace revealed, putting an end to the mystery for Horace. "Now, if you don't mind letting yourselves out, it would be greatly appreciated," she said, curtsying.

Ethan and Pastor David gathered their stuff in silence. To Grace, it seemed like they were moving slower than a toddler who'd just taken his first step. Grace strutted to the door and held it open to speed up the process.

She didn't know if there was a scripture that could correct the combination of punches thrown her way today. Hopefully, the Bible app she had downloaded to her phone would lead her to it. Pastor David and Ethan each embraced her before walking out and assured her that she would be okay. She looked over her shoulder at Horace and wondered why he insisted on breaking the rule, since her directive applied to him as well.

Once Grace heard the ding of the elevator and knew Ethan and Pastor David were gone, she turned to Horace and began drilling him. She hadn't wanted to dig into him while everyone else was around. He'd earned that much respect from her.

"Why are you still here?" Grace asked, still holding the door open by the knob.

Horace swiftly stepped up to Grace. He stood in front of her, his chest puffed up from pride or loyalty. She couldn't tell which.

"Because you don't really want to be alone," he said, tracing her jawbone with the tip of his finger. "And I don't want to leave you, Grace King." He tipped her chin upward and leaned into her, leading with his lips. First, they grazed her lips.

"What makes you think I don't want to be alone?"

Horace pecked her lips with his. "Everything about you says you don't want to be alone, from the dreamy look in those doe eyes of yours to the way your back is arched while you hold that door open," he said, subtly slinking his arm around her waist and pulling her to his body. With his other hand, he grasped her jaw tightly and pressed his lips into hers.

In that instant he infused the strength and love that those e-mails had sucked out of her back into her. The kiss was sweet enough to last until forever, and it very well would have if Grace's only neighbor hadn't decided to let her shih tzu run down the hallway without a leash on. The dog came speeding down the hallway and ran right into Grace's unit. Horace let go of Grace and scooped up the brown ball of fur before he had the opportunity to rummage through the place.

"Here you go," Horace said sweetly to the old lady who owned both the dog and the only other unit on that floor.

Once the woman disappeared down the hallway, he turned back to Grace. "Now that I saved you from that shih tzu, I know I'm entitled to at least a cup of coffee before you send me packing."

Grace smiled at the warm expression on his face and the radiance that had settled around him. He deserved more than a cup of coffee; he deserved her complete adoration. Horace had poured nothing but love into Grace, even after learning her dirtiest secrets and deeds. She didn't understand why he would even care about someone like her, with so little to offer him. Early on she had thought she was bringing more to the table, because she had a larger bank account, but there was nothing she could give him. Except herself.

Grace shut the door, went to the kitchen, and turned on the Keurig. As it warmed up, she instructed Horace to have a seat on the couch for once, instead of standing by the window.

"But I love the view. From my place I can see only into the alley behind the building and some old lady's apartment."

"Just take a seat, buster," she said, inserting the K-Cup into the machine. "Just relax, okay?"

"Okay," he agreed, exhaling deeply through his nostrils.

Once the coffee had brewed, Grace sauntered across the living room floor to him and handed him his cup. Sinking down onto her knees, she bowed her head before him.

"Grace, what are you doing?"

"I'm lying at your feet."

"Why?" he asked, holding his head back awkwardly.

"That's what Ruth did when she offered herself to Boaz. Horace, you have proven yourself to be honorable, strong, and loving. I've never had a man like you in my life. I don't think I am deserving of what you have to offer, but I want to walk this walk with you."

"Grace, as long as you're walking with Christ, I will walk with you anywhere." Horace placed his cup of coffee on the floor and kneeled down in front of her. He grabbed her hands and covered them with his own. "I can't give you what you're used to, but I can love you."

"That's what I love about you, Horace. You're not what I'm used to," she said, kissing his chin.

Cupping the sides of her face, Horace kissed her forehead, her nose, and then her lips. "Before this turns into something more, I'm going to go out that door, but first, let's pray." He took her hand in his and said, "Father God, we come before your presence with thanksgiving. I thank you for everything that has transpired in our lives, for it has led us to this moment in time. I thank you for sending Grace to Mount Carmel. I thank you for the forgiveness of sins and pray that you will use this woman for all to see how day by day you have seasoned our lives with grace, that good should come out of bad and light out of darkness because of your power, your faithfulness, and your loving-kindness. In Jesus's name, amen."

"Amen," Grace said after him, hoping that a prayer was really all she was going to need to get through this.

Chapter 36

Junell paced back and forth, biting the tips of her manicured nails.

"Stop walking back and forth, before you wear a hole in my floor," Grace commanded from beneath the cream microfiber blanket she was using to swaddle herself between sips of kombucha.

"I don't know how you can just sit there," Junell said, slapping her thigh.

Sitting and waiting was all Grace had done for the past month. She sat and waited for the right time to leave her building. Frankly, she was tired of ducking and dodging the paparazzi. She was over creeping into the building through the service entrance and entering the church through the basement, but it was either that or face the reporters and photogs, who had not stopped hounding her since she'd sat down with Diane Khan and put it all out there.

"Nothing else occupies my mind except clearing your tarnished name," Junell continued. "I can't believe that doing the right thing actually got you into more mess than when you do wrong. Grace, we have to do something."

"If my own father doesn't believe me, how am I going to change the minds of the American people?"

Grace locked eyes with Junell, and her chest swelled with fear when she saw that one raised eyebrow. She had read Junell's mind and already knew what Junell was twisting her red lips up to say.

The pictures.

Flinging back the blanket, Grace jumped up and stood toe-to-toe with Junell.

"I will not do it. It's out of the question."

"Grace . . ." Junell had turned on her "Come, let's be reasonable" tone of voice.

"No," Grace replied adamantly, with her hands folded across her chest.

Junell cuffed Grace's wrists. "Stop thinking about yourself. What about his other victims?"

Twisting her arms until she was free from Junell's grip, Grace shouted, "I'm no martyr! Please allow me to keep what little dignity I have left." Grace stomped her way back to her spot on the couch.

"You should think about it. Or at least pray on it, now that you're a praying woman."

Grace rolled her eyes and folded her hands across her chest. "You know, I'm in no mood for nonsense," she said as her doorbell rang. "Junie, did you let anyone up?"

Junell shook her head. "Maybe it's Horace. That's the only person I could see Arnie letting up here. But you stay there. I'll deal with whoever it is."

Grace moved her legs back and forth while she waited for the sparks to come flying. She felt sorry for the schmuck who thought he'd outsmarted the doorman. Arnie looked like a rottweiler but had the personality of a bulldog, while Junell, on the other hand, had proven that when it came to Grace, she was a Doberman pinscher ready to attack.

After a few nail-biting minutes on the couch, Grace couldn't take the wait; she needed to know who was at her door. She hustled to the door, snatched the knob from Junell, and opened the door wider to get a good look at the person standing there.

She was a rail-thin girl the color of eggshells, with high cheekbones coated in a dewy orange blush. Her septum was pierced, and one side of her hair had been shaved off.

"You're a little too edgy to be a reporter, you're not a member of my church, and you don't have a camera, so you're not a paparazzo. Who are you, and what do you want?" Grace said.

The girl looked down. "Grace . . . I mean . . . Ms. King, I . . . I . . ."

Snapping her fingers, Grace said, "Let's go, girl. I haven't even said my prayers yet."

"Chill," Junell said over her shoulder to Grace. "You're going to want to hear what this girl has to say."

"Javier Roberts raped me too," the girl blurted. "He took pictures of it and said that he would send them to the press if I told anyone." She pulled a manila envelope out of her messenger bag. Her hands shook as she handed it to Grace. "I was scared and didn't know what to do. I don't want this to continue. Ms. King, how do I make it stop?" she asked, her face now covered in tears, her whole body trembling.

Junell wrapped her arm around the unnamed girl and ushered her inside, while Grace remained at the door.

Grace was frozen in time. He'd done this to another girl, and now she was looking to Grace for leadership. "I can't help nobody. I can't even help myself," she mumbled.

And let us not be weary in well doing: for in due season we shall reap, if we faint not.

"Now, this time I know it is you, Lord, speaking to me. I am not built for this," she whispered to God.

No, you were made for such a time as this.

Grace ran her fingers through her short hair, massaging her scalp, until the feeling returned to her legs. With her feelings collected and in order, Grace joined Junell and Javier's most recent victim in the living room.

"What's your name?" she asked the girl after inviting her to take a seat on the couch.

"Carol Jasper, better known as the Egyptian Silk girl," she said, bowing her head, folding her hands in the center of her chest, then raising her cat eyes a few inches to meet Grace's.

"I knew I recognized you from somewhere, but I couldn't place it when Grace opened the door," Junell said, jumping up and clapping. "You know, I bought that shampoo just because of how shiny your hair looks on the bottle," she added and then turned to Grace. "Now what?"

"Let's see what Carol wants." Grace turned to Carol and kneeled down in front of her. "Carol, I know what you're feeling right now—disgust, shame, embarrassment, horror, depression, fear, and loneliness all at once. I was just seventeen years old when Javier got ahold of me. How old are you?"

"Seventeen. I was fifteen when I started working with Javier." Carol lowered her head, and a few droplets of tears fell on the manila envelope in Grace's hand. She brushed them away.

"I don't have to open this envelope to know what's in here," Grace said, squeezing Carol's hand. "Javier sent me a package just like that ten years ago. The question that we both have to answer today is, what do we want to do about it?"

Carol turned her arms over and rolled up the sleeves of her chambray top, revealing the insides of her forearms. They looked like a prisoner had been using them to count the days of a two-year bid.

"I haven't taken a job in ten months." Carol began to cry again, sucking up the mucus that was dripping out of her nose. She continued. "I've been cutting myself, and I don't want to hide anymore."

Chapter 37

"Carol, where are your parents?" Grace asked.

Carol dropped her head and focused her gaze on her scars. Grace needed to know the status of Carol's parents before offering Carol the guest room. If they were active in her life, Grace wanted them included in whatever steps they took next.

There were generally three kinds of parents Grace had encountered during her time in the business. There were the control freaks, who kept their kids on a tight leash. They had to approve of their kids' wardrobe and makeup. The children basically couldn't use the bathroom on the set without their permission. Then there were the parents who were laissez-faire. They showed up to the shoot, but they were so involved in the little bit of limelight they received, they did not even pay attention to what they were approving. Last, and most definitely least, were the hands-off parents. Those parents signed their kids' lives over to the agency, and the only thing they checked on was how many zeros were on each check.

Tapping Carol's chin, Grace asked again, "Where are your parents?"

"I think they're in the South of France, vacationing. After the big payday from the Egyptian Silk contract, they decided it was time for them to go on vacation." Tears fell from Carol's eyes and landed in the grooves of her scars. "They're touring Europe for the year. They call the house every couple of weeks. I've just been lying to them, saying things are great and I'm booking all these jobs."

"You know, when this comes out, everything is going to change for both you and your parents," Grace said.

"The thing I realized while watching your interview was we live our lives concerned about how things are going to affect people who don't care very much about our well-being. This is my truth," Carol said, holding her scarred arms out. "If you're standing with me, I think I can handle the fire."

Junell raised her hand from her spot on the couch. "May I interject?" she asked politely and earnestly. She'd been so quiet, Grace had almost forgotten she was there. "I think I know how this should be handled," Junell continued. "We have to get your agent or publicist to agree to it first, but I think I have the perfect idea. Let's host a press party at Ethan's office. We'll have Carol there. She can tell them what happened to her and unveil the photos."

"Hmmm . . ." Grace scratched the back of her neck. "Those pregnancy hormones must be really getting to your brain. Even if we show the photos, it will still be Javier Roberts's word against ours. Those photos aren't particularly incriminating in nature. That's the power of them. He can tell any story he wants. Photography is his medium, and he's had lots of practice explaining and justifying his art. If he takes a picture of a cow, he can convince people there's a bat in the photo. We have to one-up him."

"I already have," Carol said, digging into her messenger bag again. "The last time he touched me, I recorded it." After fishing around for a few seconds, she withdrew a cell phone from her bag and placed it in Grace's hand. "It's all on there," she said, with her top lip turned up. "After I went to hair and makeup to change looks, I snuck my phone on the set and stuffed it under a pillow behind me while he wasn't looking."

Junell stomped her feet and clapped her hands several times. "Thank you, Jesus! Thank you, Jesus! This is exactly what we needed. Now we can have the party, reveal the photos. Carol can share her story and play the recording for any doubters and ask his other victims to join us in seeking justice against this vile, rotten pig."

"Join *us?*" Grace asked slightly surprised. "When did this become *your* battle?"

"As soon as it became yours." Junell stuffed her palms into the couch cushions, using them as leverage to get herself off the couch. "Just as Jonathan's soul was knit with David's, so is mine with yours. From the first day I met you in the office of Fresh Faces Modeling Agency, I loved you as my own soul," she said, pressing down on her heart, then plucking away the one stray tear.

Junell went on. "Whatever bind you're in, I'm in. Whatever hole you're in, I'm in, and I have no plans of staying there. Just like it says in Revelation, chapter twelve, verse eleven. 'And they overcame him by the blood of the Lamb, and by the word of their testimony.' Let's see the scripture made manifest in our lives, girl." Junell reached out and scooped Grace into a side hug. "Now, get Ethan on the phone and tell him we need this done yesterday. Carol, baby girl, you're going to have to sleep on the couch, 'cause it's too late for me to be driving back home. Where do you live?"

"New Jersey."

"Yes, it's definitely way too late for that, and I'm too pregnant to be sleeping on somebody's leather couch." Junell rubbed her belly. "That's how I wound up like this in the first place," she said, laughing.

"Stop that," Grace said, whacking Junell on the arm.

"The marriage bed is undefiled, honey. If you know like I know, you better marry that chocolate drop as soon as possible, before you both melt from the heat," Junell said, creeping toward the stairs.

"Just toss some sheets down her for Carol please," Grace called. "Carol, you can stay the night, or however long you need. Before I call my lawyer, I just want to make sure that you're cool with what we're about to do."

Carol gripped her knees and nodded her half-shaved head.

"All righty, then. I'm going to call my guy to set everything up. You call your people when you have a chance, just to warn them. Even if they're not going to support you, let's not leave them hanging, okay, kid?"

Grace walked to the downstairs bathroom and stared at herself in the mirror. She was not who she used to be, and she was glad. "Call Ethan," she instructed her phone. "Ethan . . . I didn't expect you to pick up on the first ring. . . . Listen, I need you to send a courier over here now to pick up some photos. I need these photos blown up and put on display in the conference room. . . . Do you think it's too cold to use the rooftop deck . . . ? Ethan, don't worry about the details. Just listen to me. . . . We're going to have a press conference tomorrow morning. Make sure there are plenty of mimosas on hand and little finger foods. I'll also need some speakers to hook up to a cell phone. . . . What do you mean, you don't like how this sounds? You're going to love this."

"Good morning, Alice," Grace said as she approached Alice's desk. "This is Carol—"

"Carol Jasper, the Egyptian Silk girl. I'd recognize those eyes anywhere. What are you doing hooked up with Grace King?" Alice's caked-on, low-rent foundation cracked as she turned down the corners of her mouth like she'd gotten a whiff of rotten meat.

"We're here to see Ethan," Grace said, answering for Carol.

"You're actually on time, Grace. That's different. I'll let him know you're here."

"Take your time. We'll have a seat right here." Grace sat down in one of the fluffy peach chairs that decorated Ethan's waiting area. This was the first time since Ethan became her lawyer that she'd taken a seat in the waiting area. Alice dropped the cup of coffee she was holding as Grace reclined in the chair with her legs crossed. Carol pulled a few tissues from the holder on Alice's desk and began to dab at the coffee on the rug.

Alice shook her head. "Grace, stop playing. What are you doing? Aren't you going to bust in there, like you usually do?"

Shrugging her shoulders, Grace said, "I'm sitting down. I'll wait. All things must be done in decency and in order."

"Am I in the twilight zone or something?" Alice bent down and stuck her head under her desk, then stood up. "I didn't see Ashton under there. Which show is this for?" She laughed. "This ain't right. I never heard you quote the Bible."

In all honesty, Grace was shocked herself, but during the month she'd been trapped in her house, all she had to do was read. Unfortunately, she'd never been one of those intellectual models known for their brains and beauty. The Bible Horace had given her the day she joined the church was the only book she had in her house. Grace pored over it day and night. She had replaced her yoga with daily scripture reading. This exchange was a sign that she was actually retaining some of the knowledge she was acquiring through the study of God's Word.

"I'm doing things differently now, Alice, and I'm truly sorry if I ever offended you in the past."

"Offended me? You've done more than offend me."

"But not more than what we have all done to Jesus," Ethan interjected, placing his hand on Alice's shoulder.

Grace breathed a sigh of relief. Alice was just about to read her the riot act, and Grace wasn't sure if she was saved enough to handle that without giving her at least one good tongue-lashing.

"Good morning," Ethan said, bowing slightly in Carol's direction.

"Ethan, this is Carol—" Grace said.

"Carol Jasper, the Egyptian Silk girl," Alice said, cutting Grace off.

"Hi, Carol. Are you here to watch the fiasco, or are you part of the fiasco?"

Grace stood up and dusted off the shoulders of Ethan's cross-grained coral and gray blazer. "Hmmm . . . black trim," Grace noted, lifting the lapel. "This is a nice suit. This won't be a fiasco. You'll be glad you set this up, Ethan."

"I wish you'd just tell me what's going on," he replied.

Grace shook her head. "I can't. Now, let's get upstairs. I want to be seated when the paps get here."

Ethan escorted the ladies to the elevator and stuck his card in the slot on the elevator panel to gain access to the rooftop deck.

When the elevator doors parted, Grace two-stepped like she was auditioning for *Glee*. The scent of fresh flowers engulfed her. Small bouquets of burgundy Kung Fu tulips, dark orange roses, red carnations, and baby's breath lined the aisle between the many chairs that had been set up in front of a long table. The chairs were covered with beige drapes, and the photos were covered with scarlet sashes, creating this delightful autumn aura.

Grace and Carol took their seats at the center of the table. Moments later their support system arrived. Junell took a seat beside Carol, and Candace sat next to Junell. Ethan, Horace, and Pastor David flanked Grace's right arm. They had become her right-hand men.

"Thank you, gentlemen," Grace whispered, blowing kisses to each of them as the reporters filed in. Turning to her left, she signaled for Junell and Candace's attention.

"When I say, 'We want to share something with you,' I want you two to rip the sashes off the pictures."

By 9:01 a.m., all the seats were filled with reporters from across the country. Some of them were still groggy from their red-eye flights. During Ethan's introductory speech, Grace waved and winked at a few reporters from the *LA Times* whom she hadn't seen in a while.

"We've assembled you all here today to share a special announcement with you," Ethan stated with a slight smile on his face.

"Are you teaming up Grace with Carol Jasper to do a joint venture?" one reporter shouted from the middle row.

Grace pushed her chair back, stood up, adjusted the neck on her mixed-print, long-sleeve Balenciaga dress, and strutted to the podium. She blew kisses from her fuchsia-stained lips to the reporters before speaking. "Please hold all your questions until we are done. Who asked if Carol and I would be working together?"

An excited reporter jumped out of her seat, with her cell phone in her hand, and waved at Grace.

"Well, that was a good question. Actually, Carol and I worked on a similar campaign, and we called you all here today because we want to share something with you," Grace announced.

On cue Junell and Candace sprang from their seats and ripped the sashes off each picture. Gasps, squeals, and camera flashes filled the air following the picture reveal.

"Now my friend Carol Jasper is going to explain these photos to you in greater detail," Grace told the reporters.

Of course, there were some reporters who disregarded Grace's statement about questions, and at this moment question upon question was flung at them. Like a pro, Carol waited for the right one.

"Carol, why haven't you taken a job in ten months?" someone asked.

"I have not worked in ten months, because . . ." Carol paused and turned away from them.

Grace could already see the monster called memory sucking Carol's energy. She stood beside Carol and gripped her hand. "We're walking through the fire together."

Carol closed her eyes and lifted her head up at the sky, opened her eyes, and began again. "I have not worked in ten months, because Javier Roberts raped me on the set of the Egyptian Silk ad two years ago and has been doing so every time that I work with him. He took these photos and said that if I ever told anyone what he was doing, he would publish these photos and say that it was consensual. After seeing Grace on Diane Khan's show, I realized that I needed to come forward as well and stop living with this nightmare. Every day and every night I am haunted by his voice and the memory of what he did to me. I know some of you are fans of his, so all you see here is art, but I have the audio to go with the stills." Carol pressed PLAY on the voice memo of her phone and then held the phone up to the microphone before her. Her fright-filled screams and pleas for Javier to get off of her silenced the rooftop assembly.

"Turn it off," a reporter yelled from the back row. "Please turn it off."

Carol turned it off and switched places with Grace at the mic.

"Believe what you want to believe," Grace told the reporters. "Even after seeing the miracles that Jesus performed, many still doubted He was the Son of God, but truth is truth, and what you believe cannot and will not change it. Javier is a monster preying on the young girls who go unguarded in this business. Today Carol and I stand together, and we ask any other girl who has been victimized to come forward. We will stand with you . . ."

"Through the fire," Grace and Carol said together, holding their hands in the air.

Chapter 38

After the press conference was over, the whole crew gathered in Ethan's office. They rallied around Grace, patting her on the back and lavishing her with praises.

"I'm proud of you, babe," Horace said, squeezing her tightly and planting a kiss on her cheek.

"I knew you could do it," Junell said between bites of a croissant that was left over from the food that was served.

The conference table in Ethan's office was littered with leftovers from the event. Between the unveiling of the photos and Carol's announcement, not many people had been concerned about stuffing their faces with slices of Gouda.

"Guys . . . guys." Grace waved her hands in the air to get everyone's attention. "I'm not the brave one here." She walked a few paces to Carol, who was staring out Ethan's window with her forehead and fingertips pressed to the glass. Placing her hands on Carol's shoulders, Grace spun her around to face them all. "This is the face of today's hero. If Carol had not shown up at my door, I would still be sitting on my couch, ducking and diving from reporters. Let's give it up for Carol," Grace said, leading the group in a slow clap.

"Ca-rol! Ca-rol! Ca-rol!" they all chanted as they surrounded Grace and Carol.

Alice poked her head through the door. "I'm sorry to interrupt the party, but you have a call, Ethan."

Ethan waved his hand. "They can wait. We're celebrating the first of many victories."

"You're going to want to take this. It's RAINN—the Rape, Abuse and Incest National Network—on line one, and they want to talk to you about working with Grace."

Grace covered her mouth as she looked up to the sky. "You're a wonder," she whispered to God, placing her hand on her heart to slow the rapid beat that now thudded in her chest. She reached for Horace and clutched the sleeve of his solid black V-neck tee.

"Grace, what do you want me to do?" Ethan asked.

"Take it," Grace replied.

Ethan picked up the phone, and they all held their breath as Ethan nodded and repeatedly said, "I have to discuss that with my client." He paused for what felt like hours but was only about thirty seconds. "Thank you for contacting us. This sounds like a wonderful venture, and I will let you know my client's decision within twenty-four hours," he stated very matter-of-factly, revealing no emotion to the party on the other end or to those in front of them.

When Ethan placed the phone back in the cradle, Grace took her place at the head of his desk.

"Well?" she said.

"Well, RAINN wants to use you as the face of their twenty-fifteen Speak Out against Sexual Violence against Women campaign."

"What?"

"You heard me, Grace. They want to make you the face of their national campaign against sexual violence, and I think you should take it. This is a blessing. If you take this, millions of women across the country will find the courage to speak up about being raped, and this is what we need to take care of that little 'probation being revoked' situation. I can file a motion in the morning to have your probation amended in light of what has been revealed. I will petition the court to have the original order for you to attend anger management amended and to have your participation in this campaign count as a substitution."

"Can you do that?" Grace asked.

"Of course he can," Candace chimed in from the seat beside the table. "My man knows how to work the system, and you now have an advocate who is seated on the right hand of the Father ready to intercede for you."

"Hallelujah!" erupted from Junell's stuffed mouth. "Don't start, girl. You're going to have me slain in the spirit up in this office."

Everyone cracked up at Junell's stuffed-mouth out-burst.

"Well, babe, tell the man what you're going to do," Horace prompted Grace, massaging her shoulders.

"Ethan, I think we're going to take this party to the streets and let you get to work. You've got motions to file, offers to accept, and travel plans to set up for me," Grace stated, with a large grin spread across her face.

"Ethan, are you going to spend all day on the phone?" Grace whined, tapping on his desk with the toe of one of her four-and-a-half-inch steel-gray Guiseppe Zanotti pumps.

Ethan held up one finger and mouthed the words "one minute" to Grace.

Grace scrolled through her Google alerts. Three months after she had come forward, girls were still crawling out of the woodwork, accusing Javier Roberts of sexually assaulting them on the set. Today's headlines were PHOTOGRAPHER'S LIST OF VICTIMS LONGER THAN A ROLL OF FILM and RAPIST TALLY REACHES TWENTY.

Swiping her finger across the screen of her phone, she shifted her focus from the bad news to the throng of RSVPs she'd received for Junell's baby shower. With the pain of her past buried in a grave, it was time for her to focus on new life. It wasn't easy at first, looking at things and picking out decorations, but Grace was able to find the perfect party planner to help her pull off a Shel Silverstein–themed baby shower for Junell.

"I'm sorry," Ethan said after hanging up the phone. He folded his arms on his desk, between several stacks of folders. "What do you have to do that is so important?"

"I have a meeting today with the premier executive event planner, David Tutera. I was so blessed to have caught him in between events. He is in charge of everything."

"Who?"

"David Tutera, of *My Fair Wedding.*"

"Doesn't ring a bell. Listen, I got an offer for you," Ethan stated, trying to change the subject.

"I can't believe you've never heard of David Tutera. While we're on the subject, I have not yet received your RSVP for the shower, and it's in two weeks." Grace continued opening her e-mails as she spoke.

"Hello. I've been busy here." Ethan held a stack of folders in the air. "You and Carol opened up a firestorm. I've got all kinds of actresses and models asking for me to represent them now. I have contracts to review and negotiate."

Grace placed her cell phone facedown on the desk to avoid any more distractions and focused on what Ethan was getting at. "Isn't that what you've always wanted? Some clients besides me?"

Resting his forehead in the palms of his hands, Ethan shook his head from side to side. "It's overwhelming *and* inspiring. I'm thinking about setting up my own firm, Grace."

"What do you need me to do?"

"Nothing." He laughed. "That's not why I called you down here. I've got an awesome offer for you. I mean, out of this world. I've already done the negotiations, so all that we're waiting for is your approval." Ethan reclined in his chair and rested his right ankle on his left knee, exposing a pair of hot pink and navy checkerboard socks.

Grace scooted to the edge of her seat, placed her hand in the middle of her legs, and held on to the chair, waiting to hear what the offer was.

"Lifetime wants the rights to produce your biopic. You'll get script and cast approval, and they've asked that you play your older self. How's that sound?"

"Lifetime?"

"Yes, Lifetime."

Grace fell back in her chair and stomped her feet rapidly. "I have to tell the girls." She picked up her phone and began composing a text message to Junell, Candace, and Carol.

Ethan snatched the phone out of her hand. "What is wrong with you? That is not how we conduct business. You can't send out a mass text message, and you haven't even signed on."

Snatching her phone out of Ethan's hands, she continued typing. "Of course I'll do it. Tell them I want Carol to play the young me. I really want her to start working again. She stopped cutting herself, but she hasn't fully returned to normal activities yet."

"Is she still staying with you?"

"Yes. Her parents rented some cottage in France, and they said they can't break their lease. Can you believe how absurd they're being?"

"You know, Grace, I always wanted to say this to you, but I never thought I'd be able to. I am really proud of you. I am inspired by the way that you latched on to God and have not hesitated one bit since then."

"Well then, my next announcement is going to blow you out of your socks. I'm thinking about applying to Nyack College to pursue a degree in Christian counseling. They have a location in the city now, so I wouldn't have to go all the way to Nyack to make this happen."

With all the time Grace had on her hands now, she'd had plenty of time to meditate on the Word of God and figure out what her calling was. It wasn't modeling or acting. All the experiences she'd had would be useful in directing other people on how to rely on the Lord to heal them of their myriad issues. Through the power of Jesus Christ, Grace had not drunk, snorted, or sniffed anything except water and perfume in the fragrance department at Macy's. College wasn't going to be easy, considering she hadn't even finished high school, but she was willing to put in the work necessary to fulfill her purpose, even if that meant she had to get a GED.

"Doesn't that mean you have to get your GED first?" Ethan asked.

"Yes, it does, which is precisely why I can't hang around here with you any longer. I've enrolled in a GED program I found out about through the public library, and I have to be there in half an hour, and I have to meet David this afternoon. Ethan, are you coming to the shower or not?"

"Yes, Grace King. I will go anywhere that you want me to go," Ethan said as he rose from his chair and bowed.

Chapter 39

Grace didn't know why sweat was pouring out of her armpits. Her ruffled sleeves were wetter than the deck of the *Maid of the Mist* at Niagara Falls.

"What's wrong?" Horace asked, coming up behind her and embracing her.

"I'm sweating profusely."

"Normal. It's not every day that you host a baby shower for the who's who of prime-time television."

"It's not normal," Grace insisted, her lips twisted into a frown. "You're not supposed to sweat in organza. Especially not Isabel Marant," she said, lifting a piece of the thin white frock with her hand.

"Look on the bright side, babe. If you go put your back against the wall and hold very still, you'll fit in with the decorations," he joked.

Grace freed herself from his tender embrace. "Don't you like the decor? It's simple and chic," she said, stroking the black-and-white wallpaper, which consisted of blown-up images from *Where the Sidewalk Ends*. She'd gone through a lot to have the hall transformed into the setting of a Shel Silverstein book. "Junie loves Shel Silverstein. I think it's a great way to welcome the baby to the world. Come check out the tables." Taking him by the hand, Grace dragged Horace to the nearest table.

Horace cocked his head from left to right as he gazed at what appeared to be the stump of a tree that had been chopped down but was actually a table. The brown stump with its dull bark stood in sharp contrast to the clean white-and-black decorations. Grace ran her fingers around the circles that made up the table's top, and smiled at him.

"We're eating on stumps? You're paying this guy a bajillion dollars for tree stumps? You know I work in construction, right?"

Grace popped Horace in the gut. "It wasn't a bajillion dollars, and this is the stump from *The Giving Tree,* and all the cups are supposed to be the apples."

"What are you talking about?"

"You never read *The Giving Tree?*"

Horace shook his head.

Grace placed her hands on his cheeks and rose up on tiptoe to kiss him on the lips. "You were deprived as a child. I'm going to read the book to you tonight."

"Grace, I love you."

"Don't start getting mushy on me. The guests are arriving." Grace plucked a vintage compact mirror from her clutch and gave herself the once-over. She slicked down the hair at her temple. Even though she'd just had her hair freshly cut and permed, it was still misbehaving. Next, she ran her finger across the top row of her teeth and reapplied some lipstick.

"Are you done getting beautified?" Horace asked, spinning Grace around to face him.

"Yes, Horace, but you know, as much as I want to play with you now"—she placed both of her hands on his chest—"we don't have enough time for romance."

"How about forever? Is forever enough time for romance?"

"What are you saying, Horace?"

"I'm saying that all this baby clothes shopping, talk of safety gates, and christening got me thinking about the day Horace Jr. is born. I've been wondering what my family is going to look like, and every time I close my eyes,

I see you. When I met you, Grace, you were a beautiful mess, and I have had a front seat to your transformation. Now you're a wonderfully whole woman, and I want to walk the rest of this journey with you. Every day won't be like this, but I promise all our days will be filled with love and warmth."

"Horace, I've been thinking about walking away from the limelight, anyway," she said, closing her eyes. The flashing lights of the camera were losing their appeal, and whiskey was no longer her favorite drink, although she enjoyed the wine they served for Communion probably a little bit more than she should. All that she wanted now was the things she'd given up a long time ago, a family, friends, and her sanity. There was no way she was giving up her shoes, but she could do without the rest of the junk she'd purchased with her shoes. "I could definitely take a walk on a simpler road," she said, opening her eyes.

Horace got down on one knee.

"Horace what are you doing?" Grace squealed, covering her eyes as Horace dug his hand into a pocket of his dark gray slacks.

"I'm asking you to transform one more time for me." He drew her hands from her eyes and opened the lid on a black, heart-shaped ring box. Through her tears Grace could barely see what the ring looked like. "Grace King, would you please do me the honor and become Mrs. Horace Brown?"

Fanning her face rapidly with both hands, Grace screamed, "Yesss!"

Cheers and screams broke out all around her. Grace had been so focused on what Horace was saying, she had nearly forgotten where she was, and had not noticed the small crowd that had assembled around them.

Horace slid the ring onto her finger. "Well, are you going to kiss your man or what?"

Junell waddled to the right side of Grace and began leading the crowd in a chant. "Kiss him! Kiss him! Kiss him!"

Ethan and Candace stood to the left of Grace and joined in the chant. Carol appeared behind Horace with a cell phone in her hand, prepared to take a picture. Grace bent over and pressed her lips against Horace's. Horace grabbed her by the waist and pulled her down onto his bent knee. The crowd of guests began to clap.

"Horace, I can't believe you," Grace whispered in his ear.

"What can I say? I love you, Grace King."

"Help me get up."

Horace hoisted Grace to her feet by the waist.

Grace waved her hands in the air. "Thank you, everyone, but today is about welcoming my goddaughter, Millicent, into the world. Please check out the bookmaking stations to create a great picture book or fairy tale for Millicent, and make sure you hit the photo booth." Grace turned to Junell and rubbed her belly. "I'm sorry about this distraction. I know you're thinking this is classic Grace King trying to steal the show, but I had no idea about this. I'm—"

Junell put her hand over Grace's mouth. "I knew all about this." She lifted Grace's left hand and held it in the air. "Just who do you think picked out an oval-shaped, diamond-encased, six-pronged, braided pavé band, one representing how the two of you became one? By the way, it's a little shy of a carat. Angle it downward and most won't notice."

"Junie, you helped him pick this out?"

"Yes, either it was me or my mother, and you know Mama June was trying to give you her antique bridal set."

"I can't believe you did this for me."

"Believe it, baby! We all love you."

"Congratulations, Gracie," Candace said, kissing Grace on the cheek. "We all do love you."

"Wait a minute." Junell held up her hand. "Before the next lovefest begins, can someone get me into that chair? I have elephant ankles." She lifted the bottom of her maxi dress a few inches. "You see, Patrick won't be back from Dubai until next week, so it's just me, Epsom salts, and these ankles."

Grace and Candace both helped Junell wobble to the white and pink wicker chair in the corner of the room. Junell plopped into the chair.

"Thank you, ladies," she said.

"No, thank you," Grace said, kissing Junell on the forehead and then Candace. "All of you really helped me to see that there was some truth to what this woman said to me right after she slapped me. My life has been seasoned with grace."

Discussion Questions

1. In chapter one Grace questioned how her friend had managed to escape the photographers' lenses. Have you ever gotten into trouble with a friend and borne the brunt of the consequences? What impact did that have on the relationship?
2. During the discussion of the terms of Grace's probation, Ethan requested that they stop for prayer. What is your stance on mixing your faith with workplace interactions?
3. Grace refers to Ethan's zeal for converting her as the "honeymoon phase." What are your thoughts about those who actively try to convert someone to Christianity?
4. Early on, readers are introduced to Grace's alcohol problem. Do you think that something should have been done sooner to help her? What steps would you have recommended?
5. Who do you think is most responsible for Grace's alcohol and drug addiction?
6. What are your views on abortion?
7. There is a clear attraction and chemistry between Grace and Ethan. Do you believe that Ethan is over Grace?
8. The Bible instructs Christians "to be angry and sin not." Have you ever struggled with controlling your anger? In what ways has your faith helped you control your temper?

9. At first Grace was hesitant about pursuing a relation-ship with Horace because of his financial situation. What are your financial prerequisites for a relation-ship?

10. Horace was unwilling to enter into an "unequally yoked" relationship with Grace. Do you find that to be true for most Christian men?

11. When Grace began modeling, she was taken advan-tage of by a photographer. What are your thoughts on children entering the entertainment business at a young age?

12. Are there any points of trauma or situations in your life that have held you hostage or have held you back from being who God intended you to be?

13. Grace was able to find a purpose for her pain. Have you found the purpose for the pain in your life? Are you walking in that purpose?

14. What are your predictions for Horace and Grace's future together?

About the Author

Nigeria Lockley possesses two master's degrees, one in English secondary education, which she utilizes as an educator with the New York City Department of Education, and a second in creative writing. *Born at Dawn* is Nigeria's first published novel. Nigeria serves as the vice president of Bridges Family Services, a not-for-profit organization that assists student parents interested in pursuing a degree in higher education. She is also the deaconess and clerk for her spiritual home, King of Kings and Lord of Lords Church of God. Nigeria is a New York native who resides in Harlem with her husband and two daughters. Join her online at www.nigerialockley.com.

UC HIS GLORY BOOK CLUB!

www.uchisglorybookclub.net

UC His Glory Book Club is the spirit-inspired brain-child of Joylynn Ross, Author and Acquisitions Editor of Urban Christian, and Kendra Norman-Bellamy, Author for Urban Christian. This is an online book club that hosts authors of Urban Christian. We welcome as members all men and women who have a passion for reading Christian-based fiction.

UC His Glory Book Club pledges our commitment to provide support, positive feedback, encouragement, and a forum whereby members can openly discuss and review the literary works of Urban Christian authors.

There is no membership fee associated with UC His Glory Book Club; however, we do ask that you support the authors through purchasing, encouraging, providing book reviews, and of course, your prayers. We also ask that you respect our beliefs and follow the guidelines of the book club. We hope to receive your valuable input, opinions, and reviews that build up, rather than tear down our authors.

What We Believe:

—We believe that Jesus is the Christ, Son of the Living God.

—We believe the Bible is the true, living Word of God.

—We believe all Urban Christian authors should use their God-given writing abilities to honor God and share the message of the written word God has given to each of them uniquely.

—We believe in supporting Urban Christian authors in their literary endeavors by reading, purchasing, and sharing their titles with our online community.

—We believe that in everything we do in our literary arena should be done in a manner that will lead to God being glorified and honored.

We look forward to the online fellowship with you.

Please visit us often at:
www.uchisglorybookclub.net.

Many Blessing to You!

Shelia E. Lipsey,

President, UC His Glory Book Club